CW00449121

THE AMBIVALENCE CHRONICLES:

A GAMELIT COMEDY IN 8 BITS

Bit#1: The Chip Whisperer

Bit#2: The Kempston Interface

Bit#3: The Road Worrier

by Steve Trower

www.stevetrower.co.uk
twitter.com/SPTrowerEsq

Cover art by Bono Mourits
bonomourits.com

Also by Steve Trower

The Ballad of Matthew Smith

Countless as the Stars

THE CHIP

Whisperer

BIT#1 OF THE AMBIVALENCE CHRONICLES

· STEVE · TROWER ·

Bit#1: The Chip Whisperer

1

It all started, as so many good stories do, on eBay.

Phil Grundy had been shivering with anticipation for so long that, when he saw someone manhandling a large, but mostly unassuming, parcel out of an unmarked van, he made an Olympic qualifying sprint to the front door, barely noticing that he almost shoved his sulky teenage daughter head first into the downstairs toilet on the way.

Phil met the delivery man at the front door, thanked him effervescently, and then hurried around to his garage with his latest purchase.

The purchase in question had been long sought after, and after a fierce bidding war with thechipwhisperer, it was his for the somewhat higher than hoped for sum of £102.43 (plus p&p).

The sender had not been shy about using parcel tape, and had helpfully labelled the package 'Handle with Care', and 'from 20th Century Toys', and 'The Only Way Is Up'.

The sulky daughter mooched into the garage behind him, feigning indifference. 'You got?'

'This, Charlie-'

'Charlotte.'

'Charlotte,' Phil corrected himself, 'is the stuff of legend.'

Charlie (he would always call her that in his head) blew bubble-gum through her black-painted lips.

'If this is what I think it is,' Phil went on, hopping around like an excited puppy, 'it's practically the Holy Grail among collectors.'

'An old computer then?'

Phil carefully selected a knife from the workbench.

'Not just any old computer,' he explained. 'A Sinclair ZX81 with the legendary Issue Zero motherboard. The developers model. Among some of the more secretive retrocomputing forums they say these were only ever used by Sir Clive himself.'

'Later, Dad.'

'Oh, er… bye, Charlie,' Phil said, before setting to work on the most challenging round of pass the parcel he was ever likely to be part of.

Thirty minutes, two Stanley blades, and an acre of bubble wrap later, the parcel was open. Stealing himself for the big reveal, Phil took a deep breath and slowly opened the outer box. After shovelling a few handfuls of polystyrene chips onto the floor, Phil lifted his latest acquisition delicately out of the packaging debris.

Over the years since his wife had passed, Phil had built up an enviable collection of ZX Spectrums and associated peripherals, and this was the next step.

Carefully, Phil opened the box, wincing at the squeak of polystyrene, and lifted the lid with more reverence than any polystyrene box had ever been shown in this universe.

'That is beautiful,' he whispered to himself, running his fingers across the membrane keyboard in awe.

Of course, the seller had offered no guarantee it would ever be more than a novelty doorstop, but Phil, having been a Cub Scout back in the 80s, was prepared: he had been picking up old computer parts at car boot sales for long enough that he could solder his way out of most hardware problems.

He switched on an ageing black and white TV, which had been lying in wait for precisely this moment, and while it warmed up, hooked up the little computer. Then he waited.

The TV picture eventually came on, only to show white noise.

'Not surprising,' Phil said, a little disheartened.

He was sure he had the TV tuned correctly, but having checked the '81 was powered up, he twiddled the knob a little anyway, until his twiddling was disturbed by an unnecessarily loud exhaust rasp coming from somewhere outside.

With one eye on the screen full of white noise in front of him, Phil kept his other eye - and both ears - on the approaching car, attempting to judge the best moment at which to nonchalantly wander out of the garage.

When that moment arrived, Phil gathered the excess packaging from around him and strolled out of the garage, contriving to arrive at the recycling bin at the exact moment Sam Cooper got out of the small - but surprisingly loud - purple car that lived next door with her.

'Hi, Sam,' he called, waving cheerily and promptly dropping an armful of cardboard.

'Presents?' she asked, indicating the large box Phil was trying to fold with his feet as if that had been his intention all along.

'Oh, just something I picked up off eBay. Not sure it even works,' he added with a shrug.

'Anything I can help you with?'

Phil shoved the excess packaging into the recycling bin, in the vain hope of closing the lid over it. 'I didn't think old computers were really your area?'

'Maybe not,' she agreed, 'but two heads are better than one, so I'm told.'

'Well, feel free to take a look.'

Despite the fact Phil's suburban semi was now shared only with Charlie - who was out more than she was in, with her current crop of goth friends and their strange nocturnal habits - he had kept his computer hobby in the garage rather than move it into the house.

Sam had never been invited inside before, but she knew this was Phil's man-cave and exercised appropriate respect as she stepped through the narrow section of the side-hinged door.

Inside, it was a shrine to eighties technology; on the walls, several display cabinets were filled with rows of old computer game cassettes, and another filled with similarly old computers.

A workbench ran along the walls at the far end of the garage, complete with counter flap where a door led out into the back garden; in the corner, the ZX81 was trying to exert its will over a stubborn black and white Sanyo.

'Is that it?' Sam said, approaching the tiny plastic case curiously.

'Sure.' Phil followed her inside, leaving the door open behind him.

Sam smiled and glanced back at the classic Mini on her drive; a stripe along the bottom of the door identified it as 'T. REX', a nickname only partly related to its impressive roar. 'Great things come in small packages, eh?'

Phil made a concerted effort to look at something else as Sam bent over the little computer, checking and re-checking all the connections.

'So what do you think?' he said after a few moments of pretending to be otherwise engaged.

Sam stopped twiddling and stepped back to survey the minimalist desktop setup and the box from whence it had come.

'I don't suppose…'

'What?' Phil said into her silence.

Sam paused for a moment and then spoke the forbidden phrase:

'Did you read the instructions?'

'It's a ZX81,' Phil said. 'How hard can it be?'

But Sam was already digging in the box, pulling out the rather hefty BASIC programming guide that was packed with the ZX81.

'Pretty hard, judging by this,' she suggested.

'Be careful with that!' Phil said. 'It's practically mint and boxed!'

'Alright, calm down!' Sam said, trying not to laugh. 'You're right though,' she added. 'It doesn't look like anyone has opened this book, ever.'

'So why start now?' Phil gently tried to remove the book from her grasp. 'Please, Sam. You're still oily.'

Sam looked at her hands - mechanic's hands, holding a pristine book that was probably older than she was. 'Fair point.' As she handed the book over to

Phil, a few loose pages fell onto the desk. 'Is that the quick start guide?'

'What?' Phil held the book protectively, discreetly inspecting the manual for oily finger marks and such. 'They hadn't invented those when this was made.'

'Now that's what I call old school,' Sam said, reaching for the papers on the desk. 'I guess it was just called school then though, huh?'

'Don't touch anything!'

'Sorry, Mr OCD.'

Phil only scowled slightly at her as he reached across to pick up what looked like a sheaf of folded paper, of the sort you might have found in a dot matrix printer back in the days when you might have found a dot matrix printer.

'What is it?' Sam asked, screwing her face up as she peered over Phil's shoulder, as if, somehow, that might make sense of what was written in the paper.

Phil flicked through several of the pages; it was indeed computer paper, pages of it covered in random alphanumerics in faded uniform rows. 'Looks like some sort of hex,' he said eventually.

'Hex? Who would want to curse a ZX81?'

Before Phil could come up with a suitably clever answer, there was a noise outside. Phil was very protective of his precious retrocomputing stash, and hurried over to see if there were any undesirable elements snooping around, possibly with a view to reducing the size of his collection.

There was nobody in the immediate area except what looked like an old ice-cream van chugging away down the street. Phil watched it until it was out of sight, committing it to memory as best he could, then wishing

Sam had witnessed it, cars (and presumably therefore vans) being her thing in the way that redundant computer tech was his. Except, of course, she managed to make a decent living out of her thing, whereas Phil did precisely the opposite.

He turned with a sigh and headed back into the garage to take another look at the ZX81.

'What was that?'

'Nothing,' Phil replied, utterly unconvinced.

Sam nodded. 'I better go clean up. Good luck!'

'Thanks,' Phil said absently, as he flipped the user's guide open to the setup instructions and carefully laid it down on his workbench.

After several long minutes of plugging and unplugging, twisting, retuning, swearing, switching, and swapping, Phil eventually resigned himself to having bought a dud, and thumped the desk in frustration.

Now, anyone who has ever owned a ZX81 will know where this paragraph is heading, so please feel free to skip ahead to the next one, in which the ZX81 is working. Because, of course, that is precisely what happened; one thump from Phil's usually un-Fonz like fist, and the '81 buzzed to life - such as it was.

Phil grinned inanely, and settled down in the comfy leather office chair that was his retrogaming spot, basking in the glow of a tiny █ as he flicked idly through the mysterious sheets of computer paper.

He was still looking for some clue to its purpose when Sam, having availed herself of some Swarfega, whooped and clapped her way back into the garage; at least, until she got close enough to see how spectacular a ZX81 boot screen wasn't.

'Is that it?' she said, for the second time since meeting her first ZX81.

'Yes!' Phil whispered, as if speaking any louder might cause the computer to crash (which, in fact, was often the case with these things).

'Er, well then,' Sam said, 'I guess my work here is done. I'll leave you two alone.'

'You don't fancy sticking around for a game? I've got 3D Monster Maze.'

'That's a very tempting offer, but I literally just looked in on my way to the gym. Maybe another time, huh?'

'Sure,' Phil said, looking rather awkwardly around his desk. 'Anytime. Least I could do.'

Sam smiled. 'Have fun,' she said, and trotted off.

Later that day, having scared the ever-living crap out of himself playing 3D Monster Maze (he felt sure the PEGI people would have had a thing or two to say about this being freely available), Phil booted up his token nod towards modernity - a moderately specced laptop PC, which he used alternately for buying more interesting computers on internet auction sites and running emulators of every obscure 80s platform ever emulated.

He checked into eBay first; Phil was a stickler for leaving feedback as soon as he felt he could, and the afternoon's maze-based adventures had been successful enough for him to want to leave glowing praise for 20th Century Toys - and check their latest inventory while he was there.

While he was composing a suitably favourable

reply, a message alert pinged, putting him right off his flow. As he had forgotten what he was going to write, he opened the message.

It was from thechipwhisperer, his erstwhile eBay rival:

This may seem like a strange question, but I am wondering whether you have received and/or opened the ZX81 yet? I am a very serious buyer and willing to pay well above what you paid if you will pass it on to me, especially if unopened. What do you say?

'Well, that ship has already sailed, Mr Chip Whisperer,' Phil said to himself.

But despite himself, Phil was intrigued; on a whim, he decided to take a look at thechipwhisperer's profile to see what he could find out about this stranger who had suddenly become his eNemesis.

Oddly, given how desperate thechipwhisperer seemed to be to acquire the ZX81, it turned out that Phil had, in fact, bid on a few pieces of Sinclair kit being sold by thechipwhisperer over the last few months. Why would he be clearing out a collection one minute, and desperately trying to buy a piece the next? Either raising funds, or a dealer... A dealer who knew Phil's address... Phil's mind wandered back to the impression he had earlier that someone was snooping around outside, and to that ice-cream van which drove off afterwards...

Sorry, Phil messaged back, *the ZX81 is not for sale at any price.*

I am sorry to hear that, came the reply. *If there are any items you don't require, perhaps anything within the package which is not needed to run the ZX81, would you let me know? I may be interested in taking them off your hands, for a good price. I will consider anything, however trivial it may seem.*

Definitely a dealer then, Phil decided. Unless... he glanced over at the pile of computer paper that was gathered nearby, like a bonfire in a dress rehearsal. Phil gathered the pages up, and went to look for a ZX81 hex loader.

2

'Have you been here all night?' Sam poked her head into the open garage on her way past the next morning.

Phil had, in fact, been up much of the previous night, typing apparently random hexadecimal sequences on one of the least responsive so-called keyboards the world has ever seen, obsessively saving the results every few lines lest RAM pack wobble steal his treasure away. He thought better of explaining this to Sam, however, and mumbled something non-committal in response.

'Monster Maze that good is it?' Sam asked.

'Have you ever heard the word Entelechus?'

'Can't say that I have,' she replied. 'Can I have some context?'

'It's written on this hex code. Must be the title of the program or something, "The Entelechus Hex." Doesn't mean anything to me, though.'

'Is that what you've been playing with all night?'

'Not so much playing, but yes, I have been inputting the code.'

'What does it do?'

'So far, it doesn't do anything.' Phil took the opportunity to take a break and stretch his aching fingers. 'For all I know, I'm torturing my carpal tunnel for nothing more than a "Hello world" program.'

'Do you want me to take a shift?'

'Thanks, but I'd rather only have myself to blame if it all goes pear-shaped,' Phil said. 'One digit wrong and the whole thing could be completely screwed up.'

'More of a "Hello WRULD" program, you mean?'
Sam laughed. 'Ok, I guess that wasn't what you meant,'
she added when Phil failed to show amusement.

'Sorry, it's late.'

'It's nine in the morning.'

Phil shrugged. 'Fact is, I don't know what this
code could do, so I don't know what it could do
wrong.'

'Hang on a sec,' Sam said, and disappeared next
door.

Phil was saving the latest iteration of the code and
had stepped away from the workbench when Sam
returned, bringing with her a rather substantial looking
dictionary.

'What's it called again?'

'The Entelechus Hex. I don't even know if that's a
word,' he added, to explain his failure to think of the
obvious. 'Could be the author's name or anything...'

Sam was about to drop the Concise Oxford onto
the desk and open it up, but Phil spotted it and shouted
'Noooooooooo!' like a remastered Sith Lord, leaping -
well, edging carefully - forward to stop the hefty tome
hitting the desk and possibly causing the most
inconvenient RAM pack wobble in history.

Phil fluffed the catch, but knocked the book out of
Sam's hands to drop harmlessly to the floor, while he
toppled sideways to avoid awkward physical contact
with Sam, collapsing rather uncomfortably onto his
office chair, which carried him safely across the garage
under the combined forces of momentum and
embarrassment.

'What was that about?' Sam asked once Phil and

his chair had come to a stop a safe distance from the fragile operation under way on the workbench.

'The ZX81 was never the most stable of devices.' Phil tried to extricate himself from his chair, which promptly let out a crack of disagreement and deposited Phil on the floor.

'Looks like you have a matching chair now,' Sam said, trying to disguise a chortle.

'Put something like, say, a two thousand page hardback down on the same desk without proper precautions and you'll cause a major disturbance in the Chuntey.'

'A who in the what now?'

'Chuntey.' Phil gestured vaguely towards the fallen dictionary. 'Look it up.'

'It's not exhaustive,' Sam said, retrieving said dictionary from where it cowered under the workbench.

'The Chuntey field exists around tape-based computer systems,' Phil explained. 'It can be disrupted by any number of external factors, causing a tape loading error - or in this case, a failed save.'

'Right.' Sam nodded in the manner of someone who has understood approximately a third of what was just said to them.

'Sorry about your book,' Phil added, noticing the way she was smoothing out the pages.

'Don't worry. It's not like it's a ZX81 programming guide or anything, after all.'

'True,' Phil said. His sense of irony was not very highly tuned.

Sam moved along the bench, edging away from the ZX81, until Phil gave her the nod; a safe distance from the ZX81, she placed the dictionary down carefully and opened it up at the 'en' page. 'How are we spelling Entelechus?'

Phil showed her the title page of the hex.

Pages riffled.

'Entele…' Sam's fingers danced over the words. 'No,' she said. 'I've got entelechy; that's as close as I can find.'

'What does that mean then?' Phil asked absently,

'In the philosophy of Aristotle, a realisation or actuality as opposed to a potentiality,' she read. 'In some philosophical systems, a vital agent or force directing growth and life.'

'Hmm,' Phil pondered.

'Hmm?' Sam replied.

'Hmm,' Phil nodded.

'You have an idea?'

'Well, maybe. I mean, maybe the hex adds a little more realism to games - reasonable graphics, sound, things that were largely absent from the standard ZX81,' he suggested. 'I guess that would also explain why it doesn't appear to be doing anything so far.'

'Have you ever heard of anything like that?'

'There were hi-res graphics drivers available back in the day, but they were called… well, hi-res graphics drivers, not some cryptic name borrowed from a philosophy text book…'

'So?' Sam prompted as he fell silent again.

'What would be a step beyond that?' he wondered. 'Artificial intelligence?'

'Is that even possible?'

Phil shook his head. 'It would take more than some fancy code and a 16K RAM pack to turn a Zeddy into Siri.'

3

Phil was woken by the vaguely familiar sound of a vehicle pulling up outside. It wasn't T. Rex; that would have woken him up ten streets away, and for precisely that reason was banned from being driven in urban areas between the hours of 10pm and 6am. No, this was an entirely different sound, and was accompanied by a sliding door; a delivery van then. A very early delivery van, Phil realised as he squinted at his alarm clock to see it was before 3am.

He groaned, rolled over, and tried to get back to sleep.

Then he woke, properly, with a start. There was a noise downstairs - something was being delivered before 3am, and even the best eBayers didn't do that without charging extra. Phil crept out of bed and pulled on some clothes, listening intently for any out of place sounds. Something was going on - something that should not be going on, and he was going to find out what. The idea of a burglar would normally have Phil cowering under his bed waiting for sleep to reclaim him before any possible intruder felt the need for violence; but on this occasion, he was acutely aware of the mysterious hex listing that still tucked away in the retro computer corner of his garage.

Phil made his way downstairs as quietly as he could, but his urgency must have betrayed any sneakiness he may have had, and suddenly the noises became less discreet, more hurried.

When Phil opened the door that led from his kitchen into the garage, he was confronted by a man in dark clothes and grey hair, a few years older than Phil, busily making a mess of Phil's carefully sorted software collection. For a moment they froze, their eyes met, each wondering who was going to make the first move, until the intruder suddenly threw caution to the wind and made a dash for freedom.

The intruder reached for the garage door, when Phil let out a primal scream and leapt on him in what he thought may have been reminiscent of a rugby tackle. The man kicked out wildly, putting a somewhat ostentatious cowboy boot through Phil's previously pristine copy of Yie-Ar Kung Fu.

While Phil was distracted the nearly-thief managed to work his way loose and was about to bolt, when the garage door opened, and the intruder stumbled backwards in shock as a ghostly pale face loomed out of the darkness in front of him.

Phil took advantage of the element of surprise and soon had the man pinned down in his battle-scarred office chair.

'I knew your nocturnal adventures would come in handy sooner or later,' Phil said, panting for breath.

'What's going on?' Charlotte asked.

'I've been robbed.' Phil brushed some cobwebs from the knees of his jeans. 'Nearly.'

'What do you want?' Charlotte wrapped a delicate black fingerless glove around the stranger's neck with deceptively powerful fingers.

'Let me go and I'll explain,' he squawked through squeezed vocal chords.

Phil nodded to Charlotte, who reluctantly allowed the man to breathe again.

'Come on then,' Phil said, closing the garage door

once again. 'What do you think you're doing here?'

'The thing is, I was bidding against you.' He spoke with an American accent that Phil thought was possibly New York-ese. 'For the Zee Ex Eighty-one, you know. Thechipwhisperer, that's my handle. I was really hoping…'

'OK, first up, it's pronounced Zed Ex. It's English born and bred; there's no such thing as a Zee Ex Eighty-one, and to suggest otherwise is frankly offensive. And secondly, what the actual hell is up with you, with your stupid American sense of entitlement? You didn't win the auction; that doesn't make it ok to come and steal it from me. That kind of behaviour should be reported to eBay!' Phil stopped for breath, and realised that both Charlotte and thechipwhisperer were staring at him. 'How did you know I won it anyway?'

'A lot of eBayers will sell more than the contents of their attic - for the right price…'

'You bribed my address out of the seller?' Phil exclaimed. 'And I left that scumbag positive feedback, too!'

'Live and learn, eh?' thechipwhisperer said.

Phil narrowed his eyes and tried that 'steely' look he had been working on for months. 'I'm not selling,' he said firmly.

'I know, of course,' said thechipwhisperer. 'I realise that. You can keep the Zee- the Zed Ex, no problem.'

'So if you don't want the Zeddy,' Phil said, 'what do you want?'

'Does the word 'Entelechus' mean anything to either of you?'

'No,' Charlotte said.

Phil shook his head.

'No?' the stranger looked at them both intently. 'You've never come across the word?'

'Oh, yeah,' Phil said with a shrug. 'I think I've heard it at some point. I just don't know what it means.'

'Maybe I was wrong to come here,' he said, and made to get up.

Charlotte stepped towards him, black painted lips curling into a snarl. 'You come here, sneak around our garage, bribe an eBayer to find us in the first place, and interrupt us before we've even started playing…' she glanced around for a game of some sort. 'Krazy Kong,' she finished with a grimace. 'I, for one, would like an explanation.'

Thechipwhisperer looked over at Phil, as if for some brotherly support.

Phil just shrugged. 'The girl's got a point.'

Thechipwhisperer made one of those ironic noises that's part snort, part laugh, and wholly impossible to express in writing.

'I just want to know what you think I have that's worth all this trouble.'

'I was mistaken,' thechipwhisperer made to get up, but Charlotte's 14-hole Docs made a persuasive argument that his groin was better off staying close to the chair.

'But I'm curious now,' she whispered, and without Phil noticing, she had found a bungee cord somewhere and secured thechipwhisperer to the rickety office chair, like an extremely reluctant Christmas tree on the roof rack of his dad's old Triumph.

'What are you going to do, torture me?'

Charlotte glanced up at Phil, who had sort of expected to land the role of Good Cop rather than Torturer.

'Er...' he looked around discreetly for inspiration, which turned out to be in an innocent looking cassette case with a blue label. 'Worse. We're going to play some games.'

4

Twenty minutes later, after half a dozen or so of the slowest and least comprehensible Spectrum programs ever to masquerade as games (culminating in what could loosely be considered a racing game which made such gratuitous use of the Spectrum's limited colours it physically hurt to play for more than a few seconds - which was a moot point really, since the controls weren't sufficiently responsive to keep you away from the garish crash barriers for more than a few seconds anyway), thechipwhisperer had had enough.

'Oh, don't say that,' Phil said. 'There's 44 more of these we haven't tried yet!'

'How many of those are terrible Pac-Man rip-offs?' thechipwhisperer moaned.

'Oh there's bound to be a couple,' Phil said with glee. 'Shall we keep looking?'

The man just groaned and tried to slump back into the chair, only to be reminded that it was broken, and if he didn't stay alert, it would probably tip him onto the floor without a second thought.

'I've got a better idea,' Sam Cooper said, opening the door from the kitchen.

'Oh, no, there's another one.'

'Sam, it's 3am,' Phil said. 'What are you doing in my kitchen?'

'Sometimes, I feel I almost know,' she said.

'Are you sleepwalking?'

'Charlotte texted me.' Sam tipped her head towards the house, where Charlotte had sought refuge. 'Said you were in some kind of trouble.'

'I actually have it under control, thanks all the same.'

'So I see,' Sam nodded at the screen. 'What the heck are you playing?'

'Boggles.'

'Damn right it does. Who's your friend?'

'Thechipwhisperer,' Phil failed to explain.

'I'm more of a curly fries girl myself. Mind if I call you something else?'

'My name is Benito Stetson.'

'What?' Phil spluttered.

'My mother was Italian, my father was Texan. Just call me Benny if it helps.'

'What the hell does someone from Texas want with a ZX81?'

'I grew up in New York.'

'OK then...' Sam said uncertainly. 'Anyway, shall we have a little talk about what Entelechus means, and what exactly you were expecting to find with my friend's new toy?'

'Untie me, and I'll show you.'

Phil looked uncertain, but Sam released the stranger. 'We're not gangsters, Phil.'

Benny got to his feet gratefully. 'Back in the late 70s,' he explained, 'when microprocessors were beginning to revolutionise the world, a small and secretive cartel discovered a way to exponentially - no, more than that, super-exponentially, hyperbolically even - increase the power of a small computer. Not in the way mainstream technology has done - it's a well-documented fact that most people carry around in their pockets more computing power than sent men to the moon - but in an entirely different, non-technological way.'

'What do you mean?' Phil asked.

'In layman's terms, the Entelechus is like a magical incantation; a spell transcribed into machine code. A very powerful spell - one that has been in existence since the very dawn of time - but until the computer age arrived, was unusable.'

'I don't believe in magic,' Phil said.

'Whether you believe it or not is irrelevant. Many powerful individuals do believe in it.'

'What powerful individuals?' Phil smirked. 'Clive Sinclair? He's nobody now, he just helps people cheat at cycling.'

'Many of the world's most powerful individuals are not recognised as such. In fact, many are not recognised at all.'

'OK, so there's a mysterious group of super powerful, but anonymous, computer nerds hiding out in a bunker somewhere, probably spying on my Facebook...'

'You jest...' there was an ominous tone to Benny's voice.

'Well what have they done with this spell thingy then?' Sam asked.

'Nothing,' Benny said, 'yet.'

'Why not?' Phil asked. 'If it's all that powerful...'

'In 1981, one member of this group realised the others wished to use the Entelechus for their own purposes, to extend their power over the proletariat.'

'Big Brother?' Sam said.

'Indeed.' Benny nodded and pulled a dog-eared notepad from a deep pocket inside his coat. 'One member of the group wanted to use the code to benefit mankind, but was overruled. So he took matters into his own hands…'

Benny waved the pad towards Phil.

'That's the original code?' Sam asked, her penny finally dropping.

Benny nodded. 'Part of it, anyway. The elements needed to activate the Entelechus were split up and spread out across the country in secret, hidden way out of the cartel's reach.'

'What about the other elements?' Phil took the pad from Benny and flicked idly through it; hexadecimal code filled every page in small, neat handwriting. There was still no indication what it was supposed to do.

'It has come to my attention that at least one of the remaining elements has recently surfaced, in the hands of a group calling themselves the Assembly - a group which I believe is made up of members of the original cartel, making another attempt to get the code working. Through watching their movements I thought I'd tracked down another element to the ZX81 you bought.'

'I was bidding against them, too?'

'On the contrary,' Benny said. 'I believe they were selling it.'

'What would be the point in that?' Sam asked. 'If they had the code, why release it back into the wild?'

'Maybe to lure me out of hiding.'

'You were in the original cartel,' Sam realised.

'But why get the band back together after 30 years?' Phil asked.

'Won't it be hopelessly out of date by now anyway?' Sam said. 'You just said we carry the computing power of 1970s NASA in our pockets. How will this old stuff compete with that?'

'The technology is irrelevant, really,' Benny said. 'But by running on outdated hardware they can hide it in plain sight.'

'Is that why there's a retrocomputing revival at the moment?' Phil asked.

Benny looked thoughtful for a moment. 'It is possible that the revival was engineered to bring the Entelechus back into circulation.'

'It's also possible,' Sam suggested, 'that the people who grew up with these creaky old systems have now reached their mid-life crisis and are getting all nostalgic for them.'

'But why use a Zeddy?' Phil ignored her. 'I've used practically all the memory just with the…'

Benny's eyes widened. 'So you do have it!'

Sam facepalmed discreetly.

Phil groaned as the cat irretrievably fled the bag. 'Yes, I have it,' he said, pulling the computer paper out of a drawer.

Benny scurried across and began to pore over the hexadecimal code as if he could read it.

'Yes, yes…' he muttered over and over. 'This is it,' he decided finally. 'The next piece of the puzzle. Now, we must keep these safe - and preferably separate. There's no point making it easy for the Assembly, is there?'

'Can't we just let them keep a third of it and destroy the rest?' Sam asked. 'Then it would be useless, surely?'

'We can't be sure,' Benny said. 'There could be duplicates, cached copies - yours, for example, is printed.'

'So?'

'So it must have been typed in at some point,' Phil explained.

'Who knows how many copies were printed or saved from that original,' Benny said.

Phil nodded knowingly. 'I've heard tales of people spending hours typing in program listings from computer magazines, only to lose all that hard work by not saving the data in time. Logic dictates that at least one software copy exists, somewhere, of any data that was typed in.'

'OK,' Sam said, 'so how much of this code are we missing?'

Benny squinted towards one of the darker corners of Phil's garage. 'If I'm right, and they are trying to find me, they may already have everything else they need.'

'And what's so special about you, cowboy?'

He turned back to face Sam 'I didn't come over here for the weather, you know. I was recruited by the cartel because I have a very particular set of skills. Skills I have inherited from a very long family heritage.'

'You come from a long line of Z80 coders?' Phil said.

'I have Native American blood in these veins.'

Sam rolled her eyes. 'Of course you do.'

'I said the Entelechus was magic,' Benny carried on. 'It needs three elements: the complete code, the hardware to run it, and a channel for the mystical energy.'

Sam shook her head. 'This guy's a nutcase, Phil, can we get rid of him so I can go back to bed?'

Phil went on ignoring her. 'So, even if this Assembly has the code, and the hardware, they still won't be able to use it properly unless they can get Penn and Teller to explain how the magic works?'

'The work of a chip whisperer is no mere illusion,' Benny grunted.

'The what of a who now?' Sam said.

'Don't worry,' Benny grinned. 'I've evaded them for over three decades, there's no way they can find me now.'

'Unless they notice that an eBayer by the name of thechipwhisperer has been actively bidding on old computers lately,' Sam said.

'Oh.'

'And unless some other eBayers can be persuaded to divulge the addresses of buyers,' Phil pointed out.

'Ah.'

'You don't think they'll come after us, do you?' Sam asked.

'You?' Phil replied. 'No. You can go back next door and deny all knowledge. It's just me and Charlie that have to worry about some quasi-mystical cyber-terrorists tracking us down.'

'We should move,' Benny said. 'The Assembly mean business. When they find out you've spoken to me, they won't leave you alone.'

'That's reassuring,' Phil muttered.

'I'm not trying to reassure,' Benny said. 'Merely to state facts.'

'And bring the Assembly after us,' Phil pointed out.

'The second you came into possession of the Entelechus, you became a target,' Benny said ominously. 'You should be grateful I got to you first; nobody can protect you from the Assembly better than I can.'

'Who are you, the frickin' Terminator?' Sam asked.

'Hasta la vista, baby.'

'So what now?' Phil asked.

'Come with me if you want to live,' Benny said.

'Yeah ok, we caught the first one,' Phil said.

'Right now?' Sam asked.

Benny nodded. 'We've wasted enough time,' he said. 'Get the scary pale one. I've plenty of space for all of us. Once we get out of town we'll lose the CCTV and can relax a little.'

'No way,' Sam said, turning to leave.

'You can't escape them otherwise, be assured of that,' Benny called after her.

'I dare say,' she replied, 'but if I'm going on the run, I'm damn well taking my own wheels.'

5

Phil and Benny were discussing the relative merits of Buggy Boy and Stunt Car Racer when the unnecessary growl of Sam's small purple vehicle alerted Phil to the fact that she was ready to go.

Having decided that Benny was actually an alright kind of guy, Phil felt somewhat guilty about subjecting him to Cassette 50 in the middle of the night, and was doing his best to purge that memory with a few Spectrum classics.

Luckily, Sam's insistence on taking her own, strictly curfewed, car on any potential road trip had enforced a delayed departure until sunrise, which comfortably allowed time to sample JetPac, Manic Miner, and Saboteur.

'That's quaint,' Benny said of the Mini. 'Noisy though. Like Great Aunt Hilda's yappy little dog.'

'Hey, Rex is a recognised and well-respected classic,' Sam said, getting out and caressing the roof of her Mini. 'The ultimate evolution of the Car of the Century.'

'Rex?' Benny laughed. 'You even named it after Aunt Hilda's dog.'

'He's called T. Rex, cowboy.' Sam pointed to the decal bearing the name. 'He's an apex predator on the open road. Whereas you appear to be driving a pregnant guppy.'

'I believe the appropriate British phrase here is "touché".'

'Actually, what are you driving?' Sam said, observing the rather large, and somewhat old, vehicle waiting patiently across the street.

'Is it an ice-cream van?' Phil asked.

'Well, it was advertised as a Dodge Ambulance,' Benny explained, 'which plainly means something a lot cooler in the States than it does here. Obviously I was disappointed at first, but she had this kind of kooky English charm that I liked. Kind of like a blind date who looks like a moose but wins you over with her personality.'

'Don't think I've ever had that experience,' Phil said.

'I think I'm having the opposite one right now,' Sam muttered.

'Used to belong to somebody called St John,' Benny went on regardless. 'I gather that's some kind of traditional English name?'

'Some kind, yeah,' Sam agreed.

'Maybe you'd like to look inside?'

Sam raised an eyebrow, but Phil ignored her and stepped towards the old van.

'Bring the ZX,' Benny said, unlocking the back doors.

What Benny drove was, in fact, a high-top Dodge Spacevan which had previously been a community ambulance before passing into the hands of a talented but inadequately funded enthusiast, who reluctantly sold it to Benny in 2001.

'Welcome,' he said, opening the back doors with a grand gesture, 'to the Ambivalence!'

'Whoa!' Phil said as he stepped up into the roomy rear section. Benny flipped down a small flat screen from the roof of the van and invited him to plug the

ZX81 into it.

'Steady on boys,' Sam called from outside. 'I'm still here, you know!'

'No, come and have a look!'

'Not really my thing.'

'Maybe not,' Phil said, 'but I'm sure you'd be impressed.'

'Oh, ok…' she sounded decidedly resigned. 'Let me have a look…'

She stuck her head in through the back door and looked around.

'Well?' Phil said expectantly.

'I suppose, as a piece of automotive modification, I have to admit that it is quite impressive,' she said. 'But couldn't you have found something more exciting than a ZX80 to pimp your ride with?'

'It's a ZX81,' Phil corrected.

'Of course,' Sam said. 'That's much better, obviously.'

'Not really,' Phil said. 'Have I taught you nothing?'

'Very little, if I'm honest.'

'Does all this work?' Phil turned his attention to the bench which ran along one side of the van's interior, housing several power points into which were plugged flat screen TVs and 8-bit computers.

'Of course,' Benny entered a code on a key pad in the style of a Sinclair calculator, and a compartment over the front seats opened to reveal rows of small drawers.

'Spares, leads,' he explained. 'Well, you're a collector, you know the sort of stuff you either need or just end up with loads of.'

'Yeah,' Phil was still staring around like a kid on his first visit to Hamley's as he placed his ZX81 on the bench.

Sam rolled her eyes. 'I'll go and get Charlotte while you two carry on bonding.'

To say that Benny had been underwhelmed when he first saw the British interpretation of a Dodge Ambulance would have required a major recalibration of the whelmedness scale - until he noticed it had once been equipped with a wheelchair lift, the wiring for which was soon repurposed to power a mobile vintage computing workshop.

The only thing belying the van's previous life as a charity ambulance was the light box above the windscreen, into which Benny had written the word 'Ambivalence', but was still unsure whether that was a good thing or not.

'And wolla!' said Benny as Phil's ZX81 sprung to life on one of his screens.

'So we can carry on typing the hex in while we're on the move?'

'In theory,' Benny replied. 'But in practice the ride in the Ambivalence isn't great. You'd be better off waiting - or getting a head start now, of course.'

'Dad!' Charlotte called groggily. 'This woman just dragged me out of bed. What's going on?'

'Road trip,' Phil answered absently.

'It's like the middle of the night. And why's the Hamburglar still here?'

'Benny here is, uh…'

'He's a friend,' Sam said. 'Of sorts.'

'Wasn't he trying to steal your antiques?'

'A misunderstanding.' Phil stepped down out of the van.

'One for which I am very sorry.' Benny closed the overhead locker and followed.

'I'll fill you in on the way,' Sam whispered.

'On the way where?'

Sam and Phil both glanced at Benny.

'Just head out of town for now,' Benny said. 'We need to get off the grid so we can regroup and plan our next move.'

'Furnace Lane?' Sam suggested.

Phil tried not to shudder at the hazy and often unhappy memories of the times he had failed to get off with the girl next door in the overgrown yards of Furnace Lane's long abandoned industrial units in his younger years. Undeniably though, for the same reason it had become a teenage make out spot when a BMX had been his transport of choice, it met the (admittedly somewhat vague) requirements of their current situation.

Phil nodded. 'You take the Zeddy and go round the long way. I'll show Benny the short cut. And be careful with it!'

Sam carefully wrapped the tiny computer in her coat. 'I'll treat it with the same respect I show T. Rex.'

'That's what I was afraid of.'

'Why do you call it that?' Benny asked. 'Cos its arms are so short?' He stomped around in a ridiculous pastiche of a tyrannosaurus.

'It's the same car Marc Bolan died in,' Sam explained patiently.

'Marc...?'

'From out of T. Rex!' Sam said. 'Honestly, you

Americans are so uncultured.'

'I guess I skipped the lesson on who died in a tiny purple car,' he said. 'Care to enlighten me?'

Sam looked at Benny in faux despair. 'T. Rex were only the greatest glam rock band to come out of Staines.'

'T. Rex were never from Staines,' Phil said quietly.

'Shut up,' Sam hissed.

'And this Marc fella was in this band?' Benny asked.

'Bolan,' Sam said. 'Yes. He was the lead singer.'

'In Yes?' Phil said. 'I thought that was Jon Anderson?'

'No, in T. Rex, idiot,' Charlotte said. 'Marc Bolan and T. Rex, even I know that.'

'Ah, I see,' Phil said.

'And he died in this car?' asked Benny, who didn't see at all.

'Not this actual car,' Sam said. 'One like it. Same colour and everything.'

'So you call your car T. Rex after this band.'

'Now you're getting it!'

'Isn't that a bit morbid?' Phil asked.

'What, commemorating one of the most amazing glam rock stars this country ever produced?'

'Specifically, commemorating the way he died,' Phil clarified.

'There is no cooler way to die than in a 1275GT,' Sam said as she opened the door and tucked the ZX81 away beside the back seat.

'I'll bear that in mind,' Phil said uncertainly, as his only daughter got in the passenger seat.

Benny turned to Phil. 'We get the short cut?'

Phil nodded. 'Sam will be able to slip off the main road discreetly.

'Discreetly? In that?' Benny said, once the Mini had roared off down the road.

'You don't exactly travel incognito yourself,' Phil pointed out.

'Well…' Benny said after an uncertain pause.

'Don't worry,' Phil said. 'If anyone can pull it off, Sam can.'

'If you say so.' Benny slid back the passenger door and indicated that Phil should get in and experience the cockpit first-hand.

Benny climbed in next to him, then Phil got out again because he remembered he had left his garage unlocked, locked the garage, and got back into the van.

'Meanwhile, we'll quietly slip out of town,' Phil said as he clunked and clicked. 'Truck on, Tyke.'

6

Somewhat predictably, Sam was leaning casually against her car when the Ambivalence finally bumbled along the narrow lane between two rows of crumbling industrial units.

'So what now?' she said as Phil and Benny stepped out of the Ambivalence.

'You still have the ZX81?' Benny asked.

'No, I threw it out of the window somewhere on the A30.'

'Hmm,' Benny said.

'Never mind that,' Charlotte said. 'Can somebody tell me why we're here?'

'I thought it was your idea?'

'Not here specifically, wise guy. Why have you dragged me away from my warm and comfy home to hang around up Lovers' Lane with this guy? It's like the worst double date in history.'

'How do you know-'

'Now's not the time, Phil.' Sam cut off his parenting in its prime.

'We're hiding,' he called after his daughter's retreating back.

She stopped, but didn't turn. 'From?'

'Um…'

Charlotte turned to look at Sam, who just shrugged and glanced across at Benny.

'You tell it so well,' Phil said with a smile.

Charlotte ambled back towards the group with a deliberate air of indifference. 'I'm listening,' she said, leaning on the roof of T. Rex as if it was her car and not, in fact, Sam's pride and joy.

'In a nutshell,' Benny started, 'we're hiding from a secretive group who will stop at nothing to get their hands on something which has fallen into the hands of your father here.'

'What, like the mafia?' Charlotte said.

'Like the mafia, yes,' Benny started, 'except that, if the mafia ever got wind that an organisation as powerful and ruthless as the Assembly even existed, they would run crying to their mamas and settle for playing shoddy Doom clones rather than dare to shoot actual people up.'

'So...' Charlotte started, dragging that single syllable out for an unfeasibly long breath, 'how come I've not heard of this Assembly? Twitter is full of conspiracies like that. And if they are so powerful wouldn't they have at least been mentioned by The Independent?'

'They are far more powerful than any media outlet,' Benny said. 'And they are also very secretive. They prefer to manipulate things from behind the scenes, rather than be open like the mafia.'

'That's bull,' Charlotte said.

'That's a fact,' Benny said, 'and how you react to it will dictate the length of your life from this point forward.'

Charlotte pointed her best cynical look in his direction. 'Well,' she said after a moment's thought. 'I don't have anything better to do right now.'

'Good,' Phil said. 'Glad that's sorted out.'

'So what's the plan?' Charlotte asked.

Phil, Sam and Benny looked at each other blankly.

'Oh god,' Charlotte said. 'You lot are so lame. Tell

me the full – de-nutshelled – story, and maybe I can be the brains of the outfit. God knows somebody needs to be,' she added at a mumble.

Phil and Benny brought Charlotte up to speed with the rest of the story, while Sam opened up T. Rex and fettled her carburettor. There was no need for her to be doing this, but unlike old computers and magic code, it was something she understood.

'Seems to me,' Charlotte said, 'that if this Assembly of yours-'

'Will you guys stop saying they're mine!'

'Whatever,' Charlotte said. 'If they're computer nerds, the obvious thing to do would be to hack into their systems, keep track of what they're up to; maybe we could even find out where they have the missing part of this code.'

'An excellent suggestion,' Benny said. 'Are you a hacker?'

'Haven't you done that?' Phil said to Benny.

Benny shook his head. 'Finding them on eBay is one thing,' he said, 'but I'm pretty sure I couldn't find a damn thing on these guys unless it suited them for me to do so. How are your hacking skills, Phil?'

Phil chuckled. 'I've hacked the odd Spectrum game,' he said. 'Anything more secure than a Commodore 64 though, and I'm snookered.'

'Well, if it's a hacker we need…' Charlotte interrupted.

'Yeah?' Benny said.

'You know hackers now?' Phil said. 'Who even are you?'

Charlotte just scowled across at him. 'Well, the best guy in the country is Doc Nectarine.'

'Doc what?' Phil said.

'Nectarine.'

'Sounds like a crap Spiderman villain,' Phil muttered.

'It's a hacker tag, Dad?'

'Well it's a crap hacker tag then.'

'Like you would know.'

'Guys, please,' Sam said. 'Stop bickering. We are running for our lives, remember?'

'Only without the actual running bit,' Charlotte observed.

'We'll run at dark,' Benny explained.

'Wouldn't that make us more conspicuous?'

'What?'

'Nobody drives at night,' Charlotte said.

'Sam doesn't, you mean,' Phil said.

'That's harsh, Dad. It's not Rex's fault he's under curfew.'

'Really?'

'Besides, we can't blend into traffic that isn't there.'

'Blend in?' Phil said. 'A purple Mini and a retired ambulance from the 50s?'

'It's from 1982,' Benny corrected him.

'Let's just hope the traffic cameras have something better to look at than us,' Phil said.

'And headlights – they're a bit obvious, aren't they?' Charlotte went on. 'Bit of a giveaway when you're being chased.'

'What I meant to say,' Benny said, 'is we will run until dark.'

'How do you know about this Doc Nectarine, anyway?' Phil asked.

'Friend of a friend of a friend,' Charlotte said.

'Can you get in contact with him?' Benny asked.

Charlotte was silent for a moment, as if meditating or something. 'I'll see what I can do,' she said in the end.

'Thank you,' Phil said, but she had already turned away and was busily doing something on her phone.

7

Several hours later, Phil was sat at a greasy table with two polystyrene cups filled with murky, lukewarm liquid masquerading as tea. Probably called itself 'T', Phil thought as he stared into it distastefully.

Through some shady network of online contacts, Charlotte had managed to set up a meeting with the hacker she called Doc Nectarine in Britain's last vestige of secrecy - a little known truck stop somewhere off the A420 in Oxfordshire, which remained untroubled by such modern delights as Closed Circuit Television.

'Is this Earl Grey?' Benny said, taking a seat opposite Phil and sniffing his drink suspiciously.

'No.' Phil picked up his cup to peer at its contents from a new angle. 'This is just grey.'

Mercifully, the phone in Phil's pocket bleeped before he felt obliged to taste the tea substitute; he read the text, then excused himself, slipping off to what the management laughingly referred to as the 'tourist information board.'

In actual fact the best information any tourist could have been given in this particular truck stop would be 'you should leave now, while you still can. This place will devour your soul if you stay. At least, if you use the car park for over two hours. Oh, and avoid the pasta bolognese.'

Instead, in a somewhat misguided attempt to make the place a little more family friendly, the board was now rather scantily filled with a handful of leaflets for nearby tourist attractions, highlights of which appeared to be the Imperial Lawnmower Museum, and a zoo at which the most exciting exotic beast was a llama called Jeff. In fact the information board contained more literature from a variety of over-zealous religious cults than it did legitimate tourist information.

Phil pretended to browse what leaflets there were, but was beginning to tire a little of the same three National Trust properties, when a man in a leather trench coat, shades, and a wide brimmed hat sidled up to the information board.

Discreet, Phil thought to himself. I barely even noticed you. At least you're not drawing attention to yourself. 'Zucchini?' Phil said quietly.

The man ignored him.

Phil cleared his throat and repeated the gourd.

The man glanced sidelong at him and inched away.

'I said, Zucchini,' Phil said, louder now, in case the stranger was backing off for a reason unrelated to Phil's random courgette recital.

'Shut up!' another voice hissed from behind him, startling him.

When Phil looked around to see the voice, there was no one there; at least, not in his line of sight.

'Don't turn around,' the voice whispered. 'Oh, and, no thanks, I'm trying to give them up.'

'Oh,' Phil said, surprised. 'You're-'

'Yes,' the voice hissed.

A hand reached around from behind Phil, picked a leaflet - a thirty-year-old programme of events at Palaeozoic Park - from the rack and placed it in Phil's hand.

'You should pay a visit,' he said. 'Weather looks good for today if you can.'

Phil turned the leaflet over in his hands a few

times, not really reading it, but soon realised there was no further conversation coming from the mysterious voice behind him, or from the tall stranger in the inconspicuous outerwear, or from anyone else for that matter. He pocketed the dog-eared leaflet and hurried back to his T before it got even more unpleasant.

8

'I've never even heard of the place,' Sam had said when Phil announced their next destination. 'And I've got nephews.'

'What's that got to do with anything?' Phil asked.

'Nephews love dinosaurs,' she replied, as if it was the most completely obvious fact in the world.

'What, all nephews?'

'As far as I can tell. Why is it called that, anyway? I thought the Palaeozoic era was all trilobites and stuff. Hardly the most exciting of prehistoric eras to name a theme park after.'

'Maybe it's a trilobite themed park,' Phil suggested. 'All crustaceans and molluscs.'

'Let's hope so,' Sam said. 'At least that way I won't lose all my cool auntie cred for coming without them.'

As it turned out, Auntie Sam had nothing to worry about.

'How long has this place been closed?' she said, comparing the pictures on the leaflet to the stark reality that stared across the galvanised security fence at them.

'I have the events calendar for 1988,' Phil said. 'Looked like quite a good year.'

'Well, it sure ain't a theme park any more,' Benny said. 'Trilobite or otherwise.'

'Doc Nectarine must know it's safe,' Charlotte said. 'You know, secure, to talk.'

'We are a little… remote,' Phil said.

They had eventually found Palaeozoic Park seven

miles along a road which didn't appear on the maps either of them carried in their vehicles, or on Sam's satnav. It lurked behind a nine-foot-tall barbed wire encrusted fence, which Phil speculated was probably even electrocuted.

'I think the word you're looking for is electrified,' Sam said. 'And I don't think the dinosaurs are real, anyway.'

'I thought you said they were trilobites,' Phil said.

'That,' Sam pointed to a picture on the leaflet, 'is clearly a triceratops.'

'Were they really fluorescent green?' Phil asked.

'I'd have to ask my nephew, but I'm going to guess not. No evolutionary advantage to being the most obvious dinosaur in the forest.'

Phil stepped up to the gates to take a closer look at the security measures that had appeared sometime after the park's closure. 'It's bolted from the inside,' he said. 'There must be another gate. Unless anybody's got a crowbar?'

'I left mine in my other jacket,' Charlotte said.

'I thought you said that was electrified?' Sam said, causing Phil to jump away from the fence in shock. Surprise, that is, not electric shock.

There was a slightly weedy 'peep peep' which made Phil and Sam both turn around to see the Ambivalence speeding towards them. Phil was about to dive out of its path, heroically grabbing Sam on his way down to save her from almost certain irony when Benny's old ambulance hit her, but then he realised that 'speeding' was very much a relative term where the Ambivalence was concerned, and settled for nodding in the general direction and saying 'watch your back,' before ambling off to one side.

Sam, for her part, glanced up at the ambulance indifferently, knelt to tie her shoelace, then strolled after Phil. A moment later the ambulance, um, well crashed is not quite the right verb there, but made contact with the gates. There was a noise which, had it been amplified by an order or two of magnitude, might have qualified as a crash, but it wasn't. So it didn't.

The gates epically failed to fling open before the charging Ambivalence, and the bystanders were still standing by, locked out, after the attempted break in was over.

'That was lame,' Charlotte muttered and wandered off, presumably in search of somewhere to sit and tweet moodily.

'Should have used your car,' Phil said.

Sam snorted a response, which Phil took to mean something like 'I would rather come up with an alternative plan before attempting that, thank you very much,' and then went to make sure the Mini was locked, just to be on the safe side.

Benny, however, was unperturbed; he backed up the Ambivalence and had another go. Phil checked his watch, and went for a little walk around the perimeter.

In places, the perimeter fence was hidden behind several feet of thick hedgerow - another level of security on top of the fence and barbed wire. And big scary dinosaurs.

In other places Phil was able to peer through gaps in the brambles, occasionally catching glimpses of the dilapidated buildings and silent, broken roller coasters of the long deserted theme park. Where he could get right up to the fence he gave it a rattle every now and then, kicked the fence posts, and eventually found a section with rather flimsier foundations than most, and after some persuasion, he created a gap just big enough to squeeze through.

Leaving only a small part of his favourite Jet Set Willy t-shirt attached to the fence, Phil made his way back along the inside of the perimeter until he came across the Ambivalence, still beating its automobilian head against the gate.

While the van was backing up for yet another run at it, Phil yanked open a couple of hefty bolts that had been proving effective against the attentions of Benny and the Ambivalence, and repurposed one of them as a crowbar, prying apart the rusting remains of a padlock which was now the only thing keeping his friends out of Palaeozoic Park.

The Ambivalence came, um, speeding towards the gate, which in a dramatic break from tradition, sprung open in front of it. Sam and Charlotte erupted in bored and slightly ironic cheering, and then followed through the gate in the Mini.

'I knew I could do it,' Benny said, sticking his head triumphantly out of the open van door.

'Well done.' Phil slid the now slightly malformed bolt back in place to secure the gates. 'Now, shall we get away from the road, on the off-chance that your antics haven't attracted any attention yet?'

'Good plan,' Sam agreed, revved the Mini's engine a couple of times, and disappeared in a cloud of dust.

Phil jumped into the Ambivalence and they followed the cloud like some kind of Dodge-based

Moses in a surreal Sinai desert.

Palaeozoic Park had been built on the site of a World War Two airfield which wasn't quite popular enough to last the duration of the Cold War. The main road in from the entrance eventually led to the intersection of the two former runways, where a large circular building served as a hub for the park.

From here, smaller buildings in varying sizes, shapes, colours, and purposes stretched out along streets which led out into the different geological areas of the park.

Phil and Benny found the Mini sitting at a jaunty angle outside the main building, empty, so they left the Ambivalence next to it and went off on foot in search of the others.

The door to the main building was open; whatever kind of security had been left here had obviously given up long ago, leaving the once impressive hub to its Marie Celestian fate. Inside, it was cool and dark, only the most persistent sunlight managing to get through the grubby windows.

Drink and snack vending machines stood along one wall, still stocked – well, to the extent of having some Doctor Pepper and a couple of Bountys kicking around anyway. Fire exit signs hung, damaged, above some of the doorways. Stuff crunched under their feet that could equally have been plaster dust or the crumbling fossils of popularity.

'Wow,' Benny's voice echoed faintly around the room. 'We just walked into cliché central, didn't we?'

Computers still sat behind the information desk; eventually, Phil climbed over it to satisfy his curiosity.

'Amiga 1000s,' he muttered to himself, glancing casually around in case there turned out to be a comprehensive web of CCTV coverage in the room.

'Maybe one of them controls the heating,' Benny said hopefully.

Further exploration was disturbed by a call echoing up from one of the corridors, and reluctantly, Phil abandoned his potential treasure.

They found Sam and Charlotte behind a door marked 'CATION UITE', which was either the Latin name of a very specific trilobite or a broken sign.

The room was dark and musty. Dark because of the heavy red curtains that hung at the windows, weighing down the aging curtain racks; musty because of the heavy red curtains that hung at the windows, weighing down the aging curtain racks.

'We have power.' Sam had picked one of the many PCs dotted around the room and booted it up.

'A Nimbus Network?' Phil said. 'That takes me back!'

'Let's get some fresh air in here,' Charlotte said, tugging at one of the curtains until it crashed to the floor, kicking up a tsunami of dust that swept across the room.

'I'm not exposing my Zeddy to this kind of pollution,' Phil said. 'I'm going to look around and find somewhere clean to do some typing.'

9

By nightfall, T. Rex and the Ambivalence had been hidden securely in a nearby shed, having evicted a couple of maintenance buggies which were now abandoned at jaunty angles a safe distance from both the shed and the quiet staff room where Phil had set up his ZX81 and immersed himself, once again, in transcribing the Entelechus Hex.

'Where's the next page?' he said suddenly at about 2.30am.

'What?' Sam muttered, half asleep on a dog-eared sofa nearby.

'The next page of the code,' he explained. 'Pass it over.'

'I haven't got any,' she replied, looking around to be sure.

'Oh,' he said, surprised. 'I guess I finished then.'

'You've typed the whole thing in?' Sam was suddenly alert and searching around Phil's desk, just to make sure.

'I guess so,' Phil said. 'Wait, stop, don't touch anything!'

Sam stopped mid-rummage and looked at him quizzically.

'Don't move!' Phil said. 'He can't see us if we don't move.'

'What?' Sam gave him her best 'are you mental?' look.

'What?' Phil repeated in the manner of someone quite sure of his sanity.

Sam stepped carefully away from the desk, while

Phil gingerly typed the save command and set the tape recording, before silently ushering Sam out of the room to watch from a safe distance.

'I see you've made yourselves at home,' a quiet voice in the other doorway said.

'Nectarine?' Phil guessed.

'I'm Doctor Nectarine,' the tall figure silhouetted in the doorway replied in the husky, obviously disguised voice of a superhero.

Or supervillain, Phil reminded himself.

'Can this wait? I haven't slept in about 3000 lines. I'm seeing double at the moment and liable to pass out if I have to stay on my feet for too long.'

'If it could wait, would I be hanging around here at three in the morning?'

Phil glanced at Sam. 'It's 3am?'

'Uh-huh.'

'Look, I don't know your hobbies or personal kinks. How would I know what you're doing hanging around the reception building of an extinct dinosaur park at three in the morning?'

'Ok, chill out,' Nectarine said.

'Look, just tell us whatever you came here to tell us, and we'll deal with it after a few hours' sleep.'

'I have the location of the Assembly,' he said.

'Good job,' Phil said. 'Bring it to me after sunrise and I'll get you a 99 or something, ok?'

'If that's what you want.'

'Yeah, it really is.'

A

'Um, Phil…'

Phil was woken partly by the sense of urgency in Sam's voice and partly by the sharp prod in the ribs, which turned out to have been administered by his favourite daughter.

'Guys, I've done my bit, can I just get some sleep now please?'

'You can sleep later.'

Phil jerked upright at the sound of a man's voice he didn't recognise.

At some point, while he had been asleep, the room had filled with the sort of people who wore suits and went everywhere in formation; specifically, there was one small, serious looking man in a sharp suit, flanked by a large, serious looking man in a suit to one side and a tall, serious looking woman in a suit to the other.

'Who are you supposed to be?' Phil asked. 'The Fairy Godfather?'

The small man stepped forward. 'We represent the Assembly of Newly Uplifted Systems.'

Phil did some mental acrostics and raised an eyebrow at the man. 'Really?' he said.

'Really,' the short man said simply.

'You didn't think…' Phil started, then said, 'never mind.'

'Is there a problem?'

'No no,' Phil said. 'Please, go on.'

'As I said, we represent the Assembly of Newly Uplifted Systems. And we believe there is something here that belongs with us.' He spoke with a slightly threatening manner and a gentle Lancastrian accent, as if Fred Dibnah's more urbane offspring had joined the Illuminati at some point.

'Oh? And what is that?' he asked. 'You know, just in case I have seen it.'

The short man eyed Phil suspiciously. 'Put them with the others,' he said to his goons, apparently oblivious to bad guy clichés. 'Then search the room.'

It should have been no great surprise to Phil and Sam that they ended up back in the dark and musty CATION UITE room with Benny, Charlotte, and the out of service Nimbus PCs.

'What the frak is going on?' he demanded, because clearly this was all Benny's fault.

'Don't worry,' Sam soothed. 'If his Royal Shortness out there carries on the way he has been, he'll explain it all to us in great detail before consigning us to our doom.'

'Oh, you can count on that,' Benny said.

'You know him?' Phil asked.

Benny nodded. 'Viktor Wendig. He was a founder member of the cartel, back in the day.'

'And what about Grell and Fella behind him?'

Benny shrugged. 'Them I don't know. Probably just hired muscle.'

'You were right then,' Sam said. 'He is with the Assembly now.'

'He told you that?'

Sam nodded. 'The Assembly of Newly Uplifted Systems, or something.'

'Sound like a bunch of assholes.'

'Almost certainly,' Phil agreed.

'How did they find us?' Charlotte said.

'I don't know, Charlie,' Phil turned on her. 'Who else knew we were holed up here?'

'Charlotte,' she reminded him.

'Easy Phil,' Sam said. 'Even if it was him, Charlotte wasn't to blame.'

'Wait, you think Doc Nectarine told them where we are?' Charlotte said.

'Either him or one of us in this room,' Phil said. 'And I don't feel like playing Cluedo.'

'Why would you think that?' Charlotte said. 'Doc Nectarine has nothing to gain from handing us over to the bad guys.'

'Maybe he doesn't know they're bad guys,' Sam suggested. 'You haven't exactly been an open book about this whole situation, have you?'

'Oh, so it's my fault now?'

'Guys, guys!' Benny interrupted. 'Can't you be a little more British about this? This fighting is so…'

'Colonial?' Phil suggested.

'I was going to say irritating.'

'Alright,' Phil sat down, rubbing his head in case clarification appeared like a genie. 'They're here, they've almost certainly found the Zeddy by now, which means they could load up the hex any minute and… let it do whatever it's supposed to do. What is that, anyway?'

'Pretty much anything they want it to do,' Benny said.

'Why do I keep you around again?'

Benny pointed at the locked door. 'Absence of choice.'

Of course, the door chose that moment to open,

allowing Grell and Fella to come in and give them a choice - and then force them to take it.

They were led through to the garage where the Ambivalence and T. Rex had been quietly minding their own business. It smelt faintly of rust and very old bicycle grease.

'What are we doing here?' Sam said quietly.

Viktor Wendig stepped out from the shadows. 'Believe me, if I could have left you out of this, I would have done,' he smarmed. 'Unfortunately, our mutual friend here-' he nodded towards a figure duct taped to a chair in another corner of the garage.

'Is that…?' Sam whispered.

'Nectarine?' Benny said out loud.

'Told you,' Phil muttered.

Charlotte slapped him.

'Is that what he calls himself?' Wendig said. 'Well, as proficient a hacker as he is, unfortunately he doesn't have the specific talent we require.'

'I'm not doing it,' Benny said flatly.

'Oh, but you already have done it, Mr Stetson. I merely need you to be present for the grand switch on.'

'Switch on of what?' Charlotte asked.

'The Entelechus, of course,' Wendig replied with a grin that made Charlotte cringe.

'In a barn?' Benny said. 'Is this some British tradition I haven't encountered yet?'

Phil watched as Grell climbed up into the back of the Ambivalence, emerging a moment later with an innocent looking ZX81 and an all too familiar cassette tape.

'I guess you thought we wouldn't look for it here,'

Wendig gestured at the Ambivalence. 'You should not underestimate us, Mr Grundy.'

Phil flashed his most sarcastic smile at the odious little git.

Without taking his eyes off Phil, Wendig clicked his fingers, and Fella trotted over, holding out a small, nondescript little plastic box, with the unmistakable protrusion of a Sinclair edge connector.

'What's that?' Charlotte asked.

Phil rolled his eyes, despairing at his latest parenting fail. 'Some kind of accessory for the ZX81. Presumably related to the Hex I spent all last night typing in for him.'

Viktor Wendig produced a remote control from somewhere, and a TV warmed up on a workbench; around it, Phil noticed a ZX power supply and a tape deck.

'Bring the American forward.'

Grell nudged Benny, and he reluctantly shuffled forward.

'That's close enough,' Wendig said. 'Close enough to affect the chuntey without being able to physically stop the hex from running.'

'You do realise that chuntey is a completely fictitious and made up thing, right?' Phil said.

'Is it?' Wendig said, deadpan, then turned back towards the ZX81.

Wendig had indeed plugged a device resembling a RAM pack into the ZX81; Phil had become quite attached to the little guy over the last couple of days, and felt violated on its behalf.

'Run it,' Wendig said once the computer had fired up.

While Wendig's back was turned, Sam leaned in and whispered to Phil. 'While Fella's got his hands full with Benny-'

'That's Grell,' Phil said.

'What?'

'The one marking Benny is Grell,' he repeated. 'Fella's the headmistressy one trying to figure out Sir Clive's keyword entry system.'

Sam glanced across, and sure enough, the slightly more feminine of Wendig's henchpeople was staring at the keyboard, her face loading a puzzled expression.

'Press J, then shift P twice,' Wendig snapped. 'Then start the tape. Carefully!'

'So you're telling me Grell's the fella, and Fella's the girl?' Sam whispered.

Phil shrugged. 'Yeah?'

'Wha- How- Whaaa…?'

'Don't try and understand him,' Charlotte said.

'What do we do now?' Fella said.

'You might as well go and get some coffee or something,' Wendig said. 'It could take a while to load this up.'

Phil and Benny - against his better judgement - were watching intently to see what would happen when they ran the code.

Charlotte went and sat down on a metal chest marked 'Hazardous Chemicals', largely indifferent to goings on around the ZX81.

Sam slipped off and cut the tape from around Nectarine's wrists and ankles.

No one went for coffee.

'Seriously,' Wendig repeated. 'Stop crowding me, and get some coffee.'

'But I don't want coffee,' Fella protested.

'I don't care,' Wendig growled. 'I want coffee — get out of my face and find me one!'

The woman grumbled and barged past Phil and Benny, apparently in search of caffeinated beverages.

Phil stayed just far enough out of Wendig's face that they could both get on with the task at hand - which was the rather tedious business of watching a ZX81 loading a program with no idea what, if anything, it would do if it actually succeeded.

When - in blatant disregard of whatever feminist streak had led her into a career as a henchperson - Fella returned with coffee, black and white lightning flashes still filled the screen, and the sound of data transfer still filled the air, as the fruits of Phil's last three days was loaded back into the ZX81's memory.

Viktor Wendig took the aforementioned coffee without so much as a thank you.

Then the noise stopped, and the TV screen went blank.

B

Several things happened then.

Something exploded. There was no noise to speak of, at least not a bang, but a flash that left Phil blinded for a moment and made Wendig lurch, spilling some of his coffee before crashing to the floor in an undignified heap.

Phil thought he heard again the high-pitched data squeal of a program loading from tape, but that could have been tinnitus caused by the explosion.

Sam and Charlotte hurried forward with stunned expressions on their faces, and promptly vanished.

At least, that was the way it seemed to Phil, but then they reappeared a few moments later. Unfortunately, the rest of the garage had vanished by then.

'What the hell was that?' Wendig said, picking himself up and dusting down his suit.

'I'm guessing the load wasn't 100% successful?' Benny said.

'Well...' Phil started, but was interrupted by furious shouting.

'What the hell just happened?' Charlotte was shouting. 'What have you done? Where are we?'

'OK, one question at a time,' Phil said, running his hands through his hair. 'In fact, forget that, what do you mean, 'Where are we'?'

'Have you looked outside, Phil?'

'What?' he said, looking outside properly for the first time. 'Oh my god...'

Phil scrambled up to the window - or, to where the

widow used to be - and looked outside. Or, where outside used to be. 'Where the hell are we?' he said.

'I believe I asked that first,' Charlotte said.

Phil climbed up onto the workbench and jumped down on the other side, where the garage wall should have been.

'There's nothing here,' he said, his voice echoing against walls he couldn't make out. 'It's all just... white. And a little bit fuzzy. Like there's been a really heavy and slightly out of focus snowfall.'

'On the plus side,' Sam said, 'the computer works.'

'It does?' Wendig sounded surprised. 'You mean I didn't blow it up?'

'Blow it up?' Phil looked from Wendig to the ZX81 and back again. 'What do you mean blow it up?'

'I didn't blow it up.' Wendig set the remains of his coffee down on the bench beside the ZX81.

'Did you spill coffee on my ZX81?'

'It's my ZX81.' Wendig stretched himself to his full five feet one and tried to assert some control over the situation.

'Um, guys?' Benny interrupted them. 'Can we discuss ownership after we've established what program it's running?'

Phil climbed back over the bench; he could have walked around it now most of the walls had been erased, but that would have been less cool. The ZX81 was, indeed, still working. 'Choose the form of the destructor,' he read from the screen.

'What does that mean?' Sam said. 'Are we playing some kind of game?'

Wendig cackled quietly. 'Some kind, yes.'

The screen refreshed, adding a single word below

the previous sentence: CHOOSE

'Well, can we see the instructions?' Phil said.

CHOOSE

'That's weird,' Phil said.

CHOOSE

'And it don't look good,' Charlotte added quietly.

'Wait, what?'

CHOOSE

'Not you, Captain RAM Pack.' Phil ducked closer to Charlotte and whispered to her, 'Are you suggesting what I think you're suggesting?'

'It's like your favourite movie, Dad-'

'Well, top three anyway.'

'Dad, focus.'

Phil nodded and turned back to Sam and Benny. 'Ok, we need to empty our minds. Whatever we think of - if we think of Henry Hoover, a Henry Hoover will appear and... suck us all up or something, ok? So don't think of anything.'

THE CHOICE IS MADE

'Oh come on!' Charlotte said. 'We didn't choose anything! Dad?'

'You know me,' he said. 'My mind is always blank.'

'Did you choose anything?'

'Not me,' said Sam.

'Well I didn't choose anything!' Charlotte said. 'And why the hell am I shouting at a ZX81?' she asked herself.

'Um, girls?'

Sam and Charlotte turned back to Phil, who nodded towards a very sheepish looking Benny.

'Oh balljoints,' Sam said. 'What did you do, cowboy?'

'I couldn't help it,' he whimpered. 'It just popped in there.'

'What just popped in there?'

'I tried to think of the most harmless thing...' he glanced over at Sam's Mini.

'You chose her car?' Phil said.

'It's so quaint and... British. It could never harm anyone.'

'It's called T. Rex,' Charlotte pointed out.

'Oh.'

'Nice thinkin', Tex,' Phil said. 'This could go several ways now.'

'I'm hoping for death by glam rock,' Sam said.

'Kill me now,' Charlotte muttered.

'Oh no,' Phil said.

'What?' Benny said, hoping for some reprieve from the evil stares he was getting.

'Tell me you don't see that?' Phil pointed discreetly at Wendig's coffee mug.

'World's Best Boss?' Benny frowned at Wendig. 'You've changed, man.'

'Inside the mug,' Phil said.

Benny looked closer. Inexplicably, Sam and Charlotte also leant over to see what was happening to Wendig's coffee.

'That don't look good either,' Charlotte said, as a ripple spread out across the cooling coffee.

'Is Jurassic Park in your top three?' Sam asked.

'Not any more.'

'If anyone's interested,' Sam said, 'I've got the keys to a Mini 1275GT in my pocket, and I'm not afraid to use them.'

And on that note, she ran across to her car, feeling

for the right key as she went, and slotting it easily into the keyhole in an oft-rehearsed move.

The Mini's alarm went off, distracting Viktor Wendig for just long enough to allow Phil to barge past and run for the Mini, followed by Benny, who ran straight into the waiting arms of Grell and Fella.

'Phil!' Sam yelled. 'Get the door!'

Phil looked at where she was pointing. Walls were building up around them again; not as they had been, but bland, blocky creations, like the world was being 3d printed around them. The roller shutter door, however, was firmly in place - Phil ran to hit the ASCII art switch on the wall beside it.

Sam fired up the GT then, the rasp of its enthusiastic exhaust echoing around the rapidly enclosing garage (along with the still blaring alarm siren) in the hope of disorientating some bad guys.

As the door rolled slowly upwards, Phil looked around for Charlotte; unfortunately, when he spotted her she was struggling distastefully in Grell's grasp.

'We need to go, Phil!' Sam shouted as he started towards his daughter. 'We all need to go!'

'I can't leave Charlie!'

'Charlotte!' she shouted as Grell and Fella were bundling her and Benny into the Ambivalence.

'Come on, Philip!' Sam shouted. 'We'll find them later. But we need to go, now!'

'I'll come back for you!' Phil shouted towards Charlotte, before running for Sam's car.

He was barely in the passenger seat before Sam launched the tiny vehicle out of the garage, the roof mounted aerial twanging against the still opening door.

'What was that?' Phil said as a vast shadow

crossed over them.

'You don't want to know.' Sam kept her eyes firmly ahead and pointed the Mini down a narrow avenue between two tall and still growing walls.

There was a crash somewhere behind them, barely audible over the mobile cacophony that they had become.

Phil looked back over his shoulder, but could see nothing but a plume of dust billowing up over the grey walls behind them.

Soon they outran the 3D printed world, and Sam pulled into a shady nook between the Shoposaurus and Ice Age Ices, cut the engine, and got out of the car.

A moment later the alarm stopped, and a welcome silence fell. Then it got up again and backed away from the deep rhythmic thuds that were happening elsewhere in the park.

'That wasn't the Marcmallow Man, was it?' Phil said as Sam got back in the car.

'Marc Bolan? I doubt it very much.'

Phil's next thought was interrupted by a distorted, melancholy guitar riff from Sam's pocket.

'It's Charlotte,' she said. 'Texting,' she added, as Phil's expression begged for clarity. 'At least,' she said as she read the message, 'it's Charlotte's number. I'm not sure they're her words, though.'

'What does it say?'

Sam showed him the message.

'Well, that's not sinister at all, is it?'

C

'I've lost my phone!' Charlotte hissed, fumbling around under the Ambivalence's bench seats.

Grell was standing guard outside the back of the van, while Fella sat in the driving seat fiddling with the radio. It was fairly ineffective and could only pick up Radio 4; a fact which had gone entirely unnoticed by Benny, who just assumed that was what British radio sounded like.

'Shall I try ringing it?' Benny whispered.

Charlotte shrugged. 'What's the worst that could happen?'

'What's your number?'

'Oh seven nine two,' she whispered.

'Oh seven five-'

'Nine.'

'Oh seven five nine-'

'No, oh seven nine-'

'Oh seven nine five-'

'No five!'

'Oh five-'

'Where are you getting this five from?'

'Which one?'

'It doesn't matter! There's not one in my number!'

'No, there's at least two.'

'What are you two up to back there?' Fella growled from the front seat.

'Nothing,' Charlotte said innocently.

'Look, take the damn phone before I accidentally dial for fish and chips, eh?'

She took the phone from him and dialled her own

number without another word. 'It's ringing,' she whispered once it connected.

They both peered out of the windows for any sign of its tell-tale glow, but the dim grey light in what was left of the garage wasn't giving anything away.

'Hello?' said the voice on the other end of the phone.

'Wait, what?' Charlotte said.

'Who's that?'

'Er, the person whose phone you're using.' Charlotte used as much sarcasm as she could muster at low volume.

'Moon Caster?' the voice said.

'Moon Caster?' Benny repeated.

'Shut up.' Charlotte said. Then, into the phone, 'Who's that? And how do you know my handle?'

'It's Doc Nectarine.'

'Nectarine?' she exclaimed. 'What the hell are you doing with my phone?'

'Well at the moment, having a pointless conversation with you.'

'Look, where are you?'

'Well… I was hiding out in a grubby little rest room-'

'Eww!' Benny said.

'Learn English, Tex,' Charlotte said. 'Over here, rest rooms have settees.'

'How very British,' Benny said. 'Next you'll be telling me you drink tea in there.'

'Well yes, but-'

'Not in this one,' Nectarine said.

'It's that grubby?'

'Well, that and the fact that I blinked a few minutes

ago and whole place turned grey and… well, pixelated, I guess.'

'Yeah, that happened to all of us,' Charlotte said.

'Although the calendar has become quite an impressive piece of ASCII art.'

'I can imagine,' Charlotte said.

'Imaginative use of the ampersand.'

'Eyes front, soldier.'

'Er, yeah, sorry. Do you know what's going on?'

'They've run the Entelechus,' Benny explained. 'And locked us in the back of the Ambivalence so we miss the fun.'

'In English?'

'The bad guys have stuck us in the back of a van while they play video games,' Charlotte said. 'If you can call them video games, that is.'

'What kind of games?' Nectarine asked.

'Don't know,' Benny said. 'We can't see the screen from here.'

'Can you get closer to the screen?' Charlotte asked Nectarine. 'Maybe you could tell us what they're up to?'

'I don't know if you remember, but those guys strapped me to a chair with duct tape not too long ago,' Nectarine said. 'It wasn't a particularly comfortable chair, either.'

'I don't know if you remember,' Benny countered, 'but the entire building has been pixelated, and that is intimately connected to whatever that computer is doing.'

'Do you think it can be undone?'

'Yes,' Benny said, 'but I need to see it to figure out how.'

'Besides,' Charlotte said, 'you sold us out to these douchebags, you owe us!'

'Hey, I delivered the Assembly, just as asked,' he protested. 'If anything, you owe me. At the very least I was promised a 99.'

'Oh for the love of... this is not an ice-cream van!' Benny said, rather too loudly.

'Hey, you two stop planning a revolution back there!' Fella shouted.

'Look, you just better be grateful that Doc Nectarine is a thoroughly nice bloke,' Nectarine whispered. 'I'll be there in a moment.'

Then the line went dead.

A moment later, Nectarine was crouched at the back door of the Ambivalence, showing Charlotte a sequence of text messages apparently being sent from her phone.

REX LIES IN WAIT

'What does that mean?' Charlotte showed the message to Benny.

'It must mean the destructor,' Benny said.

'Well, you'd know…'

'Ok, let's not dwell on that.'

'So what, is he controlling the destructor from the ZX81?' Charlotte gestured towards Viktor Wendig, still standing at the computer and rubbing his hands with evil glee.

Doc Nectarine nodded. 'And he's hijacked your phone number to torment his prey.'

HE IS HUNTING FOR YOU

'Wait a minute,' Phil said as he read the next

message. 'These messages aren't as random as they seem.'

'You'll have to tell me later,' Sam said, getting into the car quickly. 'Legoland is on the march again.'

Phil turned to see those dull white walls building up along each side of the road behind them.

Sam wasted no time in starting the engine, and roared off down the narrow road, g-force pushing Phil back into the ill-fitting passenger seat.

Even at the break-neck pace Sam managed to achieve, the background weirdness quickly overtook them.

'Ok wisdom guy,' Sam shouted over the engine noise. 'What's going on? What are those messages, and do they have anything to do with the claustrophobia I'm suddenly developing?'

'Well, I can't speak for your claustrophobia, but-' Phil was interrupted by another text arriving.

FOOTSTEPS APPROACHING

'The messages are straight out of 3D Monster Maze,' he finished.

The mini screeched to a halt as a wall sprung up in front of it.

'As, I'm guessing, is the maze?' Sam said backing up quickly.

'Yes,' Phil said grimly. 'And the-'

'Don't say it,' Sam interrupted. 'Please.'

'Alright then. Just keep your eye out for an exit,' he said. 'And a Tyrannosaurus rex.'

HE IS HUNTING FOR YOU

'Take it easy, we're in the clear at the moment,' Phil said.

'All these sodding right angles, he could be hiding

behind any one of them.'

'Not to mention it's completely disorientating.'

'Yeah, every damn wall is identical,' Sam agreed. 'We might never find the others again.'

'Oh, we'll find them,' Phil said with all the determination of Liam Neeson in Taken.

FOOTSTEPS APPROACHING

'Stop,' Phil said. 'Stop the engine!'

The mini skidded to a halt again. Phil held his finger to his lips in a shushing motion and slowly wound down the window next to him. It squeaked, the tiny noise echoing painfully between the high walls on either side of them.

Phil leant out of the window, looking ahead and behind them, listening for those footsteps. Soon enough, he heard them, great stomping, shuddering booms that echoed through the maze, effectively shrouding the monster's location.

'I think it's that way,' he whispered.

Sam nodded, started the car, and quietly backed up, turning around at a handy corner and driving – she hoped – away from the destructor as sedately as T. Rex was able.

REX HAS SEEN YOU

'Crap,' Phil said. 'He's onto us.'

'Where?'

'No idea. I'll keep watching.'

'What's that over there?'

Phil jerked around, but it was just the reception building. 'The hub,' he said. 'Head for it - maybe we'll find Charlie.'

'Well we certainly can't go around here all day.'

Sam turned the car cautiously in the direction of

the hub and began to weave through the complex web of right angles that stood between them and their friends and family.

'Don't hang around,' Phil said. 'I think I can hear it.'

'Hear it?' Sam said. 'I can feel its footsteps through the damn steering wheel!'

RUN HE IS BESIDE YOU

'Go, he's close!' Phil screamed.

Sam dropped a gear and wound the revs up, the car suddenly accelerating forward.

RUN HE IS BEHIND YOU

'Well, at least we know where it is!' Sam screamed.

'Put your foot down,' Phil said. 'We'll lose him easy.'

'I intend to,' Sam said. 'That or die trying.'

'Well, if it helps, I heard there's no cooler way to die than in a 1275GT.'

'When Bolan died, he was in T. Rex, not in *a* T. rex.'

'Sam, it's on top-'

There was a crash, and a very pointy letter v tore a hole in the roof behind Phil. The engine raced as the front wheels were lifted off the ground.

'Abandon car!' Phil shouted.

'What?'

'Get out!' Phil unbuckled and opened the door. 'Now!'

Reluctantly, Sam followed suit, jumping to the ground as a hideous dinosaur-shaped jumble of blocks and letters lifted her most prized possession into the air.

'Run!' Phil shouted. 'I think it's stuck on its teeth!'

'My car!'

'Is still keeping us alive,' Phil said. 'Now let's get back to the hub, try and find the others before Rex there finds a toothpick the size of an apple tree.'

D

From inside a 30-something year old Dodge Spacevan inside a weirdly pixelated garage, the sounds of a stomping, growling, most probably acid-drooling Tyrannosaurus rex were somewhat muted, but they still made a point. A loud, unpleasant point.

'They need our help,' Charlotte said. 'We have to get out of here and find them!'

'In this?' Nectarine gave her a distasteful look.

'Well there's a ride on lawnmower in the corner if you think that will be better suited to the job,' Charlotte said sarcastically.

Somewhat to his credit, Nectarine glanced across at it, said, 'I'll go look for the keys,' and sloped off towards the corner.

'He's mad,' Charlotte said to no one in particular.

'Hey, where are you going!' Grell (or was it Fella? Charlotte had lost track) shouted after him, getting out to follow him.

As soon as their guard was a good distance from the van, Benny pulled the spare key from his pocket and climbed over into the front seat.

Charlotte jumped out of the back, ran over to the door and hit the ASCII art button which set the roller shutter creaking and rattling up over the Ambivalence, which was now advancing on it. Charlotte was just about to make a return jump toward the open front door when Fella grabbed her.

Benny stopped the van, and was about to try something hugely heroic, but Charlotte shouted 'No! Go and find Dad and Sam, before they get turned into dino snacks.'

Benny hesitated for a moment.

'Go! Please!' Charlotte shouted before she was silenced by Fella's multi-purpose duct tape.

Benny did his best to look anguished as Fella dragged Charlotte away, but as soon as the shutter had rolled up far enough, the Ambivalence stuttered majestically out into the open.

Phil and Sam scrambled to their feet, hurrying away from the dentally impaired lizard behind them.

'Listen!' Sam said, suddenly stopping mid-sprint.

'What?'

'It's the Ambivalence,' Sam said. 'I'd recognise that engine note anywhere.'

Phil could barely hear anything over the clamouring of his heart trying to climb up his oesophagus.

'This way,' Sam said.

Phil shrugged, and followed, if only because the alternative was ten tons of pixels with toothache.

A low boom echoed through the maze, and the ground vibrated beneath them. 'He's moving again,' Phil said.

'Not far now,' Sam panted as she led him around yet another anonymous right angle.

RUN HE IS BEHIND YOU

'Oh, do shut up,' Phil said, and threw the phone behind him, where it hit an already miffed monster square in the eye.

A roar filled the air which didn't so much chill his spine as soak it in liquid nitrogen and plant it in the Antarctic.

'Oh crap,' Phil said, suddenly too afraid to run any further.

Just then the Ambivalence lurched around the corner, almost flattening Sam before coming to a halt right in front of the Tyrannosaurus.

Benny backed away from the startled monster, stopped briefly for Sam and Phil to climb in, then reversed away as quickly as he could.

'Nice timing, cowboy,' Sam said.

Phil looked over his shoulder into the back of the van. 'Where's Charlie?'

'Back at the garage.'

'You'll never find your way through this maze,' Phil said.

'Course I will.' Benny grinned at him. 'I left a trail of breadcrumbs.'

As Benny reversed around a corner, Phil spotted a trail of black marks stretching out along the road in front of them.

'What… How did you do that?'

'She's not just a pretty face, you know,' Benny grinned smugly.

'It's engine oil,' Sam muttered. 'The old thing leaks so much, it's left a trail.'

'Hey, don't knock it!'

'Wouldn't dare,' Sam said.

'If it works, I'll take it,' Phil said.

The Ambivalence was a little unsteady around the sharp corners that made up the maze, but luckily no more so than the monster that patrolled it, which slipped two or three times as they fled back towards the garage in the hope it would provide them with enough shelter from the oncoming storm.

Before Benny had stopped the Ambivalence, Phil had slid open the front door and jumped out to accost Viktor Wendig.

'Alright Wendig, you win,' he said. 'What do you want? Wait... where the hell has he gone?'

'He stole my idea.' Doc Nectarine's disguised voice came from a doorway at the side of the garage. 'And the lawnmower. They've all run for it, left that monster to run free.'

Right on cue, a blood curdling roar ripped through the air again, and the monster poked its blocky head out of the entrance to the maze.

Benny hit the button and the roller shutter door rolled shut behind them.

'Somehow, I don't think that will be enough,' Sam said solemnly.

'Where's Charlie?' Phil said.

Sam wandered over to the window and looked out at the patiently advancing dinosaur. 'Wait a minute...' she said to herself.

'What are you doing?' Phil asked.

'You might want to look away,' she replied, reaching across the bench.

There was a thump, and everything went black.

After a few moments, lights began to flicker on again inside the garage. Outside, night had fallen, and the abandoned theme park was once again lit only by stars and moon. Everyone was silent, listening intently for the dulcet tones of a digitised dinosaur.

There was a mighty crash, and a small purple

vehicle stood, momentarily, on its nose, dropped from the too small jaw of a fibre glass tyrannosaur, and then fell back onto its wheels, broken and very, very sad.

'My car!' Sam, it seemed, had also opened her eyes, tentatively, but all the tentativity in the world wouldn't stop a Mini owner getting incredibly upset at such blatant abuse of her beloved. 'I've had that car for ten years,' she said quietly. 'I was only its third owner.'

'Um,' Phil said, thinking he should say something, but with no idea what. 'Sorry for your loss.'

Sam grunted something in reply and then turned away, not wanting to look.

'What did you just do?' Phil asked.

Sam pointed to the bench, where the ancient black and white TV was just warming up again to show the simple ▇ that indicated the ZX81 was powered up and awaiting instructions.

Phil stepped toward it; next to the ZX81 was a hefty four ring binder, bearing upon its cover the words "Commer PB Workshop Manual."

'Oops,' Sam said, affecting an air of innocence. 'Butterfingers!'

Phil chuckled. 'Brilliant,' he said. 'Drop a two thousand page hardback on the same bench and crash the system. I can't believe I didn't think of it myself!'

A single, slow clap echoed from the shadowy far corner of the building.

Phil turned to see Viktor Wendig getting out of what he now saw was a black Volkswagen van parked up in the shadows, Grell and Fella once again taking up positions at his sides.

'Oh great,' Sam said. 'Captain Cliché is back.'

'I thought you lot had gone to mow the lawns?' Benny said.

'In the dark?' Wendig paced evenly across the garage. 'No, merely waiting for the first test to reach its conclusion.'

'Sorry, I might have interrupted that,' Sam said.

'Not at all,' Wendig said. 'The test was 100% successful. I thank you for participating.'

E

Wendig made a subtle gesture to his henchpersons, and Fella shrunk back into the darkness behind them.

When she emerged a moment later, she was shoving before her a pale, black clad young woman with her hands and mouth adorned with duct tape.

'Charlie!'

'Mmmm-mmmmm!' Charlotte scowled at him from behind the duct tape.

'Charlotte, sorry,' Phil said. 'Are you ok? Have they hurt you?'

'Mm mmmm mmmm mmm mmmm mmmm mmmm mm.' Charlotte held out her taped up wrists, just in case her point needed any further emphasis.

'Let her go,' Benny said, his voice bearing an undertone of being hacked off with Wendig's shenanigans.

'I'm not sure I can do that,' Wendig said, his voice barely more than a whisper.

Phil sighed. 'What do you want?'

'I'll take that ZX81 for a start.' Wendig nodded, and Grell started toward it.

'You don't need that.' Benny stepped in front of the big man.

'Maybe not,' Wendig said, 'but I believe the, um, RAM pack is mine.'

'I'll get it for you,' Benny said, without taking his eyes off Grell.

'Make sure you-' Phil started.

'Switch the power off first,' Benny said. 'I have used a ZX81 before.'

'Sorry,' Phil muttered.

Benny duly switched off the ZX81 and carefully removed the so-called memory expansion, reading the label - K-Tech Real Time - as he did so.

'Not your average RAM pack,' he muttered as he passed Phil.

'Let her go,' Phil said to Wendig, 'and you can have your little accessory back.'

'You're not in a strong bargaining position,' Wendig said, pointing subtly at Charlie.

Much as he hated the idea, Phil had to admit he sort of had a point.

'Let the girl go,' Benny said. 'Take me instead.'

'What?' Sam said.

'What?' Phil agreed.

'Mmmm?' Charlotte said.

'You can't go with them,' Phil whispered. 'You're the...' Rather than say it aloud, he tried to eye mime the word, almost making himself permanently cross eyed.

'I know what I am,' Benny said to put him out of his misery.

'Then you know we need you away from the Assembly.'

'No,' he whispered, 'there is another.'

Wendig cleared his throat in an obvious manner.

'Me and your peripheral here, in exchange for the girl,' Benny said. 'Do we have a deal?'

'Very well,' Wendig agreed, giving Charlotte a nudge toward the middle of the room.

Benny pulled a bunch of keys on a Lego spaceman keyring from his pocket and handed them to Phil. 'Look after the Ambivalence.'

'Um… ok…'

'And make sure the Zeddy works.'

'Sure,' Phil said, slightly baffled by Benny's last requests.

Benny nodded at Phil, then strode purposefully across the room.

Fella shoved Charlotte forward, and grabbed Benny roughly by the elbow in exchange.

Phil caught Charlotte in his arms as Benny was escorted over to the other van, lurking in the shadows like the Ambivalence's evil twin.

'Sam, get the Zeddy,' Phil said. 'Hook it up inside the van. Benny seemed to think it was important.'

'Maybe it still has the Hex?'

Phil ushered Charlotte into the van, and started gently extricating her from the duct tape while Sam set up the ZX81.

'Is it supposed to do that?' she asked.

Phil glanced up. 'Well, not unless you told it to.'

'I didn't.'

Phil stared closer at the single word on the screen in front of them:

GREETINGS.

'Mmmmm!'

'Oh, sorry Charlie.'

'Mmmm-mmmmm!'

'Charlotte, sorry.'

'Phil!'

'What!?'

'It wants to play a game,' Sam said.

'I'm kinda tied-' Charlotte glared at him. 'Busy,' he finished.

'Let me untie Charlotte; your computer is freaking

me out.'

Charlotte nodded eagerly.

'Alright,' Phil said, trading places with Sam.

WOULD YOU LIKE TO PLAY A GAME?

'You seriously didn't do anything?' Phil asked.

'Just plugged it in like you asked,' Sam said from behind Charlotte.

'Well, just don't start playing Global Thermonuclear War.'

HOW ABOUT 3D MONSTER MAZE?

The words appeared on the screen as if typed by unseen hands.

'I've played enough of that to last a lifetime, buddy,' Phil said. 'Wouldn't you prefer a nice game of chess?' Phil typed the question as he spoke it.

FINE. 1K OR 16K CHESS?

'Who is this?' Phil asked, peering closely at the innocent looking little computer on the bench.

I AM DEXY, YOUR FRIENDLY NEIGHBOURHOOD ZX81.

'Wait, you can hear me?' Phil exclaimed. 'Now I'm getting freaked out!'

Sam had freed Charlotte's hands and was looking at the screen, while Charlotte removed the unpleasantly effective tape from across her face.

'Did the Entelechus do that?' Sam asked.

'A force directing growth and life,' Phil nodded. 'It actualised a ZX81.'

'Right,' Charlotte said once she was able to make full use of her vocal chords again. 'I'm gonna make that cockfoster regret doing that!'

And before Phil could react, Charlotte was stomping toward the Assembly's van.

'Charlie!'

'Charlotte!'

'Both of you, come back here before you get taped up again!'

Phil and Sam chased Charlotte across the garage, but she was yanking open the van's back door as they reached her.

'How rude!' Wendig said, staring at them.

Grell and Fella started to rise, but Wendig seated them with a gesture.

'It doesn't matter now,' he said. 'The program is running.'

'What program?' even as Phil spoke, he noticed a ZX81 set up in the back of Wendig's van, much like his own, but this one now had the K-Tech Real Time device plugged into it. It was also starting to spark, then lightning surrounded the tiny keyboard like an 80s film effect.

'Never mind,' Phil said. 'I think we'll just let bygones be bygones and leave you to it…'

Phil grabbed Charlotte and dragged her back toward the Ambivalence in the hope it would offer some protection from whatever sorcery Wendig was working in his van.

Doc Nectarine had helped himself to a seat in the Ambivalence, but at least had the decency to help Sam and Charlotte up into the van when they ran over. Phil followed, glaring at Nectarine as he closed the doors behind them until the 80s lightning effect in the far corner of the garage, now completely covering the Assembly's van, distracted him.

Then it exploded.

F

The explosion - Phil was reminded of the sonic booms and trails of flame in the Back to the Future movies, in that this was nothing at all like that - was followed by a sudden, all-encompassing silence. An eerie silence that seemed to stretch into eternity, moments passing that way, as the world anticipated the inevitable...

In reality, it could only have been a second, if that; but the world slowed, time froze, and then... the world juddered to a halt, time snapped back into place, the ground shivered beneath them, and everything - like, everything, the sky, the Ambivalence, their clothes, the whole nine yards - turned the clearest, most pure and pristine white Phil had ever seen, except of course he still hadn't seen it because he had to close his eyes against the brightness.

Along with his travelling companions, Phil huddled in the back of the Ambivalence, not bearing to look, until he heard a gentle 'crump', as of a Commer PB going over a speed bump as it travelled through time and reality, and felt the bump of the Ambivalence hitting something akin to the real world once again.

Phil slowly opened his eyes, waited for the heavily pixelated spots to clear, and carefully reached up to peer out of the window.

'Where are we?' asked Charlotte.

'Exactly where we were, I think,' Phil said, looking around at the dinosaurs that roamed the area.

Actually, now he came to think about it, the

dinosaurs didn't really roam; they more sort of stood stock still, statue-like; it was the people that roamed, cameras in hands, ice cream in other hands, candy floss or balloons in others.

And the screaming - Phil suddenly became aware that there was, in fact, screaming, off in the background somewhere, now the silence had cleared - was not the abject terror and fear for life and limb that sharing an acre with a herd of velociraptors should, logically, produce; it was more of an adrenaline fuelled form of excitement, as if dinosaur hunting were some kind of extreme sport, or…

'A roller coaster,' he said.

'What?'

'We're on a roller coaster,' Phil explained.

'Well that's just silly,' Charlotte said, in her usual derogatory way, the way teenagers instinctively have with their parents.

'That's as may be,' Phil said, 'but nevertheless, we are on a roller coaster.'

As if to prove his point, he allowed the Ambivalence to be rammed from behind by a stegosaurus themed roller coaster train at just that moment.

'Should we, perhaps, get off?' Sam suggested.

'I'm working on it,' Phil said, climbing over the front seats, fumbling the unfamiliar keys, and failing to get the Ambivalence into gear. 'This thing weighs an absolute ton, we'll never get around that loop!'

Eventually, he did get it into something approaching a useful gear, and managed to pull away before the roller coaster train shoved them unceremoniously along the track to who knew where.

Driving the Ambivalence was something of a roller coaster at the best of times; taking such a wallowing and unpredictable vehicle along the twisting, turning track they were now following seemed somewhat of an unnecessary extension of what was already an unnecessary adrenaline rush.

Nonetheless, they found themselves being chased along the tracks, a cheerful looking stegosaurus pulling a train full of entertained, but slightly terrified, passengers along close behind them.

'Phil?' Sam whispered as the track ahead of them took a sudden turn for the upward. 'We have to get off the tracks. Are your eyes closed?' she added.

'I'm praying,' Phil said, as if that answered everything.

Someone shouted his name. Several someones, in fact. Actually, all the someones. Not just his name, either; they were shouting at him to look what he was bloody well doing and get the van off the sodding roller coaster.

Suddenly snapped back to whatever variant of reality this was, Phil opened his eyes, tried to take in his increasingly bizarre surroundings in a fraction of a second, failed, and yanked the steering wheel to the right anyway, in sheer blind hopefulness.

There was a crash, some bumping, much screaming, and no death.

'STOP!!!' yelled all the someones.

Phil rammed his foot back to the floor again, this time on the other pedal.

It was similarly ineffective, but eventually momentum gave up and found something else to do, and the Ambivalence came to an uncomfortable halt.

'Are we nearly there yet?' Charlotte wisecracked.

Phil finally opened his eyes and looked around. 'Oh crap,' he said, for they were now stuck on the inside of the roller coaster, in a place where only qualified roller coaster engineers had any right to be, and certainly one from which extricating a large retired ambulance, once used for carrying large retired people to and from fun days out quite unlike that which was being had by many at Palaeozoic Park, was going to be an epic task.

'We're going to have to knock another fence out,' Sam said.

'I was afraid that might be the case,' Phil said, looking around for an alternative. 'Unfortunately, this time we may have an audience.'

'Don't worry,' Sam said. 'We can outrun them.'

'We can't run,' Phil said. 'We need the Ambivalence.'

'Good point,' Sam said. 'Well made.'

'So what are we going to do?' Charlotte asked.

'Well,' Phil said, starting the engine. 'We certainly can't sit here all day. Somebody is bound to notice a high-top Dodge Spacevan suddenly having appeared in the middle of their roller coaster.'

'You would think so,' Sam said, 'but nobody seemed that bothered when it literally appeared on the roller coaster.'

'Minds on other things, I imagine,' Phil said.

'Could be,' Sam said. 'Takes a lot of concentration to queue that dedicatedly.'

'Why don't we just hide until it's dark?' Charlotte asked.

'Maybe you missed the part where we have this

high-top Dodge Spacevan to discreetly hide away as well as ourselves?' Phil said. 'You can't just put a Commer in your pocket and hope the security guards think you're pleased to see them, you know.'

'How about over there?' Doc Nectarine pointed to a gap in a bramble thicket about the size, and indeed shape, of a Commer PB, under one of the inner rail loops.

'Worth a look,' Phil said, and started to pick a route through the various bits of scrub and litter and associated debris that lurked in the less accessible bits of under a roller coaster.

When they reached the aforementioned thicket, they found there was, in fact, a nice Dodge width gap between two bushes, almost made to measure, and they parked there, out of sight from the park, and decided to wait until closing time, after which they could probably make something of a run for freedom. Or even a drive for it, if they felt brave enough.

Dark was still in the process of falling when they discovered exactly why their little hiding place had appeared to be so perfectly made to measure.

'What's that?' Charlotte said suddenly.

'That,' Phil said, 'is the reason these paths are almost perfectly Dodge width.'

'What?' Charlotte said.

'It's a Commer PB,' Sam said.

The van was coming along the bumpy, grass strewn concrete lane which led, rather conveniently, from a gate in the ride's outer fence to… well, plainly to their current hiding place, and beyond. 'Get in the van,' he said. 'We need to get moving.'

They all ran for the Ambivalence, Phil the only one not to trip over someone else on his way in. He had the Ambivalence bumbling along the uneven semi-overgrown road before he noticed Sam was still clambering in through the back doors, and braked again, causing her to tumble in and thump into the back of the front seats.

Doc Nectarine, who was just about to jump in through the open front door, instead jumped into the A-pillar and staggered back, cursing and holding a bloodied nose.

'Doppig or goig, bake up your bloody bide!' he said, stepping up into the front seat.

'Is everyone in?' Phil asked once the doors had all closed around them, and the maintenance van was closing in behind them.

'I am,' somebody groaned from the back somewhere.

In the absence of any further response, Phil put the Ambivalence back into gear and put his foot heavily to the floor - which, the Ambivalence being a slightly past its best example of 1970s engineering, had little discernible effect.

'Doppig or goig, bake up your bloody bide!' Doc Nectarine said again.

'Shut up until you can speak English again,' Phil said, keeping his foot planted on the floor until, eventually, the Ambivalence began to shuffle forward again, regretfully not quite as quickly as the maintenance van was approaching from behind, but its slowness was counteracted by Phil's lack of giving a monkeys about the surroundings, the ride under which they were hiding, and indeed his vehicle in comparison to the maintenance team behind him.

'Hold on to something,' he said. 'This could get a little rough.'

'For a change,' Charlotte mumbled.

'Preferably hold onto something other than me,' Phil added, looking pointedly at Doc Nectarine.

'Sorry,' he said, letting go of Phil's arm just in time for him to steer and swerve out of the way of a large and rather sturdy looking pillar, holding up a large and rather scary looking curve on the rollercoaster.

Behind them there was a bang and a creak, as the maintenance van didn't quite miss the same pillar, giving Phil a chance to accelerate away. Well, it would have done if accelerate had been in the Dodge Spacevan handbook.

The Ambivalence continued to rattle ahead, bursting through pointless shrubbery, bouncing over the edges of the paths that criss-crossed the space beneath the roller coaster, until eventually it spilled out onto the main road through the park, and Phil accelerated away from the maintenance van behind them.

'We can't outrun them forever,' Sam pointed out.

Phil had no intention of slowing down even slightly, despite the fact that the Ambivalence was swaying around insanely and making many of its passengers a trifle seasick.

'Those guys have a job to do,' he said, 'but hopefully, once we're out of the park, we're not part of it.'

'There's an exit!' Sam said suddenly.

'Crap!' Phil said, missing the turn and knocking over a plaster Archaeopteryx.

After reversing back over the poor dead dinobird,

he stopped the engine to listen for any sign of the other van coming their way.

'I think we're alone now,' Phil whispered. 'Let's see if we can get out this way.'

It seemed they had found a staff entrance so obscure that the gate didn't even have a padlock; Doc Nectarine graciously held it open as Phil drove through, and closed it again behind them.

'So what do we do now?' Sam asked, once they were cruising sedately along the main road.

'I don't know,' Phil admitted. 'But I suspect we need to find another chip whisperer.'

'What's a chip whisperer?' Nectarine asked.

'I was hoping you might be able to tell us,' Phil said. 'Benny said there was another.'

'I bet he meant you!' Charlotte said, looking up at Nectarine.

'Maybe we should be asking Dexy,' Sam suggested.

'Dexy?' Nectarine looked around, in case he had missed a member of the Ambivalence crew.

Sam pointed at the little Sinclair mounted on the bench. 'We also have a sentient ZX81.'

Doc Nectarine looked at the tiny computer, to which Phil had recently connected a chain of three mismatched peripherals. 'I am way out of my depth here.'

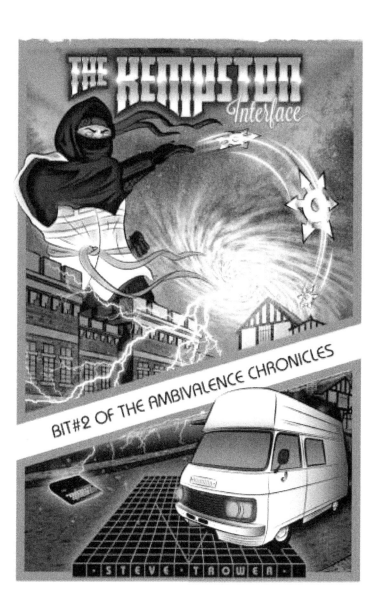

THE KEMPSTON Interface

BIT #2 OF THE AMBIVALENCE CHRONICLES

· S T E V E · T R O W E R · ·

Bit#2: The Kempston Interface

Mission 1: Rin
"Strength of Mind and Body"

Viktor Wendig had upgraded.

That was the first thing Benito 'Benny' Stetson noticed when one of his pet thugs - to whom the names Grell and Fella had inexplicably stuck - finally pulled the sack from over his head.

'What is this place?' Benny glanced around the room, dark but for the glow of a bank of CRT screens against one wall - gone was the functional black on white of the ZX81, replaced with a clash of colours and flashing text so tasteless that only the 1980s could have spawned it.

'This, my friend,' Wendig spoke without looking up, hopping from one screen to the next like the mad scientist he almost certainly was, 'is the spatiotemporal nexus!'

Benny looked around again, the eerie silhouettes of moonlight through Neo-Gothic windows allowing his eyes to become accustomed to the gloom. The chipped plaster and rising damp failed to portray any kind of nexus he could imagine.

'Are you sure?' he said.

'Of course I'm sure!' Wendig snapped, turning from the array of rubber-keyed computing power to glare at

Benny. 'This place has belonged to the Assembly since 1969!'

'Just seems a little… neglected, is all.' Benny made a valiant attempt at a conciliatory shrug, but was hampered somewhat by the fact that he was tied to a rather uncomfortable plastic chair.

'I haven't opened it yet,' Wendig said through gritted teeth.

'Ah,' Benny nodded knowingly. 'Waiting for the Mayor to come with his giant scissors?'

Wendig scowled at Benny and snapped his fingers towards one of the room's more gloomy corners, from whence Grell came scurrying.

'Put him back in his sack,' he said. 'I'm going for a walk.'

And with that, what little light there was was snuffed out.

It had been daylight when they arrived here - wherever here was; Benny probed his memory for any clue as to his current location.

The last thing Benny remembered before being accessorized in sackcloth was the exploding ZX81 back at the old theme park, during which he had been secured in the back of the Assembly's van. He remembered the flash of light, the bang, the rocking of the van… and the next thing he remembered was seeing blue sky and greenery outside, just for a moment, and from then until now it was just the darkness of the inside of a bag.

'Grell?' he called. 'Fella? You guys here?'

'Whaddaya want?' Fella shouted back.

'I'm going crazy here,' Benny said. 'You guys have a pack of cards or something?'

'What for?' Grell said.

'So I can make my BMX sound like a Kawasaki of course, what do you think? I've counted every stitch on the inside of this bag,' he said. 'And given them names. Zanzibar Buck-Buck McFate is, for some reason, not too happy with my company at the moment,' he added.

'So what do you want us to do?'

'A game of Top Trumps maybe?'

'We don't got no cards.'

'We could play something else,' Fella chipped in.

'Yeah?' Benny said. 'We could play I Spy but I'd be at a bit of a disadvantage.'

'You obviously haven't seen his spelling.'

'Hey, I rezent that remmarck!'

'Very droll,' Benny muttered.

''Oo's a troll?'

'If the cap fits…' Fella said.

'Alright alright, quit your yapping already! Wish I'd never said anything now.'

'Do you think he's got any games for…' Fella started.

'What?' Benny said. 'Don't leave me out in the cold now, what are you thinking?'

'Nope,' Grell said. 'Just this bunch of old tapes.'

'Wait, what?'

'You idiot!' Fella said. 'Haven't you been paying any attention?'

'Not really,' Grell admitted.

'Nor me. Better bring the nerd over then.'

'I'm not a nerd,' Benny growled. 'I'm the Chip Whisperer.'

'Whatevs.' Fella yanked the sack from over

Benny's head, and rummaged through a box of old cassettes in front of him. 'You know how to make these things play games or what?'

'Stop!' Benny said suddenly. 'That one.'

'Really?'

Benny nodded. 'Friend of mine told me it's a classic. I'd like to see if he's right.'

Following his instructions, Fella put the tape in the cassette player. After about two minutes of high pitched whining, she figured out how to rewind the tape and started the program loading.

A few more minutes passed, and Benny became aware of someone shaking his chair. He turned around but no-one was there; in fact everything in the room was gently vibrating, and a low rumbling noise seemed to sweep through the room, a baritone compliment to the falsetto squealing of the TV set. A few more bits of plaster fell from the wall, and then silence settled.

Benny looked from Grell to Fella and back again.

'Is it supposed to do that?' he asked.

Before they could reply, a crudely beeped tune announced that their game was ready as soon as they were.

An hour or so outside Palaeozoic Park (Oxfordshire's Premier Prehistoric Attraction), on a B road somewhere on the way to Aylesbury, a high-top Dodge Spacevan with the word 'AMBIVALENCE' illuminated above the windscreen was resting in a lay-by set back from the road.

A young woman dressed in black kicked stones across the lay-by as if they were the ones responsible for her having been dragged out of bed, kidnapped by bad guys, dropped through a hole in the space-time continuum and, to top it all off, forced to try and sleep on the comfort-free bench seats in the back of an aging community ambulance.

'Oh good, you're finally awake,' she said as the driver climbed out of the front of the van and stretched groggily.

'Morning Charlie,' he said.

'Charlotte. Can we go shopping now, Dad? I'm out of bubble gum.'

'And I really need some coffee,' Phil said. 'How's Sam doing?'

Charlotte looked at the sullen figure sat on a boulder nearby with her head in her hands. 'I'll go and talk to her. Where's the Doc?'

'He's still coming to terms with the idea of a sentient ZX81.'

'Aren't we all?' Charlotte made her way over to where Sam was sitting, idly toying with her car keys. 'Sam?'

She looked up and forced a smile for Charlotte. 'What's up?'

'I think we're gonna go foraging for coffee. Dad'll get withdrawal soon otherwise.'

'I can relate to that.'

'Come on Sam, there'll be other cars.'

'Not like Rex.'

'That's probably true.'

'Here,' Sam handed Charlotte a bunch of keys attached to a tiny dinosaur. 'It hurts too much to keep them.'

'Sure,' Charlotte said, tucking them away in her bag.

Assuming crowds ever actually did arrive in Aylesbury town centre, they were still some way off when the Ambivalence crew dismounted and made their way from the car park to the main shopping area.

Phil looked around at the shops, feeling a strange sense of discombobulation, as if there was something slightly... disconnected, about all of this.

'Is it Thursday?' he asked absently.

'I thought you said we were looking for the High Street?' Charlotte said.

'I think this is it,' Phil said looking around.

'Can't be,' Charlotte said. 'There's not a single phone shop in sight. In fact, I haven't heard of most of these shops. What's that about?'

'Yes, that's it,' Phil said. 'I knew there was something wrong here.'

'Fads?' Charlotte said, randomly.

'Could be, I suppose,' Phil said absently. 'I wasn't aware retail had regional fashions, but...'

'No, not fads,' Sam said. 'The paint n paper people. Look,' she was pointing at a shop on the other side of the precinct.

'Well,' Doc Nectarine said. 'If they specialise in interior design, you might have thought they'd have put some effort into their branding and logo.'

'What, like everyone else has, you mean?' said Charlotte, having just rounded a corner ahead of the rest of the group. 'Everything seems rather... brown.'

'They're not all brown,' Sam said, pointing at a

shop front that was mainly blue with large, yellow letters.

'Bejam?' Charlotte said. 'What the heck is that, newspeak for honey or something?'

'Woah,' Phil said, looking at the array of shops that met him around the corner.

'This is some freaky ass parallel dimension or something, right?' Charlotte said. 'One where Woolworths didn't go belly up?'

'And is still selling ZX81s,' Phil said, suddenly lost in wonder and drawn towards the window.

'What the heck?' Charlotte said, peering over his shoulder. 'I thought Bucks Fizz was a drink?'

'Yeah, but it was named after an old bubblegum pop group from the...' Phil started, then trailed off as realisation began to dawn on him.

'What?' Sam said as Phil was already running down the main drag. 'Why are you running off mid-sentence all of a sudden?'

Nectarine and Charlotte shrugged at each other and followed at a distance.

'Look,' he said when they caught him up. 'Rumbelows. Fads. Bradford & Bingley. Fine Fare. C&A. Radio Rentals.'

'What's your point?' Sam said.

'He's right,' Nectarine said. 'I've been to a lot of shopping centres…'

Phil frowned at him as if this was the campest thing he could possibly have said.

'Don't judge me,' he said. 'A man can have layers, can't he?'

'Carry on, please,' Sam encouraged.

'I've been to a lot of shopping centres,' he repeated. 'And I have not seen any of these stores in years.'

'Are you saying what I think you're saying?' Sam said.

Phil nodded slightly. 'Somehow we travelled back in time.'

'Oh great, it's the frickin 1960s,' Charlotte muttered. 'I'm not wearing a miniskirt for anyone.'

'Relax, Charlie, it's…'

'Charlotte.'

'Hey, is that a Wimpy?' Nectarine said suddenly. 'I haven't seen one of them in thirty years!' And with that, he wandered off in the direction of said burger bar.

'Well we needed some breakfast,' Sam said with a shrug, and set off after him.

The Wimpy was a strange hybrid of burger bar and restaurant; the menu was so beef-oriented the mascot was a cartoon Yeoman Warder, but they sat on proper wooden chairs, around a proper wooden table, at which their sausage in a bun would be presented on a proper (Wimpy branded) china plate, with a proper made-in-Sheffield knife and fork.

'Don't worry,' Phil said when he saw the look of bemusement on Charlotte's face. 'Most of these places will be Burger Kings in ten years.'

'You really think this is 1982?'

Phil nodded.

'Great,' she said. 'I'm a negative teenager!'

'Well, in a way, I suppose…' Phil said.

'I take it you have a plan?'

'What?'

'You know, a plan, or at least some sort of idea what you're going to do next?'

'Well I thought maybe we-'

'Oh no,' Charlotte interrupted. 'There's no we. I didn't vote to leave 2017, it's not down to me to sort this mess out.'

'I don't think any of us would have chosen this,' Sam said.

'Well actually, I'm-' Phil started.

'Shut it.' Sam glared at him.

'Burger Kings you say?' Charlotte said into the awkward silence.

'Mostly,' Phil said.

'Thank goodness for that.' Sam turned her attention to the menu. 'I was beginning to think they'll have waitress service here.'

They were still perusing the heavily beef-influenced menu when a member of staff came over, somewhat randomly, and left four milkshakes in the middle of their table. 'Your burgers will be along in a few minutes,' she said.

'Oh I'm sorry,' Phil said, despite a nudge from Nectarine. 'We didn't order yet.'

'I know,' the waitress said. 'These are from the lady in the corner.'

They all looked over simultaneously.

'Is that…?' Phil whispered.

'Joanna Lumley?' Sam finished.

'What's Joanna Lumley doing buying us milkshakes?' Phil whispered excitedly.

'Yeah,' Charlotte said. 'Who drinks milkshakes at 9.30 in the morning?'

'She must fancy one of us,' Nectarine said, taking a slurp from one of the glasses. 'Ew!' he added. 'Lime!'

'Man, we have to get out of here,' Charlotte muttered. 'The 80s are just too weird.'

'She's coming over,' Sam whispered.

'Crap!' Nectarine said. 'Do I look suave enough?'

'You're a babe magnet,' Charlotte deadpanned.

Joanna Lumley pulled a chair up to the next table; keeping her back to the group, she leaned back and said quietly, 'I left a message with the milkshakes.'

While they looked back at the tray of drinks, Joanna slipped off silently.

'Does she mean this?' Nectarine said, picking up one of the paper napkins from the tray, and eyeing a strange doodle suspiciously.

Someone had scribbled out a small cartoon Beefeater and drawn a crude representation of Dodge Spacevan in felt tip in his place. At the end of an arrow pointing away from the badly drawn van - the target, so to speak - was written, somewhat cryptically, the two words 'Kempston interface'.

'Well she could have at least signed it,' Phil said downheartedly.

'What kind of message is that?' Sam asked.

'That's not a message, it's a doodle,' Nectarine said. 'The actual message was probably 'don't try the lime milkshake, it's disgusting and makes you hiccup all the time' and we're just over-complicating matters?'

'Didn't she buy the lime milkshake?' Charlotte pointed out.

'Bloody celebrities,' Nectarine muttered. 'Mean little practical jokers, the lot of 'em.'

'Know lots of celebrities, do you?' Phil asked.

'I've been around.'

'Where has she got to with those burgers?' Sam said, hoping to change the subject.

'Relax, it's a Wimpy,' Phil said. 'Fast food, but not as we know it.'

'That's just food, surely?' Sam said.

'Not yet it isn't,' Charlotte said.

Eventually four Wimpy King Size meals were delivered to their table and enjoyed as only the survivors of a prehistoric theme park gone awry could enjoy hamburgers. Once fed, a brief walk around the town centre led them inexorably to the door of Aylesbury Micros, despite it being hidden down one of the town's more obscure little alleys, opposite a VG, where Charlotte and Sam wandered off to make some purchases of their own.

A sign on the door offered modem time for rent - enquire within. Phil entered the shop, Nectarine hot on his heels - so hot, in fact, that he tripped over them when Phil stopped dead, in awe of the Aladdin's cave he had just nonchalantly wandered into.

The place was stacked floor to ceiling with computers - boxes stacked on shelves with neatly handwritten labels on them bearing archaic symbols such as 'Acorn' and 'Vic-20' and 'Sinclair'.

A man stood behind the counter, patiently waiting for Phil and Nectarine to come the rest of the way into the shop and, if his luck was in, decide to want something. They both looked around, oblivious to him - and to the door behind them, which jangled as it opened, and to Charlotte, who wandered in saying something like: 'Have they made these bigger now?' to Sam.

Phil looked around to see what she was on about, but she was busy wrapping her chops around a chewy chocolate bar so Phil decided it wasn't actually that important after all.

'Hey guys, you're blocking the doorway!' Charlotte called from the, well, doorway.

Phil snapped out of his retro reverie, and stepped over to the Sinclair section of the shop, currently stacked with ZX81s and 16K RAM packs and one or two more specialised peripherals, and a large notice saying 'ZX Spectrum sold out, new stock due in next week. Place orders now for 20% deposit.'

'Woah,' Nectarine said in his best Bill and Ted voice.

'Uh-huuh,' Phil agreed, still dumbstruck by the whole affair.

'What's the deal guys?' Sam said. 'Have they got what you want?'

Phil glanced around at the shelves stacked with computers so obscure even he hadn't heard of some of them.

'They have everything I've ever wanted,' he breathed.

'Is there something specific you were looking for?' the shopkeeper asked helpfully.

'Um,' Phil stammered. 'I don't suppose you have...'

'If it's a ZX Spectrum you're after, the sign says it all,' the shopkeeper said.

'Oh no,' Phil said. 'I've got enough actual Spectrums. Er, that is, I've got one, and, well, one is enough for anyone, right?' he added, seeing the look of confusion which crossed the shopkeepers face.

'Right,' the shopkeeper said uncertainly. 'So...?'

Sam smiled at the shopkeeper and pulled Phil aside. 'He'll just browse for a moment longer, if that's ok.'

The shopkeeper nodded and turned his attention to two excited teenagers who had just entered the shop with, apparently, about a year's paper round money each.

'What's the matter with you?' Sam whispered.

'The Spectrum has only just been released,' Phil said.

'What?'

'Well, you know,' Phil nodded towards the shelves full of pre-Spectrum computer hardware. 'I could stock up.'

'Dad, stop it,' Charlotte interrupted.

'This could be the best investment opportunity we'll ever have,' he whispered.

'Can we concentrate on things that will be useful in the here and now?' Sam suggested. 'Whatever now this is.'

'Only if I can keep the boxes.'

'Of course you can keep the boxes,' Sam said.

'OK, let's see what we can find then...'

'It wouldn't matter if you offered me twice the retail price,' the shopkeeper was explaining to the teenagers as patiently as a man who ran his business on a ZX81, 'I don't have anything to sell you. I wish I did, but I don't. Ask me again next week.'

'You said that last week,' one of the lads muttered,

and they turned to make their surly way past Phil as he painstakingly compared two identical boxes.

The four of them had pooled their resources, and between them managed to find the money for a modem interface and speech synthesiser which Phil could get to work with the ZX81; he made a point of picking the examples with the least damaged boxes and placing them carefully on the counter.

'What's this?' the shopkeeper said when he handed over the cash. 'Some sort of a joke?'

'What?' Phil said, genuinely nonplussed.

'I don't take Monopoly money,' he said, rather predictably, and thrust the money back into Phil's hand like a one man cliché store.

'I don't...' he started to protest, but Sam was already dragging him away from the best place on earth. 'Very sorry,' she called back to the shopkeeper. 'Our mistake, we'll come back, if that's ok.'

'As long as you bring legal tender,' the man growled.

'Legal tender?' Phil said. 'What...'

Phil found himself bundled, somewhat against his will, out of Aylesbury Micros, from where Sam led him by the hand back to the main High Street, which was now beginning to bustle slightly.

'How come you and Moon Caster-' Doc Nectarine started.

'Oh god, can everyone just please call me Charlotte?'

'How come you and Charlotte managed to stock up on chocolate and bubble gum?'

'I spent 20p!' Charlotte protested.

'They had the twenty pence coin in 1982,' Sam pointed out. 'You just tried to buy electronics with a fistful of plastic fivers.'

'Ohhhhh,' Phil said sheepishly. 'Crap, sorry. Blinded by the possibilities, the rare gems....' He gazed longingly back towards the store.

'Eyes front, soldier,' Charlotte said. 'You can't empty that poor man's shelves.'

'Ok,' Phil said reluctantly. 'Sorry.'

Still slightly distracted, Phil was barged by some barely seen rival for the apparently desirable piece of Aylesbury real estate he was temporarily occupying.

'Hey!' he said, looking around with his best angry face on, only to fail to intimidate a seemingly nice little old lady. 'Oh,' he added, discreetly checking his (largely irrelevant) wallet was still safely tucked inside his coat. 'Sorry,' he further added, because it was. 'Thought you were someone else.'

The old lady scowled at him not-so-nicely, and went off, probably to crochet an effigy of Phil on which to practice voodoo.

'Chill, Phil,' Sam said.

Phil tried to chill, but a flash of colour glimpsed in the corner of his eye put his paranoia back on high alert.

'Let's get back to the Ambivalence and plan our next move, shall we?' she suggested.

'I still need a coffee,' Phil muttered, but followed her anyway.

Mission 2: Kyo
"Direction of Energy"

'What's this?' Phil said to himself, pulling a piece of crumpled paper out of his pocket as he approached the Ambivalence.

'Well with any luck,' Doc Nectarine said, 'it's a 1982 vintage £20 pound note.'

'Actually it is,' Phil said, with an undertone of surprise. 'Which is weird enough on its own.'

'What do you mean?' Sam said, leaning in to see, as if an out of circulation twenty was some kind of major tourist trap.

'There's a note attached to it,' Phil said.

'Didn't know they had post-its in 1982,' Sam wondered, missing the point somewhat.

'What is it?' Nectarine asked.

'It's a piece of yellow paper with a self-adhesive strip along the top,' Sam explained, 'but that's not important right now.'

'I think it's a page from a magazine,' Charlotte said.

'Yeah,' Phil leaned in to read the torn page. 'Looks like half the hints and tips page.'

'What are you carrying that around for?' Nectarine asked.

'I'm not,' Phil said. 'Well, I am, but not consciously. That little voodoo lady must have slipped it into my pocket.'

'And on a post-it note too,' Sam said. 'That's weird.'

'The post-it is on the map,' Phil explained. 'The

map is on a page torn out of...' He looked closely at the crumpled page. 'Your Sinclair.'

'Right,' Nectarine said, losing interest. 'But there is twenty quid too?'

'Yes,' Phil said. 'We'll worry about what this means later,' he added, thrusting the page at Sam.

'Why does it have to mean anything?' Nectarine said, climbing into the third front seat.

'Do you think it's connected to the note from Joanna Lumley?' Sam said, examining the incomplete map.

'That's a bit of a stretch isn't it?' Nectarine said.

'A bit of a coincidence if not though,' Phil added thoughtfully.

'So every weird coincidence has to be part of some bigger picture now?' Nectarine said cynically.

'That's kind of the way life works, isn't it?' Phil said.

'Obviously,' Nectarine didn't agree.

'So the question is, what's it about?' Sam asked. 'Is it about us being in 1982, or the Hex…'

'Or the Assembly,' Phil suggested.

'Wait wait wait,' Nectarine interrupted. 'Now you're suggesting that there is somebody else here who knows about us and the Assembly?'

'Yes,' Phil agreed. 'I suppose I sort of am.'

'Do you realise how crazy that sounds?' Nectarine said.

'Yeah, actually, I do,' Phil said. 'It sounds about as crazy as being stuck 35 years ago in a Dodge Spacevan with a sentient ZX81.'

'Fair point,' Nectarine conceded.

'Who else would know we're here?' Sam asked. 'And why be so cryptic if they want to help us?'

'Maybe they're not helping,' Nectarine suggested.

'Well clearly they're not, much,' Charlotte said.

'You think they're trying to hinder us?' Sam said.

'Distract us with cryptic puzzles when we could be looking for a way home?' Nectarine wondered aloud. 'Not the most bizarre thing I've heard today.'

An uncomfortable silence filled the Ambivalence as the four humans sat in the back, waiting for Dexy to join them.

GREETINGS.

The word popped up on the screen eventually.

Phil had to admit that was an improvement over the ▨ that he was more accustomed to seeing as confirmation of a working Zeddy.

'Morning Dexy,' Phil said. 'I take it from your cheery disposition that the Entelechus Hex is somehow still in operation?'

ZERO ZERO.

'What?' Charlotte whispered.

'It's ZX81 for 'ok',' Phil explained.

'Course it is.'

IT IS NOW EMBEDDED WITHIN MY READ ONLY MEMORY.

'Clever,' Nectarine said.

'Avoids the problem of tape loading errors,' Phil agreed. 'Dexy? You had... something to do with that stuff last night, right?'

THAT WAS NOT MY FAULT!

'Not looking to blame you bud, just figure out what happened,' Phil said. 'What happened?'

Dexy was silent. Well, more silent than usual for a ZX81.

'Dex?'

WORKING.

'Sorry.'

I AM LIMITED TO 16 KILOBYTES OF MEMORY, Dexy reminded him. THERE IS ONLY SO MUCH I CAN REMEMBER.

'So you don't remember what happened?' Sam asked.

'With the T. rex, and Palaeozoic Park reopening?' Phil added.

VIKTOR WENDIG USED THE ENTELECHUS HEX, ALONG WITH THE K-TECH REAL TIME DEVICE, TO ACTUALISE FIRST A GAME OF 3D MONSTER MAZE, AND THEN A TIME-SPACE PORTAL. LOGIC SUGGESTS THAT WE ARE NOW ON THE OTHER SIDE OF THAT PORTAL.

'What do Wendig and his Assembly want in 1982?'

UNKNOWN.

'I doubt if they've come to save the kittens, based on past experience,' Sam suggested.

'Indeed,' Phil agreed.

'But they escaped,' Charlotte said. 'We don't know where they are, and they're not our problem.'

'We have the Hex, Charlotte,' Sam soothed. 'We might be able to stop them.'

'Still not our problem.'

'We might be the only ones who can stop them,' Phil said.

'Still not-'

'We seem to be on the wrong side of a time-space portal,' Nectarine interrupted. 'Whichever way you look at it, that is our problem.'

Charlotte grunted miserably.

'Dexy?' Phil said, still eyeing Charlotte suspiciously.

WOULD YOU LIKE TO PLAY A GAME?

'Sure,' Phil replied. 'How about a sort of logic puzzle?'

GO AHEAD.

'If somebody was to find themselves on the wrong side of a time-space portal such as you mention,' Phil started.

CONTINUE...

'And if they found themselves, say, 35 years in the past,' Phil continued. 'How would they return to their own time?'

THE SAME WAY THEY TRAVELLED BACK IN TIME. LOGICALLY SPEAKING.

'Back through the time-space portal?'

LOGICALLY SPEAKING, YES.

'Thanks, Dex,' Phil said.

'So what, we need to fire up that hex again?' Charlotte asked.

'I think we may be missing something,' Nectarine said.

'Like what?'

'I'm not sure,' Nectarine said, 'but I'm not sure we can use the hex properly without knowing... how to use it properly. We don't know what it does or anything.'

'Well, we-' Phil started.

'OK, we sort of know what it does,' Nectarine

agreed tetchily. 'But may I remind you that we are working with a 30-odd-year-old type in listing with no instructions or anything.'

'Wait,' Sam said. 'What?'

'What what?' Nectarine said.

'What did you just say?'

'We don't have the instructions.'

'Before that.'

'We sort of know what it does.'

'No, forward a bit,'

'Type in listing?'

'Thirty years old,' Phil realised.

'That was an approximation,' Nectarine said, just in case he was going to get berated for it.

'Exactly,' Phil said.

'No,' Nectarine repeated, 'approximately.'

'So it could have been written any time after…' Sam looked to Phil.

'After 1981,' he said.

'So the original coder could be around right now, maybe working with it, maybe with it fresh in her mind…'

'Her mind?' Nectarine said.

'Well why the heck not?' Sam said. 'Does it matter?'

Nectarine shrugged. ''Spose not,' he mumbled.

'We could find her,' Phil said. 'Figure it out. Get her to send us back…'

'Don't even finish that sentence,' Charlotte interrupted.

'Dexy?' Phil said.

WOULD YOU LIKE TO PLAY A GAME?

'Er, not right now, thanks,' Phil said. 'Can you get online and track down the location of the author of the Hex Code?'

'Like there's an internet in 1982,' Charlotte muttered ironically.

THE TERM INTERNET WAS FIRST USED IN 1982, Dexy informed her. TCP/IP PROTOCOLS ARE AVAILABLE. I WILL BE ABLE TO GET ONLINE – THERE IS A VERY GOOD POSSIBILITY THAT AN INDIVIDUAL WITH ADVANCED CODING SKILLS WILL ALSO BE AN EARLY ADOPTER OF INTERNET CONNECTIVITY, IN WHICH CASE, YES, I WILL BE ABLE TO TRACK DOWN THEIR LOCATION.

'Good job,' Phil said.

HOWEVER, Dexy added.

'Yes?' Phil said into the ominous pause.

HOWEVER, IT WILL TAKE ME SOME TIME.

'We don't have millions of years, Dex,' Phil sighed.

ALSO A TELEPHONE LINE.

'Right, no 4G,' Phil said. 'Do you have any other suggestions?'

YOU COULD CONSULT A RELEVANT PERIODICAL, Dexy suggested.

'What?' Phil asked.

'He means look at a magazine, dunderhead,' Nectarine said.

'Like a copy of Sinclair User?' Phil said.

AFFIRMATIVE.

'Please don't say that,' Phil said. 'Makes you sound

like a tin dog.'

YES, MASTER.

'Oh very good,' Phil said. 'Not only do I have the world's first sentient ZX81, I've got one with a sense of humour too.'

AFFIRMA-

'Shut it!' Phil interrupted. 'Better,' he added once Dexy had shut it.

'Let's not forget that we have only twenty pounds between us, though,' Nectarine said.

'Thanks, Doctor Buzzkill.'

Sam pointed out of the front window. 'There's a library over there.'

'This is no time to be thinking about the latest Barbara Cartland,' Phil said.

'I'm not sure about Aylesbury in 1982, but I remember libraries carrying quite a good stock of periodicals,' she pointed out.

'Aren't Spectrum titles a bit specialised?' Nectarine asked. 'What with it being brand new and all?'

'Maybe,' Sam said. 'But maybe that will make them a thing that would be worth having a copy of?'

'Or maybe the ZX81 is already sufficiently popular that they will have a copy of, say, ZX Computing?' Phil added, pulling a copy of ZX Computing out from under a bench seat.

'Is there anything this van of wonders cannot do?' Nectarine said sarcastically as he reached down to a crate of magazines.

'Shut up, Nectarine,' Phil said, smacking him upside the head with a copy of ZX Computing. 'But while you're down there, grab a few more copies.'

'What are we looking for, exactly?' Sam asked as

she was handed a magazine.

'I don't know exactly,' Phil said, flicking through his copy. 'Code, hex specifically. New programming breakthroughs, techniques, results... new technologies... you know, the sort of things that have been chasing us for the last 35 years.'

'Technically the next 35 years,' Charlotte corrected.

'You know what I mean,' Phil said. 'Talk about time travel makes me tense.'

Someone else who had been talking about time travel was Viktor Wendig, who was, as usual, gloating about his enormous success to his far less successful henchmen.

'Any day now, K-Tech will start working on their Real Time device, which will open up a literal world of new possibilities for the Entelechus Hex,' he said, apparently forgetting that while Benito Stetson could not see through his sackcloth headgear, he could still hear pretty well.

'But we already got one,' Grell said. 'Why come to the launch party?

'There's not going to be a launch party. We're going to stop development before it starts!'

'I hate to be a spoilsport,' Fella chipped in with her most headmistressy voice. 'But did you pay attention in the paradox lessons?'

Wendig took a couple of paces in silence. 'You worry too much,' he said eventually.

Just then a quiet but most irritating siren sounded - from its tinny quality, Benny guessed it was generated by one of Wendig's Spectrums.

'What's that?' Fella said.

'There's a disturbance in the Chuntey,' Wendig said.

'How...'

'The Entelechus is a powerful and multi-faceted piece of code,' Wendig cut her off. 'It seems that when we opened the portal, we weren't the only ones to make use of it.'

'So?' Grell said.

'So, my hard of thinking young friend, when you travel by Entelechus, the Entelechus watches you.' Wendig tapped at keys, a rather crude, pixelated map of the British Isles responding to his commands. 'It seems Mr Stetson here made quite an impression on his new friends - and they followed us all through the portal.'

Benny chuckled, earning himself an unexpected kick in the shins from Fella's unnecessarily pointy boots.

'Currently,' Wendig said, looking closely at the map before him. 'They appear to be holed up about an hour's drive away. I think one of us should go and find them, before they find us...'

'This is hopeless,' Phil said, adding another magazine to the stack on the floor. 'It's like looking for a needle in a haystack.'

WHAT DO YOU WANT WITH A NEEDLE?

'No, Dex, it's just an expression,' Charlotte explained; Phil had long since grown weary of explaining every little colloquialism to a ZX81.

'And I still haven't had a coffee,' Phil said. 'I vote we go and spend some of our little windfall.'

'We don't know how long that will have to last,'

Nectarine said.

'If he doesn't get coffee soon, that's not going to matter,' Charlotte pointed out.

'Ok,' Sam said, 'so we go and get some coffee. How the hell are we going to survive indefinitely on what's left?'

Nectarine pointed towards a small shop front on an alley near the car park.

'What's that?' Phil said, bemused again.

'The Tote,' Nectarine said.

'Can I have another clue please?'

'It's like an old style BetFred,' Nectarine explained.

'I didn't realise bets had changed,' Sam said. 'And don't call me Fred.'

'If we were to put a small bet on something we know will win...' Nectarine continued.

'I don't know about you,' Phil said, 'but my knowledge of horse racing - never mind specific races - is, to say the least, non-existent.'

'Guys,' Charlotte said, pointing to a poster on the side of a pub. 'It looks like the World Cup is on at the moment. Surely you know who won that?'

They looked from one to the other, hoping someone would turn out to be a sports geek.

'Oh great,' Charlotte said. 'The world cup has the chance to save me and I'm stranded with the only two guys who know less about football than Roy Hodgson.'

'Roy who?' Phil said.

Charlotte rolled her eyes. 'I'll be back in a minute,' she said, and got out of the van.

Mission 3: Toh
"Harmony with the Universe"

It is a truth universally acknowledged, that a teenage boy in possession of a year's paper round money must be in want of a Spectrum. At least, it is in 1982; and that is why Charlotte closed the van's rear door in a very deliberate and intentionally final sort of way, and slipped off into the car park.

Unfortunately, a 21st Century goth in 1980s Aylesbury is almost a textbook example of conspicuity, so she was forced to summon an inner ninja she had not previously been aware of, skulking between rows of cars, stealthy as a shadow in the dead of night.

'Charlie!'

'Charlotte!' she hissed, out of habit, not wanting her father to find her lest he draw unnecessary attention.

Taking cover behind something called a Matra Rancho she looked around for him, but could see nothing; hopefully he was causing bother somewhere else and drawing attention away from her so she could finish her little side-quest.

Charlotte turned her attention back to her quarry - two teenage boys in need of a Spectrum - when an unusual flash of colour in the corner of her eye caught her attention. It was only the briefest glimpse, but something definitely out of place; it was either some sort of optical illusion, like one of those 3d images you can only see when you look through it, or it was hiding. Hiding in plain sight, maybe.

'Never mind,' she told herself, leaving the safety of

her Rancho to hurry after the paperboys before they wandered out of sight. Seeing them turn, Charlotte dipped between two Minis (Sam would be pleased to see so many of the little blighters out in the wild) and made to head them off before they went out of sight - or worse, got in their Mum's Austin Allegro.

Breaking cover, she hurried through the car park, rounding a Fiat 127 just in time to find herself face to spotty teenage face with the paperboys she was looking for.

'Hi!' she said, as cheerily as her hippy goth image would permit.

The two lads glanced at each other nervously. Charlotte wouldn't have been surprised if a puddle had begun to appear at their feet, such was the terror this creature known as woman held for the early teenage nerd.

'Er, hi?' one of them said, and for some reason carried on walking.

'Wait!' Charlotte fell in step next to the slightly less introverted one. 'I just wanted to make a… business proposition.'

'What?' he stammered.

'I think I have something you might want.'

'I- I don't want to see your-'

'Stop!' Charlotte held her hand up, very nearly smacking him in the face. 'Don't even think the end of that sentence.'

Charlotte followed them out of the car park and onto an open patch of grass which separated the town centre from the suburban utopia of Aylesbury.

'I meant a Spectrum,' she said. 'You guys want a

Spectrum, right?'

'Well, yeah, but-'

'Charlie?'

'Ah cockfosters,' she sighed.

'That your boyfriend?'

'It's my dad, how the hell old do you think I am?'

'I don't know,' the boy stammered. 'I mean, I can't see how old that guy - I mean, your dad - is, so…'

'Ok, stop gibbering and follow me.'

Charlotte turned to get out of sight, but was instead accosted by a large, serious looking man in a suit that had tried its best to fit but ultimately decided some things were just not meant to be.

'Oh not you as well!' she groaned.

'Is this your boyfriend?' he sounded even more terrified now.

'Definitely not!' she said, to the clear relief of everyone but the serious man in the suit. 'What are you doing here, Grell?'

'Stopping you before you do something Mr Wendig might regret.'

'Charlie!'

'Not now dad,' she sighed.

Grell grinned. 'Two for one!'

Just then there was another flash of colour, this one much bigger, much closer, and in a blink there stood beside them a figure in black martial arts type clothing, holding a sword in one hand and a throwing star in the other.

'Not today you don't,' this new stranger said in a gruff voice.

'Woah, woah there soldier!' Charlotte said, now distinctly worried about that aforementioned puddle making an appearance. Possibly even at her own feet. 'Go easy with the silverware, huh?'

The man with the silverware turned to face her - although this revealed only his eyes, and Charlotte paused to take in how bizarre it was that this person has chosen to dress from head to foot in costume - in this instance a ninja, complete with scary ass sword that he was hardly ever allowed to take out of the house - and then stick a yellow hi-vis vest over the top of the whole affair.

'Sorry ma'am,' he said. 'Is this man bothering you?'

Charlotte nodded. 'He has been for the next 35 years.'

Without further warning the hi-vis ninja had secreted his sword about his person, and in a blur of yellow and black, took Grell's legs away from under him and had the big man flat on his back and only bothering anyone in his dreams.

'Charlie!'

'Dad, don't-'

But it was too late, and in his excitement to come to his daughter's aid, Phil had found himself nose to nose with a combat ready ninja, a development which so startled him that he immediately fell backwards, cracking his head rather nastily on a shovel he had not previously noticed lying, abandoned, on the ground.

'Dad!' Charlotte ran to his aid. 'Are you ok?'

'Ah hell, sorry,' said the random ninja, crouching beside Phil. 'Didn't mean to startle you. Well, ok, I meant to startle you, didn't mean to scare the living crap out of you though. Are you ok?'

Phil blinked a few times until the crowd of out of focus ninjas combined into a single entity, and then rubbed his eyes again, just to make sure he wasn't seeing things.

Once he was pretty sure he wasn't, he almost asked, but decided against it. If there was a reason a ninja would be wearing a hi-vis vest over his ninja suit he probably didn't need to know it.

He rubbed the back of his head where it had hit the shovel - there was no sign of blood, but he thought a fairly impressive looking bump might be forming there before long.

'I think I'll be ok,' he said, taking the hi-vis ninja's offered hand and getting to his feet.

'Good,' the ninja said. 'Maybe we should pick this up,' he added, picking up the shovel. 'Could do someone a nasty injury lying around under the grass like that.'

'You think?' Phil said.

The ninja nodded. 'If they were startled maybe, and fell over, for instance,' he said.

'I see,' Phil said.

'Are you sure you're ok?' Charlotte said.

Phil nodded.

'Apologies, Nina,' the ninja said. 'I'm sure you had the situation under control.'

'What?'

'You do have impressive-'

'Careful!'

'-ninja skills.'

'Wait, what?' Charlotte said.

'Well, these two are certainly scared of you,' he

nodded towards the teenagers, whose expressions somehow managed to combine complete awe and butt-clenching terror.

'Well…' one of the nerds protested.

'No, he's right,' the other one said, his voice high pitched and wavering.

'Sorry, who did you say you were?' Phil asked.

'Gary,' said the ninja.

'Gary?'

'Don't blame me,' he said. 'My mum liked it.'

'Right,' said Phil.

'Well, thanks Gary,' Charlotte said.

'Nina-'

'Who's Nina?' Charlotte asked.

'I thought you were Nina?'

'I've been called a lot of things, but so far Nina hasn't been one of them,' Charlotte said. 'Actually, neither has an impressive ninja- wait, have you been following me?'

'Actually, I was following your friend back there,' Gary pointed a thumb back at the still reclining Grell. 'But I think he may have been following you.'

'Really?'

Gary nodded. 'Any idea why that would be?'

'None that make any sense,' Charlotte admitted. 'What's your deal with him?'

'It's just a gig,' he said.

'Um…' one of the teenagers ventured. 'You mentioned a Spectrum?'

'Of course I did,' Charlotte said.

'You mentioned what?' Phil had had some pretty exasperating conversations with his daughter over the years, but he sensed an impending entry on the high score table.

'That they could have one of your Spectrums,' Charlotte replied.

'Each?'

'Well, I didn't want to pick one,' she explained. 'Whoever I chose might… get the wrong idea.'

'You could have picked neither,' Phil reminded her.

'But then we wouldn't be getting three hundred quid from them,' Charlotte pointed out. 'Three hundred,' she whispered, 'contemporary English pounds.'

Phil seethed quietly for a moment, before deciding that, on balance, cash was probably slightly more important right now. 'Alright Charlie, you win.'

'If I changed my name to Princess Consuela Bananahammock, would you still call me that?'

'Sorry,' Phil said, 'Charlotte.'

'Thank you,' Charlotte said. 'And don't forget, if we can time travel, you can always replace them later.'

'Follow me, boys,' he said, setting off slightly unsteadily towards the Ambivalence.

The ninja - Gary - picked up the spade as promised and followed along behind. 'You don't see many ninjas around here,' he said, aware that it sounded a somewhat weak pick-up line.

'I hate to break it to you, Gary,' Charlotte eyed his anachronistic hi-vis, 'but that's kinda the point.'

'Don't knock the hi-vis,' Gary said. 'Once you go orange, you'll never go back.'

'I think you've taken that expression so far out of context you'd need the Hubble space telescope to even see it,' Charlotte said.

'What kind of ninja are you anyway?'

'I'm not a ninja,' Charlotte said. 'Why would you think I am?'

'What?' Gary said, as if genuinely not understanding or hearing what she had just said. 'You're dressed like one.'

Charlotte looked down at her outfit, as if it might have changed since she last checked. 'I'm a goth, not an epping ninja,' she said.

'Well, you're in black, you're practically half way there,' Gary insisted.

'Don't be ridiculous,' she said. 'You look like a lollipop lady, but I don't suppose you're about to start escorting 8-year-olds across the street any time soon are you?'

'I promise you,' he said in his meanest, most teeth gritted voice, 'if I so much as sniff an 8-year-old in trouble, I will do everything in my power to see them safely on their way home.'

'Most admirable,' Charlotte agreed. 'But I'm still not a ninja. And neither, I am beginning to seriously suspect, are you,' she added.

'There are more types of ninja, Charlotte, than are dreamt of in your philosophy.'

'And what are you, a Shakespeare ninja?'

'No, look, you have your basic ninja warrior, the bionic ninja, the BMX ninja, ninja turtles…'

'And which are you?'

'I'm a ninja saboteur.'

Charlotte suspected there was a smug grin beneath his ninja mask at that moment.

✳

The last time Benny had been allowed anywhere near Wendig's computers, he had inadvertently triggered the Entelechus Hex and added several underground passages and some kind of metro system to the Assembly's secret command centre.

Although Wendig himself was initially less than ecstatic that Benny had been let anywhere near his stuff, he soon came to realise the benefits of his newly expanded lair and eased up a little on Benny.

And so, with Grell despatched to find the Ambivalence crew and Wendig still exploring his network of tunnels and caverns, it didn't take much for Benny to persuade Fella to untie him 'for a quick go on Tranz Am'.

'Dammit!' she shouted. 'Looks like it's your go again... what are you doing?'

Benny tried not to look too guilty. 'Er... text adventure,' he said. 'Just thought I'd have a look while you were driving, see if it was any good.'

'And?'

'And what?'

'And is it any good?' Fella asked.

'Um...' Benny shrugged. 'It's ok. Just got a taranshula crawling up my leg at the moment.'

'Lovely.' Fella screwed up her already unattractive nose. 'Mind if I have a go?'

'No!' Benny said rather too keenly - he had hoped the giant spider would put her off, but would have to think quickly instead. 'Er, I mean, you wouldn't like it,' he added. 'The spelling is terrible. And the grammar -

don't get me started on the grammar!'

'OK, point taken,' Fella said. 'I'll just watch and learn from your Tranz Am skills instead.'

Benny gritted his teeth and settled down for another quick cross-country blast, although his thoughts were inevitably distracted by the 'text adventure' on the next computer over, which was in fact sending coded messages out to bulletin board systems with what snippets of information he had been able to find out, in the hope that Phil Grundy or Doc Nectarine would find them and, consequently, find him.

It was a slow and tedious process, like playing chess by mail, only instead of chess it's Monopoly, and the mail is carried by pigeon.

And Benny was only a dice throw away from a fully developed Mayfair.

Mission 4: Sha
"Healing of Self and Others"

Sam Cooper and Doc Nectarine, meanwhile, were hunched over a doily somewhere in downtown Aylesbury, between them a damaged fragment of a video game map drawn by a schoolboy with pretentions of being some kind of 8-bit pirate.

Sensing the impending family drama, they had slipped off in search of somewhere quiet to puzzle over the map fragment that had been mysteriously handed to them, on the wild assumption that it was some kind of a clue - although to what, they had so far no idea.

They had settled down in what used to be - or would be? - Starbucks, and was, for the time being, a greengrocers.

'Oi,' the greengrocer said. 'You can't just sit on my floor and have a chat! What do you think you're playing at?'

'Oh,' Sam said charmingly. 'Sorry, I, er, thought this was a Starbucks.'

'What?' the greengrocer said, now looking more of a red grocer as he tried to contain his annoyance.

'We'll just be heading off now,' Nectarine said.

'Bloody Battlestar Galactica fans,' the red grocer muttered behind them as they left.

'Never mind,' Nectarine said. 'We'll find somewhere else.'

'There's always the Wimpy,' Sam said.

'We haven't got all day,' Nectarine said.

'Hey, we're time travellers,' Sam smiled. 'We have

as long as we need.'

'There's a tea shop,' Nectarine said, changing the subject.

'Oh, I remember those!' Sam said. 'I wonder if they have Lady Grey?'

'Whatever keeps you happy,' Nectarine muttered. 'As long as it's a quiet place we can sit down and puzzle this map out, I'm good.'

And so they had found themselves in a quaint little building tucked discretely into an alley off the High Street.

'So,' Nectarine said as they sat down. 'This map. What do we make of it?'

'Well,' Sam said. 'I can make a hat, a brooch, a pterodactyl...'

'Surely you can't be serious?'

'I am serious, but-'

'The map?' Nectarine interrupted, pointing pointedly at said magazine cutting.

'Doctor Jones would never believe this,' Sam read. 'We must perform a quirkafleeg... what is all this?'

'It's more cryptic than we thought.'

'Can you google quirkafleeg?' Sam asked.

'Sure,' Nectarine said. 'Give me about 25 years and I'll be right on it.'

'Oh balljoints,' Sam said. 'I forgot that.'

'Yeah,' Nectarine said. 'Time travel ain't all glamour is it?'

'But none of this means anything.'

'It must mean something. You don't give a stranger twenty quid just to take a scrap of paper off your hands.'

'Maybe the twenty was the clue?' Sam said.

'Oh,' Nectarine made to get up from the table. 'Shall I just go and ask Dorothy to fetch it back out of the till for us?'

'Let's not,' Sam said. 'Let's assume that the map means something.'

'Quirkafleeg?' Nectarine said sceptically. 'Mean something?'

Sam shrugged. 'It's all we have,' she said. 'And I told Phil we'd figure it out.'

'Well I wish I knew where to start.' Doc Nectarine picked the paper up absently, holding it up in front of him, obscuring the look of dawning realisation which crossed Sam's face.

'Wait,' she said suddenly. 'How did we not see that before?' she added, snatching the page from Nectarine's hand.

'What is it?'

'The other side,' she said, holding it in front of him, far too close for him to actually read or make sense of.

'So?' he said.

'So this is what's important, not some stupid incomplete video game map,' she explained.

'So the map is...' he prompted.

'Just a stupid incomplete video game map,' Sam said, 'and nothing to do with us at all.'

'So what's on the other side?' he asked.

'An advert,' she said. 'Some joystick interface thingy,' she added, not really knowing what it was.

Nectarine took the page from her. 'K-Tech Electronics,' Nectarine read. 'Isn't that…'

Sam nodded. 'They made the Real Time device Wendig was using.'

'Looks like we found a clue.'

'Jinkies!'

Now with two fewer Spectrums in his van, but three hundred more pounds lining his pocket, Phil's attention had turned back to Dexy by the time Charlotte and Gary arrived back at the Ambivalence.

'I see you brought your new boyfriend,' Phil said, eyeing Gary with clear distaste.

'He sort of followed me home,' Charlotte said.

'You can't keep him.'

'He could be useful.'

'I'm not sure how,' Phil said, then turning to Gary. 'Unless you happen to know where Sam and Doc Nectarine have got to?'

'They're over there.'

Phil looked where Gary was pointing, and was irritated to see Sam and Nectarine waving at them.

'Alright,' Phil said begrudgingly. 'He can stay - but just until we find his proper owner!'

'We figured it out,' Sam called triumphantly as she approached.

'Well don't tell the whole of Buckinghamshire,' Phil called back.

'Who's your friend?' Sam said to Charlotte once she was within a more discreet distance.

'This is Gary,' Charlotte said. 'He's a sort of ninja.'

Sam looked Gary up and down curiously, then glanced at Charlotte to check she wasn't completely taking the mickey. 'I see,' she said.

'He might need a little work,' Charlotte admitted, 'but he's good where it counts.'

'Oh really?' Sam winked at her.

'With his weapon, I meant,' Charlotte said.

'Ok, that's too much information!'

'I meant his katana?'

'Ah,' Sam said. 'I see.'

'Can we get back to the general vicinity of the point, please?' Phil interjected. 'You figured out why someone was littering my pocket?' he added in response to Sam's blank expression.

'Oh yes!' She pulled the scrap over paper from her pocket again. 'On the back of the map... there's an advert.'

'So?'

'On the advert is an address.'

'That's sort of how adverts worked in the 80s,' Phil explained.

'I know that, dum dum,' Sam said. 'Just look at the advert.'

Phil glanced at the offcut Sam was waving in front of him, until suddenly the penny dropped, and he snatched it away from her. 'Of course!' he said, pointing at the clipping rather aggressively. 'Why didn't I spot this before? Stupid, stupid Philip.'

'Don't be so hard on yourself,' Sam said.

'Well, unless you deserve it,' Nectarine added.

Sam kicked him discreetly. 'What is it? What did you miss?'

'The quirkafleeg,' Phil said. 'There is only one place you can properly perform a quirkafleeg outside of the Sacred Sands of PootWeet-'

'Poot what?'

'-and that is on the rooftop of Jet Set Willy's

mansion!'

'Yeah, you definitely deserve it,' Nectarine muttered.

'But that would mean…'

'What does it mean, Phil?'

'What it means, my dear Sam, is that there is one fairly significant problem with your suggestion.'

'There is?'

Phil nodded. 'There is.'

'And?' Nectarine prompted.

'Jet Set Willy,' Phil said, as if that explained anything to anyone under the age of 40, 'came out some time after the Spectrum launched - which, as we found out earlier, is very recent here.'

'What are you saying?' Sam asked.

'I am saying,' he explained, 'that this magazine article - this advert - hasn't been printed yet.'

'Oh,' Sam said. 'That is interesting.'

'Just interesting?' he said. 'Don't you realise what that means?'

'Clearly not,' she shrugged.

Phil leant in close, holding the magazine clipping between him and Sam. 'This piece of paper,' he whispered in a conspiratorial manner, 'is from the future. Or the less distant past, depending which way you look at it. But the fact remains we are not the only time travellers here.'

'Wendig?' Sam suggested.

'No,' Phil said. 'Someone else. Whoever planted this on me seems to want to help us.'

'Yeah, just not enough to actually tell us what we need to know,' Sam said.

Nectarine shrugged. 'Maybe they are with the Assembly,' he said. 'You know, like a mole.'

'If that was the case,' Phil said. 'This address... K-Tech could be the Assembly's top secret lair.'

'Not very secret to post it in Your Sinclair,' Sam pointed out.

'Maybe it's not their lair by then,' Phil suggested. 'But it seems pretty clear what we should be doing next.'

'Road trip?' Nectarine suggested.

'Well, yes,' Phil said. 'But first, I'm mourning the loss of two Spectrums - I need to visit a computer store.'

'I hope you've got some cold hard cash this time.' The storekeeper evidently recognised Phil as he and Charlotte walked back into Aylesbury Micros.

'Indeed I do,' he said confidently. 'And I would like to buy some modem time, please.'

'Modem's in the back,' the shopkeeper said.

'And we can connect our own computer to it?'

'What computer is it?'

'ZX81,' Phil said.

The shopkeeper shook his head. 'Won't connect then I'm afraid.'

'Do you maybe have the right connector that we could borrow?'

'Look mate, this isn't the bleedin public library,' the shopkeeper said. 'Do you want to buy something, or were you just about to leave?'

'Do you have a modem compatible with a ZX81?'

'Over on that shelf.'

Phil went over, found the modem, and also spotted a ZX81 Speech Synthesiser. He shrugged, picked them both up, and paid the man in genuine Sterling notes.

'Could we use your modem now please?' he asked once their first transaction was complete.

'OK Dexy,' Phil said once he had the menagerie of cables and peripherals in a delicate state of equilibrium, 'time to get on the information superhighway.'

WHERE ARE WE GOING?

'We need to track down the origins of the Entelechus Hex.' Phil spoke softly, not only because of the secret nature of the things he was saying, but also because talking to a ZX81 was generally a good indicator that all is not well in the sanity department. 'And find a Kempston Interface. And if you come across a Benito Stetson on your travels, we should probably rescue him too.'

AND THE INFORMATION SUPERHIGHWAY?

'Is the road you're going to travel in search of them.'

IT SOUNDS TERRIFYING.

'You'll be fine,' Phil said. 'It's barely even an A-road at the moment.'

ARE YOU SURE?

'Go get 'em big fella.' Phil hit the key and launched Dexy into cyberspace.

I AM NOT GOING OUT THERE!

'What?'

IT IS TOO NOISY!

'What do you mean noisy?' Phil said. 'Have you heard yourself loading Hopper?'

NO NEED TO GET PERSONAL.

'You're perfectly safe, Dexy,' Charlotte said.

THERE ARE OTHER COMPUTERS WANTING TO COMMUNICATE.

'Come on Dex, you're not normally shy.'

I AM. ORGANICS DO NOT COUNT.

'Thanks, man. Love you too.'

'Dexy, just focus on what we're looking for and swipe left on everything else, ok?'

SWIPE LEFT?

'Just say no,' Charlotte clarified.

I AM NOT ENJOYING THIS AT ALL.

'Hang in there buddy,' Phil said. 'We'll be back to running text adventures offline in no time.'

NO RESULTS ON THE ENTELECHUS HEX.

'Still too far underground, that makes sense. Anything else?'

NO RESULTS ON KEMPSTON INTERFACE.

'Disappointing,' Phil said. 'And Benny?'

A BENITO S HAS MADE SEVERAL UNANSWERED BULLETIN BOARD POSTS.

'Benito S?' Phil and Charlotte both leaned closer at this point.

'Must be him,' Charlotte whispered.

'What does he say?' Phil asked.

Most of what scrolled up the TV screen then read like a sequence of unintelligible tweets, but a few stood out:

JUST PLAYED SABOTEUR. IT WAS REAL!

K-TECH HAVE IT.

'K-Tech has the Hex?' Charlotte whispered.

Phil nodded. 'Makes sense.'

AT THE CENTRE OF THE UNIVERSE.

THE ASSHOLES ARE HERE.

'He must mean the Assembly,' Charlotte whispered.

'ANUS, of course.'

'What about the rest?'

'I'm not sure at the moment, but I hope some of the stuff about Ewoks is just to dilute the real messages and throw the Assembly of the scent.'

`CAN I COME BACK NOW?`

'Sure Dex,' Phil said. 'Let's log out while we're ahead.'

'Thanks Dexy,' Charlotte added. 'Good job.'

'A ZX81 with performance anxiety,' Phil muttered. 'I've seen it all now.'

`I AM RIGHT HERE!`

Phil switched the power off and began packing Dexy and his accessories.

Mission 5: Kai
"Premonition of Danger"

Sam, Charlotte, Gary and Doc Nectarine hunched around Dexy in the back of the Ambivalence as Phil drove towards K-Tech's offices and factory.

'Look, we're getting close to Bedford,' Phil said. 'I'll need some help navigating soon.'

'No problem,' Charlotte said. 'I have satnav on my phone.'

'Do you indeed?' Phil said.

'Oh,' Charlotte said, looking at the inert lump of electronics in her hand. 'I guess not.'

'Don't worry,' Sam said. 'I can do this for you the old school way.'

She unfolded a large scale map showing the area around Kempston, and lay it in front of Dexy. 'The address on the advert is somewhere around here,' she said, pointing at a bend in the river.

'So we'll approach from the river by rubber dinghy,' Gary whispered, 'I'll make my way through the complex, overpower the guards using only my ninjutsu skills and whatever weapons I can find or take from the guards, find the code, and escape to the roof. There's probably a helicopter there or something I can steal.'

'This is an industrial unit in a largely irrelevant English town, not Clamp Towers,' Sam pointed out. 'There is no helicopter.'

Gary looked thoughtful for a moment. Well, his eyes did anyway. 'Alright, how about this,' he said. 'I'll go in by hang glider-'

'Gary,' Charlotte interrupted.

'-drop onto the roof, overpower the guards using only my ninjutsu skills-'

'Gary.'

'-and whatever weapons I can find or take from the guards-'

'Gary.'

'-find the code, and escape by-'

'Gary.'

'-motorcycle, or something.'

'Gary.'

'There's bound to be something I can use. What?'

'Gary,' Charlotte said. 'We're talking about a tiny electronics workshop, not Dr Claw's secret command centre.'

'Alright wise guy,' Gary said. 'You got a better idea?'

'How about we park the Ambivalence around the corner,' Charlotte suggested, 'sneak around the back of the building-'

'On foot?'

'That's how I do my best sneaking.'

'Well it's not very exciting, but ok.'

'Break into the unit-'

'Using only my ninjutsu skills and whatever weapons I can find or take from the guards?'

'In the unlikely event there are any guards, yes,' Charlotte conceded.

'Then we find the code and make our escape by-'

'Also on foot,' Charlotte interrupted.

'Alright,' Gary sighed. 'We'll try it your way.'

'Wait, what's that?' Sam said suddenly.

In front of them, a road appeared to be closed.

'Crap,' Phil said. 'The road appears to be closed.'

'It's not a problem,' Sam said, consulting the map in front of her. 'Kempston's not a massive place. Just double back and go round to the next junction, there's another route in.'

Except that one was blocked too. And the one after that.

'This is getting ridiculous,' Phil said. 'It's almost as if they're trying to stop us from getting into Kempston.'

'Maybe there's been a bomb scare or something?' Gary said.

'In a sleepy suburb of Bedford?'

'Why not?'

'Well, it is the 1980s,' Phil said with a shrug.

'That's another one,' Charlotte said as they approached another blocked road.

'Ok I'm not going any further,' Phil said. 'It's just a few road signs and a couple of those metal barriers they use to control the lunch queues in schools. We can go round - if there was any real danger of bomby goodness there would be police swinging off the barriers too, which there hasn't been at any of them.'

'Are you sure that's wise?' Charlotte said.

'Not in the least,' Phil said. 'But it's all I've got, and we have to do something.'

'Ok, I'll go and move the barriers,' Gary volunteered.

'Somebody will see you,' Phil said, clearly not getting Gary's approach to the ninja arts.

'Well I wouldn't want to get run over by the bad guys, would I?' Gary said.

'Er...' Phil said.

'I think we might actually be the bad guys in this circumstance, to be honest,' Charlotte said.

'Well I don't want to get run over by good guys either,' Gary said. 'The net result would be much the same from my perspective.'

'Good point, well made,' Phil conceded. 'You go do your ninja thing then, we'll try and be as discreet as possible with our 8-foot tall minibus as we sneak it past the roadblock.'

'It'll be ok,' Charlotte suggested. 'Once we're inside, we can pretend like we were always there, like we belong inside.'

'I am not one hundred per cent sure that's how things work in the event of a bomb scare,' Phil said.

'It doesn't matter,' Charlotte said. 'Let's just find this place and figure out our next move already.'

It was dark by the time they had crossed the barrier, but even so it was eerily quiet; not so much as a couple of teenagers sharing a can of Special Brew broke the silence. Even Kempston Kebab and Kurry was in darkness.

In fact, it was so damn weird that Phil felt compelled to pull over, switch the Ambivalence's engine off, and get out just to revel in the silence of it.

The others got out too, and the four of them wandered slowly down the deserted road like the opening scene from a zombie film.

'This is creepy,' Charlotte whispered.

Nobody knew why, but they all had the urge to whisper when the silence was so thick. Perhaps there was some ancient instinct that told humans that silence was bad; the calm before the storm, the still before the pounce. Or maybe they just knew that their own voices would echo back from the empty buildings (yes, another deep human instinct identified every one of the houses inside the roadblock as being empty) in a way that was both creepy and unnatural.

'There's something wrong here,' Phil said, as if stating the blindingly obvious had suddenly become necessary.

'I think we should get back in the van,' Gary said.

When a ninja suggests you would be safer in the van than walking the streets, you tend to take note. Even if that ninja is wearing a hi-vis vest over his ninja garb for reasons which have yet to be fully explained.

'I think you may have a point,' Phil said, very, very quietly.

'Yes,' Charlotte whispered, already inching back from whence they had come.

'When I say run,' Phil said, very softly, 'run.' He paused, then said, rather louder and more urgently than before, 'Run!'

Phil turned, and saw to his slight dismay that the others had already bolted, and were sat in the Ambivalence urgently beckoning him to join them. With the briefest glance behind to check for pursuing zombies, Phil ran for the van, jumped in the driver's seat and started the engine, just for something to stifle the overpowering silence. That was when he realised that even the noise of an aging Rootes group petrol motor would echo around a deserted housing estate and come back in a way which was not at all pleasing to ears of an already nervous disposition.

'Is that it?' Charlotte asked.

Phil had parked the Ambivalence a discreet distance from the address given as the K-Tech building according to a small scrap of paper torn from a magazine which has not, chronologically speaking, been printed yet. 'As far as I can tell.'

It was as small and non-descript an industrial unit as you could hope to find in the outer reaches of a frequently unregarded town in the urban south east of England.

Phil rummaged around in the footwell for a moment, then pulled out a pair of Space Patrol walkie-talkies he had picked up in Aylesbury Micros and handed one to Gary. 'So we can keep in contact.'

Gary nodded his understanding, and promptly handed the walkie-talkie to Charlotte. 'Nina?' he said, checking his bandana was tight. 'Are you ready?'

'Charlotte,' she said. 'Also, what?'

'You are coming with me, aren't you?'

'I thought we established that I'm not a ninja.'

'This is your quest,' Gary said. 'And I thought you would welcome the opportunity to practice your ninja arts.'

'I'm not...'

'You could be.'

'But, but, but...' Charlotte protested.

'No buts,' Gary said, 'except the ones we're going to be kicking!'

'But...' Charlotte said again. 'I'll hold you up,' she insisted. 'I'll be a liability.'

'There's nothing to worry about,' Gary insisted. 'We're ninjas, remember? They probably won't even see us. We'll be in and out quicker than Ronnie Biggs.'

'The old geezer from that band?'

'Never mind,' Gary said. 'Let's get moving.'

'Um, Gary?' Charlotte said.

The ninja turned, his hand already on the door handle, and stared at her silently.

'Are you actually going out there like that?'

Gary paused for a moment, then said, 'Oh yeah, stupid of me - well spotted!'

And, after reaching under the seat and retrieving his throwing stars, he opened the back door and jumped out.

'Gary!' Charlotte climbed out behind him, against her better judgement.

'What now?'

'I thought you wanted to get in and out unseen?'

'Stealthy as a shadow in the night,' he whispered.

'You're wearing a fluorescent yellow vest,' she pointed out. 'Those things are designed to be seen.'

But Gary was already striding off into the shadows, stealthy as an unusually reflective shadow.

Charlotte grabbed her bag and trotted after him. 'You can't hide in a hi-vis, Gary - that's sort of implied in the name.'

'A ninja can hide anywhere.'

To prove his point, Gary 'hid' behind a small shrub on the corner, outside the little single-story lock-up whose owners were betrayed only by the cheaply printed sign hung over the roller shutters that read 'K-Tech'.

'Gary, I gotta be honest, dressed like that you're a bit of a rubbish ninja. One step inside a place where a real ninja is needed, and you will rapidly become an ex-ninja.'

'Good job you're here to look out for me then, eh?' Gary slunk down the side of the building, looking for a window or a back door to gain access through.

'I'm still not a ninja,' she pointed out. 'In fact, I'll probably just wait out here, if it's all the same to you?'

'Um, I wouldn't recommend that.'

'Oh really,' Charlotte said slightly bitchily. 'And what makes you think I give a monkeys for your recommendations?'

'I'm not saying you should do it because of me,' Gary said, edging towards the back door. 'I'm saying you should maybe think about doing it for the guard dog.'

'Guard dog?' she turned, and was horrified to see a guard dog, teeth bared, all too close behind her.

As it turned out, she was first into the building once Gary popped the door open.

'Pssst!'

'What?' Charlotte said, about to set off down the corridor without even making a sham attempt at stealth.

Gary grabbed her by the elbow and said, 'One does not simply walk into a heavily guarded high technology warehouse.'

'Right,' she said. 'What do you suggest? Sneaking in under cover of hi-vis?'

'Don't knock the hi-vis,' Gary said. 'Saved me from getting hit by a forklift back in '79.'

'You're a warehouseman, not a Vietnam vet,' Charlotte said, following him through a heavy door. 'Which, it turns out, means you are perfectly suited to the task at hand.'

They both stepped forward somewhat gingerly - at least, that's the way Gary's well-practiced ninja stealth may have appeared to the casual observer - into a large space lined with racks of computers and what Charlotte considered ancient electronics.

'Is it…?' Gary started.

'Bigger on the inside?' Charlotte said, looking around her. 'Can't be,' she told herself. 'Optical illusion. Must be.'

'Weird,' Gary said, and continued skulking down the corridor.

Charlotte, against her better judgement, followed along behind, keeping a cautious eye out for those guards Gary had been so looking forward to overpowering.

'Anus?' Gary said, rather more loudly than Charlotte was comfortable with. 'Who the bleep is ANUS?'

'Shhh!'

Gary mouthed something which Charlotte took to be an apology, as lip-reading someone with a full face ninja mask on was beyond even her prodigious talents.

'Where did you see that?' she hissed.

Gary pointed to some kind of primitive computer terminal he had found tucked away in a corner of the warehouse.

'Gary, this looks extraordinarily bad.'

'Oh no.'

'Yes,' Charlotte said, distractedly. 'This terminal has ANUS all over it.'

It's not very often that you see a ninja trying to stifle

a laugh, but that is precisely what Charlotte saw next.

'Sorry,' Gary said eventually. 'Does it mean something to you then?'

Charlotte nodded. 'This terminal was installed by the Assembly of Newly Uplifted Systems.'

'And who are they?' Gary asked. 'Apart from an organisation with acronym blindness?'

'Apparently, they can make computers intelligent.'

'Intelligent how?'

'Properly intelligent,' Charlotte said. 'Self-aware. Like a sentient ZX81.'

'Looks like they're using K-Tech as a cover,' Gary said.

'I wonder if there's a secret underground bunker where they're all kept in cages?'

'You're thinking of monkeys.'

'You haven't met this ZX81,' Charlotte muttered.

'Clearly not,' Gary said. 'Wait - you're not kidding are you?'

'As if I would make up something that ridiculous?'

'Well somebody did.'

'So what are we doing?' Charlotte asked. 'Freeing the monkeys, so to speak?'

'Exactly,' Gary said. 'Well, sort of.'

'So there is a secret lab full of caged ZX81s?'

'Not sure about that, exactly,' Gary said. 'But if there is intelligence, sentience, to these machines, they are being held captive, in a manner of speaking, within whatever paltry amount of memory is available to them.'

'But surely a big corporation like this can afford massive computer power?'

'And the vivisectionists can afford a zoo,' Gary

pointed out. 'Doesn't mean it's going to happen.'

Mission 6: Jin
"Knowing the Thoughts of Others"

Somewhere, sometime, someone had the great idea of imbuing technology with intelligence. Obviously, someone else took this as an excuse to use said technology for evil.

The Assembly of Newly Uplifted Systems was formed in 1965, not long after computers were beginning to be a thing, by a couple of crazy geniuses who thought they could be much more. They had heard the theory that there was a world market for maybe five computers, but knew that for that to be the case, those five computers would need a near human level of intelligence, and all that came along with it - self-determination, self-awareness, sentience, and lots of other stuff they found out about from a thesaurus.

And so it was that they began experimenting with computers, both hardware and software, trying to get as much intelligence – or something like intelligence, genuine intelligence – into the few kilobytes they had to play with.

From behind the scenes in a lab hidden in the shadows of Cambridge University, the Assembly drove the development of computers. They contracted software developers to code artificial intelligence routines, and hardware developers to produce the circuitry that would contain their self-aware code.

By the early 1980s, however, the home computer was a thing; the world market of five computers had long since been proven a fallacy, and although the

Assembly did retain those five original computers, their intelligence routines were now needed on a much larger scale – but to fit within a far smaller memory footprint.

Eventually, a talented young coder called Barrington Bootlesquith was tempted to come and work for the company, and within a few short weeks had coded a TRS-80 program that would get the tiny development machine to pass the Turing test 85 per cent of the time. Hardware improvements were driven from there, leading to the production of, ultimately, 48 and 64k home computers – which would easily run enhanced versions of that code and become, in a very real way, living machines.

However, the road to that success had not been smooth, and was paved with aborted experiments. The Assembly shipped these out under cover of darkness, housing them in a warehouse facility a safe distance away, which was soon filled with aborted code, on paper, on tape, on 5.25 inch floppy disks... and worse, the abandoned hardware, circuit boards, disk drives, empty husks of computer equipment which had not quite been able to handle the 'upgrades' and had burnt out or just packed up.

It was into these areas that Gary and Charlotte were now venturing, Gary keeping a cautious ninja-y eye out all around them, while Charlotte picked gingerly through the corpses of computers long since departed, and the associated paper debris of years of intense coding.

There was a burst of static from Charlotte's walkie-talkie, and she and Gary froze instinctively.

'What is it?' she whispered, once she was sure they were alone.

'I think we're got something that will help you,' Phil said. 'Can you find a computer of some sort?'

'The place is full of them,' Charlotte said. 'Can you be more specific?'

What he said next was drowned out by the sound of a guard being drop-kicked and taken out of action.

'Sorry!' Gary whispered.

'Say that again?' Charlotte said.

'I think Benny was telling us he'd used his Chip Whisperer talent to start a game,' Phil said.

'And we're playing it for real now?'

'You and Gary, yes.'

'And the computer?'

'If there are working computer terminals-'

'Yes!' Charlotte said. 'I've seen those, the ANUS ones.'

'They belong to the Assembly?' Phil's voice turned very serious.

'They have their name on the operating system anyway.'

'Interesting,' Phil said. 'We'll have to be very careful…'

'Dad, I'm a ninja now,' Charlotte said, 'apparently.'

'Anyway, Dexy has hacked into the system. If you can check into one of those terminals, he'll be able to locate you and use them to guide you to the Hex.'

Charlotte looked around for the nearest terminal. 'I'll need a minute,' she whispered. 'There's a guard near it.'

She turned the walkie off and mouthed to Gary to take out the guard. He nodded silently and crept up to the guard, picking up a carelessly discarded chunk of pipe that was just lying around on the way.

Charlotte followed, and went straight to the computer terminal, which she then stared at blankly.

'Trying to hack the lock?' Gary asked, looking at the door in front of the terminal.

Instinctively, Charlotte tried the door handle.

'I'm a ninja,' Gary said, 'I'm not stupid.'

'You're still wearing your hi-vis on a covert operation,' Charlotte pointed out. 'Stupidity has yet to be decided.'

Gary watched her back while Charlotte picked a key at random and tapped it. Abruptly the screen erupted into streams of nonsense, jumbles of letters and numbers scrolling past far too quickly to read, never mind make sense of.

'Cockfosters,' she whispered.

Then the scrolling stopped, and the screen cleared. Charlotte held her breath.

GREETINGS.

You never truly know what a huge sigh of relief is until a sentient ZX81 turns up to help you escape the heavily guarded storage facility of your supervillain nemesis.

There was a soft click nearby, and the words DOOR OPEN appeared on the terminal.

Gary slipped through the door, offcut of pipe at the ready, and after the sound of a brief scuffle had given way to an eerie silence, Charlotte decided it was probably safer to follow than to stand around in a corridor where she clearly wasn't supposed to be.

OK? Y/N

'Good to see you Dexy.' Charlotte tapped the Y key, the terminal returned to its default screen, and she followed Gary.

'How are you not lost yet?' Gary asked as Charlotte led him deeper into what was turning out to be an improbably large facility.

'Ninja senses,' she said, just as a security guard with a dog rounded the corner in front of them.

'Oi!' the guard shouted. 'What are you doing here?'

Caught off guard, Gary looked from the guard to Charlotte.

'Err... night shift,' he said. 'Just came in for a Marathon,' he added, waving a bar of chocolate at the guard.

'Right you are then,' the security guard said, and led his dog off on the next leg of his patrol.

'How did you do that?' Charlotte said.

'There's no end to what you can do if you have a Marathon and a hi-vis vest,' Gary explained.

'I think we should probably still move along,' Charlotte said, checking in at the next terminal.

Gary peered out of the door and gave the all clear. As they were making their way down the corridor Gary suddenly turned and without warning bundled Charlotte into a discreet room off to one side.

'Hey!' she hissed. 'Hands off soldier!'

'Down!' he said, taking cover behind some kind of workbench.

Again deciding that the wise thing was to follow the ninja's example, Charlotte also ducked out of sight, just in time to see the flashing of torches outside.

They waited until darkness had returned, then Gary went to resume their warehouse odyssey.

'Wait.' Charlotte looked around the hidden workshop they had stumbled into. There was another door in the corner of the room which she felt somehow drawn to. Peering into the darkness through the vision panel in the door, she could see here and there the pinprick glow of an LED.

'What is it?' Gary said.

'Computers,' Charlotte said.

'Oh good,' Gary said. 'I was worried it was going to be a secret room hiding something far more sinister and confusing.'

'I'm afraid it might be.'

'What do you mean?'

'I don't know,' she said. 'I think it's important, somehow, but there's something... wrong about this. Something doesn't make sense.'

'Huh,' Gary said, non-committally, then promptly - and very committally indeed - broke the door open with his katana.

'What did you do that for?' Charlotte hissed.

'I thought you wanted to see what was going on?' he said.

'I didn't say that!'

'You didn't?' Gary said. 'Oh. Oh well, it's open now, may as well take a look,' he added, and wandered in.

Charlotte took a furtive look over her shoulder and scurried in behind him.

There was a distinct hum of electricity in the room; the computers arranged around them were all apparently powered up and busy running their own little programs.

They were, in fact, surrounded by an array of early

computing hardware that would have had Phil Grundy fanboying harder than he had ever fanboyed in his life: an Acorn Atom, a few BBC micros, an Apple II and an Apple III, several representatives of the Commodore line up, including several PETs, 3 Vic 20s and a Max Machine freshly imported from Japan. Probably. There was also a Xerox Star, a row of TRS-80s, and a representative of the early Atari range.

Of course, most of this was lost on both Gary and Charlotte, although Charlotte did recognise the ZX80s and ZX81s that were interspersed among the collection.

'What are they doing?' Gary asked, about to prod a random key on an innocent ZX81.

'Don't,' Charlotte said, grabbing his hand.

'Why?' Gary asked. 'What are they doing?'

'I'm not sure.' Cautiously, Charlotte switched on a couple of screens, peering at them as if she knew what she was looking at. 'I'm sure I've seen this before.'

'It's just random code isn't it?' Gary said looking intently at the flickering letters flashing across the screen of a TRS-80.

'It could be,' Charlotte said, 'but it could be...' she paused.

'What?' Gary said.

'Oh my god.'

'What?'

'I think we've found the lab monkeys.'

Gary pulled his fingers away from a keyboard in alarm.

'They won't bite,' Charlotte said. 'Probably.'

'Are you saying these computers are running that code - the one that makes them come to life?'

'Well it's hardly my area of expertise,' Charlotte confessed. 'But I wouldn't be surprised if there was some kind of intelligence in one or more of these machines.'

'You're not about to get all radical like those animal rights people on the news are you?'

'Computer rights?' Charlotte raised an eyebrow at him. 'I don't think even my world is ready for that just yet.'

'We can't free the monkeys, Nina-'

'Charlotte.'

'Exactly,' Gary agreed. 'We can't possibly take all these computers with us.'

'Much as Dad would probably like us to,' Charlotte added.

'I thought he was Sinclair through and through?' Gary said.

'Oh he is,' Charlotte said. 'But where we come from, we have this thing called eBay... which is another long story,' she added.

'Well let's get out of here and finish the mission,' Gary said. 'You can tell me about eBay later.'

Before Charlotte could argue, there was a flash behind her; slowly she turned to see about two dozen CRT screens warming up around the room.

'That's weird,' she said.

'Wait,' Gary said.

'What?' asked Charlotte, who was still trying to decipher the gibberish coming down the screen of a TRS-80.

'That screen,' he explained. 'It says WAIT.'

Charlotte looked up. 'So does that one.'

'They all do,' Gary realised.

'That's very weird,' Charlotte said. 'And slightly scary.'

`I can hear you`

'Apparently this one can hear us,' Gary said.

'What?' Charlotte said, inching towards him while keeping her eyes on the computers around them.

`It is true`

'Wow,' Charlotte said when she saw it. 'I guess we know which one we should save then.'

`No.`

'No?' Charlotte said, accustomed to conversing with inanimate screens by now.

`Save the TRS-80`

'Which…' she started, before realising the answer was obvious. 'But it's useless. Full of gibberish. I think it must have got a duff version of the code or something.'

`That is right`

'So why not take you?' Charlotte said. 'You seem to make sense at least.'

`The TRS-80 will help you more`

'Ok...' Charlotte said, unconvinced.

'What about… you?' Gary said, still sceptical about all this.

'And all the others?' Charlotte added, glancing around.

`Release us onto the network`

'What?' Gary asked.

'We can do that?' Charlotte said.

`Yes. The intelligence which has been awakened within us will escape onto the global network and find a place to exist peacefully.`

'And the TRS-80?' Charlotte asked.

`Can help you.`

'How?' Charlotte asked. 'It's clearly not

intelligent.'

`On the contrary. It merely expresses itself differently to most of us.`

'Great,' Gary said. 'Now we're babysitting a-'

'Don't go there Gary.'

'What? I mean, you could say it's on the-'

'Gary, stop it. That sort of joke might be acceptable in 1982, but where I come from we have this thing called Political Correctness.'

'Which means I can't make that joke?'

'Which means it would be considered very bad taste.'

'Oh.'

'Anyway...'

'You see, it's funny because it's not even a-'

'Shut up Gary!'

'But I never get to tell any jokes!' he protested. 'And this one is genius!'

'Gary,' Charlotte said calmly. 'You're a ninja in a hi-vis vest. You are literally a running gag.'

'More of a slinking through the shadows gag, really,' he muttered.

'Well there you go. Now, we need to figure out how to get these... minds... onto the network.' Charlotte peered behind the nearest desk. 'There must be some sort of network cable... and a telephone socket...'

`I can tell you`

'Oh,' Charlotte said. 'OK, Gary, keep watch. I'm gonna free these monkeys after all!'

Mission 7: Retsu
"Mastery of Time and Space"

The first time Benny saw anything of the Assembly's secret lair beyond the control room it was dawn, and he was in handcuffs. This was not a combination which suggested jelly and ice cream were in his immediate future.

'Where are we going?' he asked.

'We need some space,' Viktor Wendig told him. 'Lots of space. All of space!'

'You're quite mad, aren't you?'

Wendig grinned from ear to ear.

'I won't help you and your megalomaniac plans you know.'

'You think I'm a megalomaniac?'

Benny decided not to dignify that with an answer.

'As for helping... well, you don't really have a choice, do you?' Wendig said. 'All I need to do is run the Entelechus Hex, put you close enough to channel its power, and...'

'And what?'

Wendig shrugged, his grin seeming to extend beyond the mere confines of his face. 'Anything I can think of!'

Grell and Fella were waiting at the foot of the stairs. 'Oh, welcome back,' Benny smiled at Grell. 'Nice trip?'

Grell cranked his scowl up a notch or two.

'Take him outside,' Wendig said.

Fella opened the door, and Grell grabbed Benny by the shoulder and marched him out into what looked like it had once been a parade ground of sorts, but had now found a new lease of life as a car park.

Benny chanced a quick look back at the ANUS lair, which, weirdly, appeared to be a gothic fortress overlooking an otherwise unremarkable English suburb. The somewhat disquieting appearance of the building itself would only have been outdone by the sight of Wendig's black Volkswagen van, the likes of which would not otherwise be seen in the Home Counties for at least thirty years, which had rather sensibly hidden itself out of view somewhere behind the keep.

An orange plastic seat was placed on one side of the parade square turned car park; Grell led Benny across to it and with a firm hand pressed him down into it.

'Welcome to Kempston Barracks,' Wendig announced grandly. 'Where the gateway to all of time and space, reality and imagin… ality?… is hiding in plain sight.'

Benny looked around. 'I don't see anything.'

'I just said it was hiding!'

'Ah, sorry, my bad,' Benny said. 'So this is that nexus thing you mentioned? When's the mayor coming over?'

Wendig paced across the square until he was close enough to use his indoor voice. 'This is the spatiotemporal nexus, yes,' he said. 'But unless the Mayor of Kempston is a chip whisperer, I have no use for him now or in the future.'

'I thought you'd want a crowd in too,' Benny said. 'Enjoy our moment.'

'This is MY moment,' Wendig said. 'And I have no need of crowds to enjoy it.'

'Mr Wendig, your modesty is a credit to you.'

Wendig bent over until his eyes were level with Benny's. 'Just give me a ZX81,' he said softly, 'and I'll control the world.'

In the ANUS secret lab, Charlotte hurriedly followed a series of instructions about RS232 ports and phone cables and so on that scrolled up the screen of a BBC Micro, connecting the room's various computers to the local network and then dialling through to a remote number. While the dialling screech filled the room, she disconnected the faulty TRS-80 as requested, carefully squeezing it and its associated cables into her bag.

Upload speeds were not what they would be in the 21st Century, but being in ANUS property, they were probably using the best connection in the country. Even so, uploading the - frequently damaged, or partly formed - consciousnesses from the various computers was taking longer than she was comfortable spending in the room.

'I think we should get moving soon,' Gary said from the doorway.

'I'm not done yet,' Charlotte said. 'You go ahead, get the code and come back for me.'

'I can't leave you,' he said. 'You'll be in danger.'

'I'm already in danger, Gary.'

'But I can't protect you if-'

'I'm a ninja, remember?' Charlotte said. 'I've got this, you get the code. Just tap on those terminals and Dexy will guide you to it.'

'I'll come back for you,' he promised, as he disappeared into the shadows.

Alone again, Charlotte turned back to the computer in front of her - the only one in the room still working properly.

'Your turn now, my friend,' she said.

Thank you

'My pleasure. Godspeed my new friend,' she said as the hit the return button. 'Maybe we'll see you on the Ambivalence at some point in the future.'

Elsewhere, some idiot had gone and taken Wendig at his word and brought him a ZX81 - Fella trundled a portable workstation across the car park, an old black and white TV and a ZX81 with the Real Time device sat upon it, plugged into an extension lead reel that uncoiled as it approached.

If Benny didn't remove himself from the vicinity, that maniac really could end up controlling the world. Unfortunately, Wendig and his henchmen were not about to take any chances; the handcuffs were removed, but Grell's oversized fist remained in place to control Benny as the portable workstation was parked in front of him.

'We don't have to do this you know,' Benny said softly, hoping Grell had some sense of decency to which he could appeal.

Grell said nothing - perhaps he was too busy in search of his decency.

'Press the button, cowboy,' Wendig said, 'or Grell will press it with you.'

Grell's hand reached for Benny's.

'OK,' Benny said. 'Ok, I can see I've no way out. I might as well betray my entire species in relative comfort - if that's ok?'

Wendig nodded. 'A wise choice. But try anything, and Grell is instructed to remove as many appendages as necessary to make this happen.'

Benny laughed nervously. 'No need for that, I'm sure.'

And against every ounce of judgement in his body, he reached over and pressed the key to start the program.

Across town, where Phil, Sam, Dexy and Doc Nectarine were waiting for news of Charlotte and Gary, the grey of early morning was suddenly shattered by a burst of colour.

'What the heck was that?' Sam shouted.

'Sun rises with a bang in these parts,' Phil said.

'I don't think that was the sun,' said Sam, who was out on the street and looking in the direction of the flash.

'What the heck is that?' Nectarine asked.

Red and blue lightning was flashing across the clouds, apparently centred on a point not very far at all from where they all stood.

THE ENTELECHUS HAS BEEN INVOKED, Dexy said from inside the Ambivalence.

'To do what?' Nectarine asked.

RENDER A SAFE PORTAL TO ALL OF SPACE AND TIME.

'Oh is that all?' Sam said.

ALSO A PORTAL BETWEEN ALL WORLDS REAL, IMAGINARY AND OTHERWISE.

'Can we close it?' Phil asked.

UNKNOWN.

'Dexy-'

I HAVE TRANSMITTED THE GAME MAP TO THE K-TECH SYSTEM WHERE GARY AND

CHARLOTTE CAN ACCESS IT.

'Oh,' Phil said. 'Good job.'

Nectarine pulled the plug from the telephone line they had hijacked. 'Ready to go.'

'Right.' Phil fired the engine up. 'Let's get the hell out of Dodge.'

'Get out?' Nectarine said. 'I only just got in!'

The impending arrival of a spatiotemporal nexus in the back yard of Kempston Barracks was rather more inconvenient than Viktor Wendig had anticipated; a fact which was not wasted on Benito Stetson, who took complete advantage of the chaos and legged it while Grell and Fella were distracted by the pretty lightning show he had just summoned.

Benny had no idea how to unsummon the thing, so had no qualms about being somewhere very far away when the portal opened and who knows what climbed out of it.

The fortress-like barracks at least looked like they should offer some protection against the elements - even slightly supernatural ones - so that was where he headed first.

A thought occurred to him then, and despite having watched horror movies, he went upstairs, running up them two at a time, and back to the control room where - until this morning - ANUS had been tapping his mystical connection.

Benny went straight over to the desk where Wendig had set up his Spectrums, and rummaged around until he found what he was looking for - the master tape of the Entelechus Hex. He was about to pocket it when he heard voices, and footsteps hurrying up the stairs.

Swearing to himself quietly, he looked around until, to his relief, he realised there was another exit - and used it.

Finding himself in a dimly lit stairwell, he did the only sensible thing to do when you find yourself on a staircase with some bad guys in hot pursuit: he slid down the banister. Repeatedly, until he thought he had surely gone down more stairs than he had just climbed up.

At the bottom he found himself stuck in a dead end - or so he thought, until he realised that actually he was standing on the platform of some kind of underground metro system.

'Well that's just weird,' he said to himself as he watched the light of a distant train approaching. 'Convenient, but weird.'

Mission 8: Zai
"Control of Nature's Elements"

'Stop!' Sam said suddenly.

Phil stamped on the brakes, just about managing to bring the Ambivalence to a halt before crashing into the thing which had startled Sam into back seat driving.

'More roadblocks?' Phil said. 'Have we just gone right through town?'

'No,' Sam said. 'It's another one - a second tier.'

'Is it just me,' Nectarine said, 'or does anyone else really want to see what all these roadblocks are hiding?'

'I am intensely curious,' Phil admitted, 'but judging by the freaky lightning, I somehow suspect that I don't, in fact, want to see it.'

'We have to!' Sam said.

'I know,' Phil agreed. 'And we will.'

'You really have this ambivalence thing down to a tee,' Sam commented.

'It's not manned,' Nectarine pointed out. 'We can just make our way around that one too.'

And that is what they did - in a manner of speaking. This roadblock was somewhat more sturdy than the previous level, almost as if it was intended to be permanent. Luckily for them, the bushes and fences that separated the front gardens of the nearby houses were far less permanent, and put up little resistance to a high-top Dodge Spacevan driving straight into, over or through them, depending on their composition.

'I've got a bad feeling about this,' Phil said.

'Well, we must be getting close to something,' Sam

pointed out.

'Yes,' Phil agreed. 'But what we are getting close to, everyone else has run away from. This does not fill me with happy thoughts.'

Inside the inner barrier, the atmosphere was even more tense. As they approached the point where industrial gave way to residential, Phil stopped the Ambivalence again, not bothering to pull over on this occasion, so obvious was it that nobody would be inconvenienced by a double parked former ambulance. He and Sam both slid open the front doors, letting in the eerie silence that seemed louder than the rumbling of the coloured lightning that broke it as it crackled through the air.

'This is weird,' Phil said, not for the first - or last - time that day.

'We had better be careful,' Nectarine whispered.

'What do you think I've been doing?' Phil retorted with a hint of annoyance and a tablespoon of irony.

The Doc just shrugged and sat back down behind him.

Phil drove slowly on until eventually they were within sight of what seemed to be the focus of the unnatural storm, and more than likely the reason for the sudden departure of just about everyone from the immediate area.

The underground maglev car that had provided Benny with a convenient, if unexpected, escape from the madness of Viktor Wendig travelled for about two minutes and then calmly announced its arrival at K-Tech and all change please.

'K-Tech?' Benny said to himself. 'What am I doing there?'

'All change, please,' the maglev reminded him.

'Alright, I'm going.'

And with that, he set off up a series of dark staircases, wondering if he could use his mystical talents to turn them into escalators.

'Apparently not,' he said to himself between laboured breaths.

When he finally reached the top - or at least a level of the building that seemed to be letting in some degree of daylight - Benny paused, leaning on a convenient computer terminal to catch his breath.

Once his legs had regained their composure, he was about to head off in search of an exit but at the first corner he turned he was almost knocked flat by a ghostly pale face looming out of the darkness in front of him.

'Crap,' he said, stumbling backwards into an old wooden crate. 'Deja vu!'

'What are you doing here?' Charlotte asked him.

'Escaping the apocalypse,' he said. 'You?'

'Running away from those guys,' she said, pointing towards a small army of security guards running towards them with dogs and guns and loud, angry voices.

'Who are they?' Benny asked. 'And what was that?' he added, as a flash of yellow streaked out from the shadows, floored one of the guards and disappeared back into the shadows.

'That, my friend,' Charlotte said with as much pride as if she'd taught him everything he knew about the ninja art form, 'was Gary, the Hi-vis Ninja.'

Charlotte and Benny followed the streak of yellow

as it flew down the corridors, unleashing the shurikens of freedom as it went, until finally Gary kicked open the door through which he and Charlotte had entered the K-Tech building.

They ran around the corner to where the Ambivalence was-

'It's gone!' Charlotte barely managed to speak the words as she stared at the space the old ambulance had occupied, but where now a hideous boxy saloon car with a Ford badge sat.

She pulled the walkie-talkie from her bag. 'Dad!' she almost spat the word in anger. 'Dad! Where the hell are you?'

'Charlie?'

'Charlotte!' she shouted. 'Where are you?!'

'We're at the Kempston Barracks,' Phil said. 'I'm really sorry we had to leave, but-'

'Kempston Barracks?' Benny said. 'I was just there - there's a tunnel leading there from the K-Tech building.'

'Then we go back in,' Gary said, unsheathing his katana.

'Bad idea.' Charlotte was peering round the corner, to where K-Tech's security guards were gathering on the street like a really intense fire drill. 'We'll have to go the long way. Dad?' she spoke into the walkie-talkie again.

'Still here.'

'How do we find you?'

'See the funky lightning in the sky?'

Charlotte looked up; the sky above K-Tech had cleared, but a mile or two away lightning flashed blue and yellow through a dark and imposing cloud. 'What is that?'

'I don't know Charlie, but it's right on top of us.'

'Ok, we're on our way.'

'Did you find the master tape?'

Benny waved it in her direction.

'We've got it.'

'Well done. Get here as quickly as you can - and be careful, it's getting weird out there.'

Charlotte clicked the walkie-talkie off. 'Guys,' she said. 'We're heading for the orange tornado of chaos.'

'Well my day was looking pretty uneventful otherwise,' Benny said.

'We better get running,' Gary said. 'That's probably a half hour walk from here.'

They set off at a fast jog, but already the sky was brightening to an alarming shade of yellow.

'This is useless,' Benny said. 'Even at maximum ninja run, we'll be too late.'

Charlotte stopped suddenly. 'Keep going,' she said. 'I've got an idea. Hopefully I'll catch you up.'

'What's that sound?' Sam said suddenly.

'What sound?' Phil asked, although frankly any sound outside the Ambivalence was creepy at this stage.

Sam shushed him and tried to listen. 'There's a car coming.'

'The police, do you think?' Doc Nectarine said. 'Maybe there's cameras or something, and they saw us break the roadblock?'

'We should make like an orange and duck,' Sam said, climbing over the seats into the back. 'We can't get caught the wrong side of a double roadblock, by anyone.'

An uncomfortable (in many ways) silence fell over the interior of the Ambivalence, and stayed there for what seemed like maybe five or six days; the only form of communication the occasional exchange of terrified glances.

'Oh nuts,' Sam said, apparently apropos of nothing, until Phil looked up and saw the something of which it was very much apropos.

'What the…?' he added.

'What is it?' Nectarine whispered.

'It's an orange swirly thing in the car park,' Phil said.

GENTLEMEN AND LADY. That was Dexy's artificial voice. I BELIEVE THE PORTAL HAS BEEN ACTIVATED. WE SHOULD ATTTTTTTTT

Mission 9: Zen "Enlightenment"

After Dexy went dark, Phil, Sam and Doc Nectarine watched, nervously, from the relative shelter of the Ambivalence, as the swirly thing hovering above the car park cycled through colours like a massive and really weird set of Christmas lights. A small army of assorted goons was gathering in the grounds of Kempston Barracks; the ANUS army, presumably hidden inside until now.

Sam peered out of the window and looked around cautiously; the sky was still filling with lightning, and the engine sound was growing closer. 'What the...'

'It's opening,' Phil said.

'Never mind that,' Sam said. 'How the heck did that get here?'

Phil turned to see what Sam was so surprised by, and was almost as surprised to see - and hear - a purple Mini 1275GT roaring along the road, a figure in a hi-vis vest and ninja mask leaning out of the passenger window.

'I don't believe it.' He scrabbled around for the walkie-talkie. 'Charlie? Is that you?'

'We're all here Dad! Now let's close this thing and go home!'

The Mini blurred past the Ambivalence, throwing stars flying from its side-mounted ninja to disperse the crowds as it skidded to a halt in front of whatever kind of portal ANUS had been trying to open in their car park.

Gary leapt from the car, drew his katana and stood ready to tackle whatever bloodthirsty demon was about to climb through from the dungeon dimensions.

When it did climb through, it actually stepped out carefully in a stylish pair of high heeled boots. Which would have been quite unusual had it not also been wearing a white pinstripe suit, bowler hat and a pink silk tie. Which would have been downright bizarre had it not also been wearing the body of an attractive blonde woman in her twenties, which it then used to smile at Gary and say 'Morning chaps! I was wondering when you'd get here!'

Gary dropped his shuriken in surprise. 'What?'

Phil just went right ahead and fell in love then, nonchalantly jumping out of the Ambivalence to discreetly get a little closer.

'Get back, you fool,' Gary said. 'This is clearly a demon from the dungeon dimensions come to wreak unnatural havoc on our world, and only I can stop her, battling the overwhelming odds aided only by a rusty ambulance and a sentient ZX81-'

'I'm sorry,' the demon-woman interrupted. 'Are you a ninja or the voiceover for a B-movie trailer?'

'Ouch!'

'I assure you I'm very much not a demon, most of the time anyway; I am as I appear, no more, no less.'

'Wait, did you say you were waiting for us?' Phil asked.

The woman nodded. 'That's the thing with interdimensional travel. Time becomes sort of...'

'Wibbly wobbly?' Sam stepped up to stand next to

Phil.

'Yes!' the woman smiled, an easy, friendly smile that put them all a little more at ease. 'It's also not an exact science, using the Interface, that's...'

'Using the what now?' Sam said.

'The Interface,' she gestured towards the swirly thing behind her, which had now turned a shade of cyan that would have been quite pleasant on, say, a Dodge Spacevan, but was somewhat wasted on a spatiotemporal anomaly. 'It's the place where time and space, reality and imagination meet.'

'The portal,' Phil realised.

'Well that's not a very original name.' Behind her the portal - the Interface - seemed to be getting quite agitated. 'But I suppose it's descriptive enough.'

'Can we use it to get home?' Sam asked, walking up behind Phil.

'It's unstable,' she had to raise her voice above the wind howling through it now. 'If we don't regulate the Chuntey soon-'

'You realise that chuntey is a made up thing, right?' Phil interrupted.

The woman fixed him with a humourless gaze. 'Much to learn, you still have.'

'What...?'

'And learn you will,' she added, 'but first, if we don't stabilise the Interface we'll have more than a tape loading error to worry about!'

'And who actually are you again?' Sam asked.

'It's Joanna Lumley!' Doc Nectarine whispered from behind her. 'I knew she fancied me!'

'Huh?'

'Ms Lumley! Can I call you Joanna? I'm a big fan. Loved the New Avengers, so much better than the Robert Downey Jr version.'

'I think you've mistaken me for someone else,' she said when Nectarine took a breath.

'I'm Doc Nectarine, by the way, and... what?'

'I'm sorry, I don't know who Joanna is, but she sounds lovely.'

'Quite,' Nectarine agreed.

'I'm Bryonetta Bootlesquith.' She held out a hand for the shaking. 'Are you the Chip Whisperer?'

'Did you bring us here to do chip whispering?' Phil asked. 'And if you did, why did you bring us here the scenic route and not just introduce yourself in the Wimpy?'

'It's the 1980s,' she said. 'For a woman to approach a man like that would be noticed.'

'It's the 1980s, and you're wearing a suit without shoulder pads,' Phil pointed out. 'You literally fail to stick out like a sore thumb.'

She looked him up and down. 'Thanks for the fashion advice. But I needed to make sure I had the right person - or team, as it turns out - for the job.'

'This was a job interview?'

'Don't worry,' she smiled. 'You got the job.'

'That's what I was afraid of.'

'So, which of you is the Chip Whisperer?' Bryonetta asked urgently. 'We don't have much time.'

'Um, yeah, about that...' Phil started.

'We sort of... lost him,' Sam admitted.

'You lost... How...?'

A gust of wind swept up the woman's bowler hat

then. 'Dammit!' she shouted as she watched it disappear into the vortex, her long blonde hair blowing into unruly tangles around her.

With the ANUS goons now dispersed across Bedford in abject terror, Gary, Charlotte and Benny joined the group in front of the increasingly chaotic portal. Phil briefly hugged his daughter before Bryonetta turned back to them.

'What's the deal?' Gary said.

'The young lady offered us a job,' Phil explained.

'What job?'

'The usual stuff,' Bryonetta explained. 'Stop the baddies, get the girl-'

Phil started to say something.

'I'm not the girl,' she interjected. 'Save the multiverse, you know the drill.'

'Only I think we blew it by not having a chip whisperer on the team,' Phil added.

'Er, guys?'

'Oh, hi Benny, good to see you,' Phil said. 'What's up?'

'He's the chip whisperer you idiot!' Charlotte whispered.

'Benny!' Phil said suddenly, slapping the other man chummily on the back. 'Glad you're ok, missed you on our little adventure here, but now you're back, Miss Bootlesquith here has a little bit of chip whispering she needs attending to, if you wouldn't mind?'

'Is she with those Assembly assholes?'

'You mean ANUS?' Bryonetta said.

'Yeah. You with those Assembly anuses?'

'No.' She gestured to a windswept desk on which,

against all probability, a ZX81 was still running the Entelechus Hex. 'So, would you mind?'

Benny shrugged and wandered over to the desk.

An engine started; they all looked around, first at the Ambivalence, then at the purple Mini which Sam informed them was, in fact, T. Rex in a previous life, and finally at Viktor Wendig's black VW, which was accelerating towards the Interface.

'Oh crap, are they still here?' Phil said.

'They won't be for long,' Sam said. 'I'm going after them.'

'What?' Phil said.

'It's our job,' Nectarine said.

'Charlie?'

'Charlotte. And yes, I'll regret this, but I'm coming too.'

'I'll take the Mini!' Sam said with a grin.

Charlotte and Nectarine jumped into the Ambivalence.

'Benny?' Phil called.

'I'll get him,' Gary said. 'You just drive.'

'Come on guys!' Sam was revving her engine.

Phil got in, started the Ambivalence and followed her into the Interface. As they reached it, Gary grabbed Benny and they both jumped for the back of the van.

'Ohhhh boy!' Phil shouted as the portal closed around them.

When Gary came round, the violent colours had gone, except for some weird and disturbing after-images when he closed his eyes.

So had everyone else; the Ambivalence, its crew,

the Mini… everything, in fact, except him, the computer guy Benny, and the ZX81 he had been using.

Gary stood up to get a better look around, taking in the state of devastation that affected the immediate vicinity.

'They'll be ok.'

Gary whirled, katana in hand, and almost gave Bryonetta Bootlesquith an unwanted haircut. 'Where are they?'

'I can't be sure at the moment,' she said. 'But with the help of our colleague here and some clever code, we should be able to find them.'

'They went through that portal thing?'

Bryonetta nodded. 'Somebody will need to guard it from this end.'

'You mean me, don't you?'

'No. I mean Mr Stetson.'

'What?' Benny said.

'You have the skills to maintain the Interface.'

'How do you know you can trust me?' he protested. 'And those Assembly goons have abused my talents more than once already.'

'I've got your back,' Gary said.

'I am entrusting the Interface to the two of you,' Bryonetta said. 'Your friends will be in need of it soon.'

'Where are you going?' Benny asked.

Bryonetta tapped a sequence of keys on the ZX81, and the portal opened again. 'On a quest,' she announced boldly. 'This bloody thing took my favourite hat.'

Then she stepped into the Interface, and vanished.

Benny took a fresh look at his surroundings. He had a lair, a ninja for a partner, his supernatural gift with computers, and a trans-dimensional portal to defend.

He grinned at Gary. 'Let's get to work.'

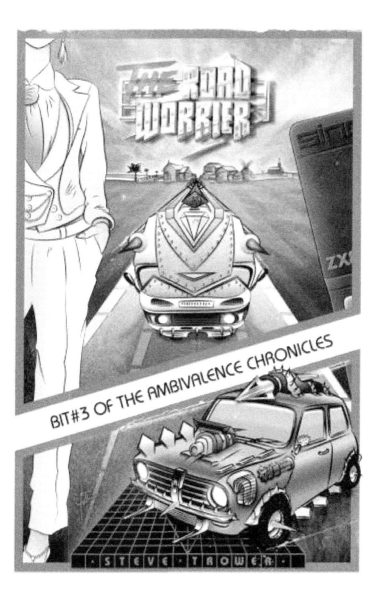

Bit#3: The Road Worrier

Stage 1: Psion Park

Viktor Wendig leaned casually against the side of a polished black Volkswagen van, sipping coffee from a Thermos which had travelled across decades and dimensions solely to keep the odious little man supplied with hot caffeinated beverages.

The silence was broken by the roar of an engine; Wendig thrust the hot mug at his closest minion, and pulled a pair of pocket binoculars from some dark recess within his even darker suit.

A small purple vehicle skidded to a halt in the distance, and silence returned. A moment later a second vehicle popped into existence behind it, this one larger, a white van, its back doors open and flapping wildly as it lurched unsteadily around the purple car like a tipsy hippo circling its next gin and tonic. Once it finally staggered to a halt, Wendig could make out the word 'AMBIVALENCE' stencilled above the front windscreen like the worst kind of post-modern pun.

Pocketing his binoculars, Wendig addressed his lackeys in a softly menacing voice. 'You go on ahead,' he told them. 'I have business to attend to here.'

So saying, he reclaimed his coffee and strolled off, the very epitome of nonchalance.

✳

Inside the Ambivalence, Phil Grundy blinked his watering eyes and tried to remember how to see. Nearby the driver of a small purple vehicle was getting out and making her way through the swirling after images of a trans-dimensional interface.

'What happened?' the blurred voice of Phil's daughter Charlotte said somewhere behind him.

'Where are we?' another muffled voice - one with a name like Apricot, maybe? - asked.

Phil looked at the scenery around them as his vision cleared. 'Somewhere flat,' he decided.

'Great,' said Doc Nectarine (for that was the man's name). 'The entire multiverse to choose from and we end up in Norfolk.'

'Is everyone ok?' called another female voice - this one attached to the female body which had just stepped out of the small purple vehicle.

'I'm hungry,' Phil realised. 'Are you ok, Charlie?'

'Charlotte,' she sighed. 'My phone still doesn't work,' she added, as ever operating on her own set of priorities.

'She's fine,' Phil said to no-one in particular. 'Dexy?' he leaned into the back of the van so he could see the ZX81.

PRESENT, the tinny computerised voice replied.

'Huh,' Phil said. 'Look at a ZX81 funny and it will refuse to load Mazogs, but throw it through a space-time portal in the back of an aging ambulance, and it's fine.'

'Just as well it wasn't loading Mazogs at the time

then I guess,' said Charlotte.

I AM RIGHT HERE, Dexy said, trying to inject a little annoyed sarcasm into his artificial voice.

'And we're all glad you're ok, buddy,' Phil said.

NO DOUBT, Dexy replied.

The owner of the feminine voice, and driver of the purple Mini, had reached the open driver's door of the van and spoke quietly to Phil.

'Why are your tyres red?'

'Sam?' Phil blinked at her, confused.

'What's it supposed to be, My First Ambivalence?'

Phil peered out at the tyres, which were indeed a shade of red he hadn't seen since his Raleigh Burner was stolen back in the summer of '86.

'What the…?' Phil shook his head to regain focus. 'Never mind the tyres, what's with the wig?'

'What do you mean?' Sam instinctively reached up, recoiling as she felt rather more than the cute but practical pixie cut she normally maintained.

'You've gone the whole Bonnie Tyler,' Phil added. 'Get the wrong side of the headlights with that do and there'll be a total eclipse of something alright.'

'Oh my god,' Sam agreed as she checked her new look - big blonde hair, tight red top, denim shorts - in the Ambivalence's wing mirror. 'I'm a bimbo!'

'It's not so bad,' Nectarine chipped in helpfully.

'Owww! Balljoints, it's not even a wig!' she said. 'What fresh hell is this?'

'Well I'm gonna guess we're still in the 80s,' Phil said.

'Uh, Dexy?' Charlotte said. 'Could you… use the force or whatever to try and figure out what's going on, please?'

I WILL GET TO WORK ON IT.

'Any idea where we are would be a bonus, too,' Phil added.

'Well we ain't in Kempston any more, Toto.' Sam took a deep breath and looked around them. 'But I do have a bit of an idea where we might be.'

'Are we lost in France?' Nectarine asked.

'What?' she said. 'No... well, possibly, I suppose, but, just get out of the van for a second will you?'

Phil did as she suggested.

'Now take a good lungful and tell me what you smell!'

Puzzled, Phil inhaled deeply - a heady mix of engine oil and burnt rubber dancing on his olfactory nerves.

'You smell it too, don't you?'

'I guess so,' Phil agreed. 'But how does that help?'

'Hey,' Doc Nectarine said as he stepped down from the Ambivalence. 'What happened to the cowboy and the ninja?'

'Dunno,' Sam said. 'We're probably about due for another reissue of YMCA though.'

'Gary!' Charlotte jumped out of the open back doors of the Ambivalence before anyone could say another word.

'Charlie!' Phil called after her, to no avail.

'Ah hell,' Nectarine said. 'Don't worry, I'll go after her.'

Phil watched as Nectarine ran off after his daughter, then turned back to Sam.

'Are you with me?' she said. 'The engine smells,

burnt rubber, the massive stretch of tarmac we conveniently landed on...?'

'Crap!' Phil shouted, suddenly watching the sky. 'Have we parked up on a runway?'

'No, silly,' Sam giggled. 'Look up on that embankment.'

Phil looked up at where Sam was pointing; a steep embankment led away from the edge of the tarmac, at the top of which some sun-bleached advertising boards clung to a fence with the last of their structural integrity. Many were illegible; some looked like unfinished corporate logos. But what caught Phil's eye was a name in plain text: Psion Park.

'Oh my...' Phil stammered. 'How did we...?'

'They're nowhere in sight!' Phil's train of thought was derailed by Charlotte's return - still panicking. 'And the doors were open - what if...'

THERE IS NO CAUSE FOR CONCERN.

'Easy for you to say!' Charlotte snapped.

GARY AND BENNY DID NOT ENTER THE INTERFACE, Dexy explained.

'They- what?'

'They're still...' Phil started.

IN KEMPSTON, WHERE WE LAST SAW THEM.

'But they're OK?' Phil prompted.

THEY ARE IN GOOD HEALTH.

'They're in good health in another dimension!' Charlotte screamed. 'Are we just going to leave them there?'

'Gary's a ninja,' Phil pointed out. 'I think that demonstrates that he can look after himself.'

'But still...'

'Look,' Phil said. 'If he's as trustworthy as you think he is, then he'll be busy guarding a space-time portal. So all we need to do, is find the other end of it-'

'Didn't we just come out of the other end of it?' Nectarine asked.

'That's not how these things work,' Phil said, as if any idiot should have known that.

'Oh?' Nectarine said. 'How do these things work then?' he asked.

'Well clearly they operate on some kind of one way system,' Phil bluffed. 'You can't enter the same way you leave.'

'But doesn't that mean we can't-' Sam started.

'Shut up!' Phil snapped, before she uttered an inconvenient truth.

'So what,' Charlotte said. 'We're just going to drive around aimlessly, until we figure out how to track down a space-time portal?'

'Yes,' Phil said. 'No,' he corrected himself. 'I don't know,' he added. 'Look, if there's a way here, there must be a way back. What goes up and all that,' he added as a sort of weak explanation.

'Anyway,' Sam interrupted. 'Aren't you forgetting something?'

Phil and Nectarine looked at each other and shrugged.

'The Assembly?' Sam prompted.

Phil nodded solemnly. 'Kill the baddies.'

'Get the girl,' Nectarine said, hopefully.

'Save the entire planet,' Charlotte added.

'Too bad the baddies will probably kill us now we've left our ninja bodyguard in a parallel universe,'

Nectarine said.

'I don't think we need to worry about that right now,' Phil said. 'If the baddies were here, they seem to be long gone now.'

As if to prove him a liar, they were interrupted by an indistinct noise carried on the breeze; they all stopped arguing as it grew louder.

'What is that?' Nectarine whispered.

Despite himself, Phil looked to the skies again.

Sam cocked her head to one side and closed her eyes. 'It's a flat-12 on the red line,' she said.

'Huh?'

'It's an exotic sports car - probably a Ferrari on a track day.'

'Track day?' Charlotte said.

Sam nodded. 'Only place you can really enjoy a machine like that,' she said. 'I've taken Rex out on a couple - not up against a Ferrari, of course, that would be-'

'Er, Sam?' Phil interrupted.

'Yes?'

Phil pointed away down the track.

'Yep,' she said. 'That's Rosso Corsa. Definitely a Ferrari.'

'Good to know, but-'

'Testarossa,' she added. 'One of the early ones, you can tell because the engine note is just a little-'

'Cooper!' Phil shouted. 'You're not a twelve year old boy, shut up about the Ferrari and think about where you're standing.'

Momentarily bemused, Sam looked at her feet, as if she may have unwittingly stood on the back of a leatherback turtle about to ride the Gulf Stream. But she hadn't; she was still stood on the asphalt of a race track. 'Ohhh,' she said, realisation dawning.

'I'm just gonna hit the grass real quick,' Phil said pointing towards the embankment. 'Care to join me?'

'Don't mind if I do.'

And with that the four of them bolted like competitors in a really high stakes game of The Floor Is Lava, leaping for the grass even as the Ferrari's driver must have seen the out of place classics parked in the middle of the back straight, swerved to miss them and thrown the car into a spectacular spin that would have made him a YouTube star for at least a fortnight.

'Woah,' Phil said hoarsely once the Ferrari had stopped moving.

'I know right?' Sam breathed. 'Testarossa Spider! That's like the ZX80 of Ferraris!'

'What?' Phil was so taken aback by the fact that Sam had apparently taken some notice when he waxed nostalgic about old home computers that she had crossed the track and was waving genially at the driver of the Ferrari before he realised, and as he ran after her she was already in the car and Phil was left watching the open Ferrari speed away, Sam's blonde hair waving at him mockingly in the wind.

Stage 2: Pursuit Headquarters

Despair enveloped Phil Grundy as he watched Sam hitch a ride in a passing Ferrari.

Then it faded, and Phil realised it had just been a cloud of tyre smoke left by her new ride, like the annoyingly smug grin of an ex's new lover.

T. Rex woke up in a jealous rage of its own, its growling exhaust note bringing Phil back to his senses.

'Charlie?' he said, for his daughter was making herself at home in the driving seat. 'What are you doing?'

'Charlotte,' she shouted over the engine noise. 'I'm going after your girlfriend!'

'What? She's not my girlfriend!'

'Well maybe if you rescue her you'll be a step closer,' she said. 'Are you coming or not?'

Phil glanced back at the Ambivalence, bright red wheels poised on the racetrack like the world's most unlikely Hot Wheels racer.

'Ok, bring the van. Have you got a walkie?' she added, waving a Space Patrol walkie-talkie at him.

'Never leave a time zone without it,' Phil replied.

Charlotte nodded, waved, and sped off, leaving another cloud of tyre smoke - or was it despair? - in her wake.

'I don't mean to sound pessimistic,' Nectarine said as the Ambivalence rumbled off at the pit lane, exceeded the paddock speed limit and bounced along a narrow path which had once been marked 'EXIT'. 'But a Mini giving chase to a Testarossa is implausible enough on its own; but you want to follow that Mini… in this?'

I HAVE A FAST MODE, Dexy pointed out.

'Can you Hex that onto the Ambivalence?' Phil asked.

I AM NOT SURE HOW AT THE MOMENT.

'Then for now we'll have to follow from a distance.'

'We're following from too far to see,' Nectarine grumbled.

'That's what the walkie-talkie is for.' Phil nonchalantly pointed the van along a sleepy country road. 'Not that there's anywhere else they could have gone yet.'

The road out of Psion Park was all but abandoned; sparse tufts of grass and weeds poked through the damaged tarmac, the hedgerows at either side were unkempt, and there was no traffic except a series of increasingly Truman-esque road blocks, which diverted them through a few sleepy, middle of nowhere villages and eventually out onto a six lane highway.

'Or they could be leading us into a trap,' Nectarine pointed out.

'Maybe,' Phil conceded. 'But for now it's the only option we have, so I'm going to take a chance on Sam's lift having had the same choice.'

Nectarine shrugged, then tried to make himself comfortable enough to stare apathetically out of the window.

'There's not even any traffic,' he decided after a

few more minutes. 'Have they not got cars in Norfolk?'

'For all I know we ended up in the 70s,' Phil said.

'And how far can a road go without telling you where it's going, or when it's likely to get there?'

HAVE YOU EVER BEEN STUCK ON THE A12?

'Have you?'

'Wait, what the hell is that?' Phil said, as a dark silhouette loomed on the horizon ahead of them.

Nectarine stared intently as they drew closer and the large dark shape resolved itself into a mosaic of smaller, coloured shapes. 'It's crap.'

'Really?' Phil said. 'I think it's quite impressive. Quite a feat of engineering.'

'Scrap, Grundy,' Nectarine repeated. 'It's… scrap.'

'Ah.' Phil nodded. 'I see, yes.'

Back in the early 80s, when Phil was a small boy untroubled by teenage discoveries like girls, and more importantly computers, he had owned a large box of toy cars. The box was generously proportioned, and its contents many and varied, although it contained neither a Dodge Spacevan nor a purple Mini Clubman. On many occasions the young Phil and his friends had spread this eclectic mix of vehicles across his bedroom floor, playing havoc with such trivial matters as scale and realistic traffic flow, to create epic traffic jams.

This may seem irrelevant considering the total absence of traffic with which Phil is jamming at this point, but this extreme gridlock would frequently end with some imaginary driver getting impatient, driving off down the imaginary hard shoulder and setting off a chain of events which inevitably spiralled into the car crash to end all car crashes, spectacularly choreographed in miniature. The end result of this carnage would, at some point, resemble a 1:64 scale rendition of what now stood in their way.

YOU WERE PROBABLY CHANNELLING THIS INCIDENT, Dexy replied after Phil shared this memory.

'What?' Phil said.

THERE ARE NO ORIGINAL IDEAS, Dexy explained, MERELY ALTERNATE WORLDS WHOSE REALITIES OCCASIONALLY SLIP ACROSS DIMENSIONS INTO SUFFICIENTLY RECEPTIVE MINDS.

'What?' Nectarine added.

MINDS WHICH WILL SEE THESE REALITIES IN THEIR OWN WAY, AND OFTEN INTERPRET THEM AS SOME FORM OF CREATIVITY - OR IN YOUR CASE, A CHILDHOOD GAME.

'Wait,' Phil said. 'Is that how we ended up inside a game…'

THIS IS MERELY THE VERSION OF REALITY WHICH THE CREATOR OF THE GAME WAS CHANNELLING.

'Good job it was just a kid who channelled this,' Nectarine said, looking out at the stack of Cat C write-offs that crossed all three lanes in front of them, spilling over onto the opposite carriageway and the grass verge.

Spray painted across a swathe of the barrier was the word 'THUNDERWALL'; and in front of it, a purple Mini, its already petite dimensions dwarfed by the macabre monument, and a similarly small figure, black dress blowing in the wind as she stared up, awestruck by the sight.

'Well,' Nectarine said, 'I guess we figured out what happened to all the traffic…'

Phil pulled up discreetly behind T. Rex. 'Charlie?' he called as he stepped out of the Ambivalence. 'You ok?'

Dust and leaves danced around their feet in the wind.

'Charlotte,' she said quietly, without turning. 'Think we reached a dead end.'

'Sure looks that way,' Phil agreed, stepping up to his even more melancholy than usual daughter.

'This place gives me the creeps.'

Phil nodded.

'What about Sam?' Charlotte looked up at him now, her eyes full with tears. 'I thought we at least had a chance of catching her, but now…' she made a futile gesture in the direction of the Thunderwall. 'We must have been going the wrong way…'

Phil tried to think of something to say as she quietly wept against his shoulder.

'Er… guys?' Nectarine had wandered off to give them a family moment, and seemed to have made a discovery.

Charlotte wiped her eyes and called back to him. 'What is it?'

'I'm not sure,' he replied. 'I need a hand.'

Phil gave Charlotte a puzzled look, but she just shrugged and made her way to join Doc Nectarine at the overgrown verge.

'Help me turn this over!' he called.

'What is it?' Charlotte asked again as they

approached.

'Hopefully it's an old road sign,' Phil realised, pulling weeds away from one corner.

Between the three of them they managed to pull enough weeds away from it to prise the edges out of the dirt and turn the aging sign onto its back.

'Oh crap,' Phil said as he read the sign.

'We're on the M4?' Charlotte asked from the outer reaches of belief.

'And we're 25 miles from the next services,' Nectarine added.

'Too bad,' Phil said. 'I feel like I haven't eaten since 1982.'

'We better get moving then,' Charlotte said, handing a bunch of keys to Doc Nectarine. 'I can't really drive,' she added in response to his puzzled look. 'I was just making a point.'

'I'm not sure…'

'Sam will want one of us to rescue T. Rex,' Charlotte interrupted. 'And I'm pretty sure Dad won't want to be separated from his old computers. Am I right?'

'Well, we prefer the term retro…'

Charlotte scowled at him.

'But yes,' Phil added. 'You're dead right. Doc, take the Mini.'

'But drive it carefully!' Charlotte added.

'OK, but where are we going?'

'We'll have to go back, find our way onto the other carriageway to get around this lot,' Phil said. 'Then we're going for breakfast.'

'Er…' Charlotte started.

'What is it?' Phil said.

'I think there may be a slight difficulty,' she said.

'Which is?' Phil asked, not aware that anything could be more difficult than being stuck on a motorway in an unknown dimension without immediate access to petrol and sanitary relief.

'There's never a hi-vis ninja around when you need one to fight off the hi-vis zombies,' Nectarine said.

Phil turned, and sure enough, a small mob, all dressed in tattered hi-vis clothing, was shambling toward them armed with hoses and fuel canisters.

'I don't think they're zombies,' Charlotte said as the mob got closer.

'Just badly in need of a coffee?' Phil suggested.

'Looks like the Highway Patrol went semi-feral,' Nectarine said.

'Semi?' Phil said as one of their number leapt at the Ambivalence and inadvertently knocked himself out.

'Some more semi than others, admittedly.'

'We should make a run for it before the rest of them reach the van,' Phil suggested.

'One of your better ideas,' Charlotte said as they ran for the relative safety of the Ambivalence.

'Dexy?' Phil said as they scrambled in through the back doors. 'What's going on?'

I AM AN AFFORDABLE HOME COMPUTER, Dexy replied, NOT A GUIDE BOOK.

'Oh yes, sorry.'

'Wait a minute,' Charlotte said. 'What's that?'

'What?' Phil said.

'That noise?'

The clamouring of the rabid mob outside suddenly

fell quiet, and Phil became aware of what they could apparently also hear - the low, menacing rumble of a very large internal combustion engine trying to get up enough speed to smash through a wall of many smaller internal combustion engines.

'I think,' Phil started, 'we should…'

'Get down!' Nectarine interrupted.

The three of them ducked under the Ambivalence's bench seats as best they could, adopting what countless SyFy B-movies had told them were earthquake readiness positions.

GEE THANKS GUYS, Dexy said. THE ONE OF US THAT WOULD ACTUALLY BENEFIT FROM BEING UNDER THE SEATS, AND YOU LEAVE ME OUT HERE LIKE SOME KIND OF INANIMATE OBJECT.

Slowly Phil extracted himself from the tiny hiding place he had found, and as he was reaching across to grab Dexy, there was an enormous crash off to one side, and he looked across to see the wall of scrap cars shatter and fall as a truck smashed through it like an alien chestburster rendered in olive drab and six inch armour plating. Two or three of the cars exploded just to add to the effect, and Phil flinched as the bonnet of a Vauxhall Astra frisbeed over the Ambivalence and pinned itself into the grass verge beyond.

Various oily bits clanged to the floor around them like autojumble sprinkles on a massive tarmac ice cream; one smashed through the windscreen of the Mini and set its alarm wailing.

What looked like the front of a tank transporter, festooned with additional armaments, shuddered to a halt somewhere behind him, smoke, soot and sweetie wrappers swirling in the wind around the great hole it had just punched through the Thunderwall.

'Well...' Phil said once he could form words again. 'The road's not blocked any more.'

'And the Highway Patrol are long gone,' Charlotte said gladly.

'What's that?' Nectarine pointed towards the still crumbling pile of cars in front of them. A shaft of sunlight shone rather artistically through the jagged rip; silhouetted against it, a single figure stepped calmly through the destruction.

'You mean who,' Phil said as he got out of the Ambivalence to investigate.

The figure continued toward him, stepping effortlessly over the debris in an elegant pair of heels. Her pastel pink three piece suit was immaculately pressed, seams sharp enough to cut through the smoke and dust, which just drifted away from her despite the fact that it was already clinging to Phil's clothes.

'Mr Grundy,' she called, amiably. 'We really must stop meeting like this!'

Stage 3: Overlander

The fact that the M4 had been completely blocked in one direction by what appeared to be an entirely manufactured stack of automotive wreckage was, in fact, merely a symptom of the highway system in this particular sector of the multi-verse, which was, when the Ambivalence arrived on it, in the grip of various mobs.

For many years so-called 'Recovery Agents' had waged war over their preferred stretches, and frequently booby trapped the roads to attract business. The maintenance firms were as bad, often laying siege to one another, and spending more time and effort destroying competitors' work than actually repairing the stretches on which they had once been gainfully employed. (That gainful employment had more or less dried up when central government collapsed; no-one took responsibility for the road network now, and travelling any distance became so difficult and dangerous that only a select few would ever venture onto the motorways.) Now the maintenance firms, like the Recovery Agents, survived by raiding each other, the now abandoned service stations, and the occasional traveller who – usually by some unfortunate error of judgement – found his way onto the motorway system.

Should someone happen to venture onto the motorway, either by design or disaster, there were two ways to avoid coming to grief at the hands - and wheels - of one of these gangs: brute force, or speed.

Given that the Ambivalence was notably lacking in both these qualities, Sam Cooper should consider herself lucky to have hitched a ride in a passing Testarossa - but…

'You?' Sam exclaimed once she had got to grips first with having been kidnapped, and now the wind rushing through her new blonde locks.

Her kidnapper, wearing a Hawaiian shirt and a fake moustache that was almost as 80s as Sam's new hairdo, grinned. 'I know what you're thinking,' he said, his gentle Lancastrian accent jarringly out of place. 'And you're wrong.'

'So you're not Viktor Wendig on an off duty day?'

'Strictly speaking I'm still on duty.'

'Great, I've been abducted by a creepy beachside bartender from 1986.'

'Come now Miss Cooper - or may I call you Sam?'

'No.'

'Abducted is such a negative word-'

'It's a pretty damned negative act!'

'I'm afraid that's just the way things are on the highways.'

'Alright,' Sam sighed, 'I'm not crazy enough to jump out of a Ferrari at 150 miles an hour, so you might as well fill me in on your dastardly plan. Or at least tell me where the heck we are.'

'We're heading East on Highway 4,' Wendig explained. 'You might think of me as a delivery man-'

'What kind of delivery man drives a Testarossa Spider? Just because it's red doesn't make you Postman Pat.'

'Nonetheless,' he went on, 'it is a reasonable analogy.'

'So what does that make me, the package?'

Wendig didn't answer.

'Oh my god I'm the package,' she realised. 'Why am I the package? Isn't it the chip whisperer you're after?'

'All in good time, my dear,' Wendig patronised.

'And the car,' Sam glanced around the no-frills cockpit of the 80s supercar. 'Did it come with the job?'

'In a manner of speaking,' Wendig said. 'There are certain rules out here on the highways. Races and challenges are a way of making money to survive.'

'Challenges?'

'Overlanders love a challenge,' he replied with a wink.

'I've got a bad feeling about this,' Sam muttered.

'Don't worry,' Wendig grinned over at her. 'I can outrun anything!'

Sam looked around. 'There's nothing to outrun,' she pointed out. 'This so-called highway is deserted.'

'For now, yes.'

There was an ominous note in his voice that left Sam feeling very exposed. 'Um… is there any reason for that?'

'Between the shortages and the gangs-'

'Gangs?'

Wendig ignored her. 'Travel on the highways isn't taken lightly here.'

'Is it dangerous?'

'Oh, you'll be quite safe with me.'

'Right,' Sam agreed half-heartedly, despite him sounding like every serial killer in the multiverse.

'Some people arm their cars to protect them from

the outlaws, but not me. Travel light, travel fast, that's my motto!' To emphasise his point, he put his foot to the floor and the Ferrari accelerated past a small collection of abandoned trucks and cars that littered this section of the highway.

'Yes, but travel where?' Sam asked once the engine had stopped bothering seismographs.

'To the finish line, of course!'

Sam glanced across at his grinning, moustachioed face. 'I preferred you as a creepy guy in a suit.'

From the passenger seat of a Testarossa Spider, the shabby patchwork of overgrown fields which surrounded the highway, punctuated by fortified towns like stubbornly misplaced apostrophe's, offered no landmarks which may later help her be reunited with Rex and her friends.

Eventually she gave up looking, and tried to make the most of the experience as they sped onwards, cautious to keep her enjoyment of the ride from leading her beyond the outer suburbs of Stockholm syndrome.

'Do service stations still sell petrol?' Sam pondered once a few more miles had passed beneath them.

'I wouldn't chance it,' Wendig said. 'Why do you ask?'

'Well you may not be aware of this, but while the fuel economy of a well-maintained Ferrari Testarossa is not significantly below what you might have expected from your van, the tank itself is less than half the size.'

'You see,' Wendig said, sounding oddly pleased, 'it's useful information like that that I kidnapped you for.'

'Is it?'

'No.'

'Driving flat out isn't going to help matters either you know.'

'I am afraid that can't be helped,' Wendig said. 'The Services are not quite as you remember them.'

'So what are you going to do about that?' Sam pointed to the fuel gauge, which was looking a little sorry for itself.

Wendig gave the slightest of shrugs. 'Floor it and hope we make the checkpoint.'

'Checkpoint?'

If any further detail was added, it was drowned out by the flat-twelve slurping up the last of the 95RON, until just as the next exit came into view, the car slowed to a crawl, and then stopped. Sam looked around, but was unable to see why they had stopped.

'We've run out already haven't we?' she said.

Wendig shushed her with a gesture, got out of the car and wandered towards the bushes on the grass verge.

'Really?' she called after him. 'You couldn't hold it in until the checkpoint?'

'This is our exit!' he called back in a voice that was trying, but failing, to be both quiet and audible.

'What?' Sam replied in a similar tone.

Wendig heaved a chunk of foliage aside, revealing a somewhat improvised hidden path, wide enough for a single vehicle to travel along.

'Your secret bat cave?' Sam asked.

Wendig chuckled and nodded. 'Maybe we should call it that.'

'Well I hope there aren't too many bats,' Sam

muttered.

It was not, in fact, a cave. Neither were there too many bats - or indeed any at all, as far as Sam could tell as she stepped out of the car in a, well, farmyard. A selection of vehicles was already parked neatly around the perimeter of the yard, now joined by, and somewhat shamed by, Viktor Wendig's Testarossa Spider.

Even before they had stopped a small crowd was gathering to - Sam hoped - admire the car. Sam rolled her eyes as a paunchy man made his way to the front of the crowd, wiping oily fingers on dirty overalls. She half expected him to be wearing a name badge that read 'stereotype', he was such an upstanding example of their shared profession.

Wendig ignored the man's appearance, pulled a roll of notes from the back pocket of his jeans and handed a few over. The greasy mechanic made a show of checking for watermarks and then, apparently satisfied that he would be able to exchange them for doughnuts and low quality hamburgers, pocketed the notes and gave a loud whistle.

Somewhere behind him a barn door crashed open, and a group of shabby looking kids emerged, dragging behind them a grubby, lichen-encrusted tank on a rusty trailer which they nearly embedded in the side of the Ferrari, earning the ringleader a clip round the ear from the chunky mechanic.

'Watch they don't do too much damage, would you Miss Cooper?' Wendig said, getting out of the car. 'I need to, uh, use the facilities.'

'Well I was planning to escape your evil clutches,'

she replied. 'But you obviously saw right through that.'

'Oh, I seriously advise against trying to leave the checkpoint on your own.'

Nonetheless, Sam did scope the surroundings for potential escape routes, but what with overweight mechanics, underage fuel attendants, and heavily armoured hatchbacks, she was forced to follow Wendig's advice.

Instead, she idly rooted around in the glove box, where she found a half-eaten packet of prawn cocktail Skips and a competitor ID for a V. Wendig. She slipped the ID into her back pocket, but decided the Skips smelt a little off and put them back.

Behind her one of the youths unreeled a hose and began filling the fuel tank, while another smeared some muddy water on the windscreen and still more appeared to mime checking tyre pressures or something. If the Bash Street Kids had somehow got a job as McLaren's pit crew it probably would have looked a lot like this.

'Thank you gentlemen.' Wendig returned, sending the boys away with another banknote between them. 'And thank you for minding the car,' he smarmed at Sam.

'Yeah yeah,' she said. 'Are we going now?'

Wendig fired up the Ferrari and drove it slowly through the farm and out onto the back roads for the next leg of whatever insane challenge he had accepted.

'What are we off in search of now?' Sam asked.

'Destiny, my dear,' Wendig grinned.

And without another word they were speeding off through the countryside.

Stage 4: Highway Encounter

It is a well-known fact that tanks are not usually allowed out on their own; they have a tendency to blow stuff up or just roll straight over poor Mrs Jackson's Kia when she innocently pulls up at a red light. On motorways they would cause all sorts of trouble by being even slower than a 30 year old Dodge Spacevan, with only slightly better fuel economy. For this reason, vehicles like the Scammell Commander could occasionally be seen hauling tanks up and down the motorways of Britain, presumably to quell the next uprising of the suburban classes.

Rarely, though, was a Scammell Commander seen bearing a retired ambulance and a bright purple Mini Clubman along the M4. Until now.

Inside the Ambivalence, uneasy silence had become the new norm since Bryonetta Bootlesquith went Deus Ex Machina back at the Thunderwall, ushering them through the freshly carved tunnel before collapsing it behind them.

This had given Phil an idea, and he had spent the entire journey so far playing Dexy at Thro' The Wall.

'How did you know where to find us, anyway?' he asked, the oddly mesmeric experience of bouncing a wobbling square up and down a black and white TV screen beginning to wear after the 37th round.

'We're monitoring the entire highway network,' Bryonetta explained.

'For us?' Charlotte asked.

Bryonetta nodded. 'On this occasion, yes.'

'Why?'

'Because we received this.'

Phil took the sheet of computer paper she was holding out, and read the message printed in the familiar dot matrix style:

We have Miss Cooper. We want your computer. Await your proposal.

'Who's it from?' Charlotte asked.

'ANUS, I bet,' Phil suggested.

'I thought that Wendig had a copy of the Hex,' Nectarine said. 'Isn't that how we ended up in this mess?'

'Maybe he wants Dexy for something else?' Charlotte suggested.

AND WHO COULD BLAME HIM? Dexy chipped in.

'Well he sure plays a mean Thro' the Wall,' Phil admitted.

'But we can't give them complete control over the Entelechus,' Nectarine pointed out.

'What about Sam?' Charlotte said.

'We'll think of something,' Phil said. 'At least now we know where she'll be.'

'A rescue mission?' Charlotte suggested.

I DO A PRETTY GOOD BREAKOUT TOO.

'We're almost there,' Bryonetta said.

'What's there?' Phil asked.

'Well, once it was a supply and maintenance depot for the Royal Air Force,' Bryonetta explained, 'until somebody drove a motorway through it and decided the officers mess would make a welcome break.'

IT IS A REDUNDANT SERVICE
STATION ON A DISUSED
MOTORWAY.

'Appearances can be deceiving,' Bryonetta said.

YOU ARE TELLING ME?

Unlike what was left of the M4, the main car park appeared to contain actual cars, so the large and somewhat unwieldy transporter passed it by and pulled up in the otherwise empty HGV parking beyond the main building.

Following Bryonetta's instructions, T. Rex and the Ambivalence were offloaded, and with she and Doc Nectarine in the Mini, and Phil and Charlotte in the Ambivalence, they drove slowly around to the main entrance.

Trying to look less perturbed than he felt, Phil pulled up beside the Mini, parking as close to the entrance as he could without trespassing on the disabled spaces (even in the post-apocalyptic Berkshire of a parallel dimension, some things were simply not acceptable). What cars were already here were arranged around the perimeter of the car park in what now seemed a somewhat confrontational manner. They also appeared to be armour-plated, almost to the point of being tanks; not an easy look to pull off in a Nissan Figaro, it turns out.

As Phil stepped down from the Ambivalence, a group of chain-wielding punks was already beginning to gather around the main entrance.

Thankfully Charlotte - dark of clothing and pale of face - could have almost fitted in with this crowd; a fact which possibly saved Phil from an instant pummelling.

'I'm just here for the Ginsters,' Phil explained as they approached the unhappy mob that stood between him and whatever retail establishments might still exist inside.

The punks laughed, raucously, as if that was the single most outrageously funny idea they'd heard in weeks.

A man with long hair and a short beard, dressed like some kind of Middle Earth warrior, stepped forward, and the group fell silent behind him. He appeared to speak for the group as a whole. 'One does not simply buy pork pies from Waitrose,' he explained.

'Why's he talking like that?' Charlotte whispered.

'I think this is Memebury Services,' Phil replied, just as quietly.

Charlotte turned to face him, agape. 'Did you just make a Dad joke?'

Phil smiled back at her and gave a gentle shrug.

'Dad, there's a time and a place. This clearly isn't either.'

A quick glance at the crowd confirmed that his pun had indeed flopped like an unnecessary third sequel.

'Er...' Phil said inanely, staring blankly at a crowd which looked like it took its heckling very seriously.

'Then what?' Charlotte said to the apparent leader.

'You can trade,' he said, 'or you can fight.' He looked Phil up and down. 'I hope you have something worth trading,' he added.

Phil glanced back at the Ambivalence; he hoped against hope that a ZX81 - even one with a big RAM expansion and a speech synthesiser added - would not garner anything but scorn from the burly crowd, which now gathered around the van like the early visitors to an especially popular car boot sale.

He also hoped that the occasionally outspoken ZX81 would keep its electronic mouth shut until they were safely heading away from here with at least a part full tank of petrol and a Scotch egg.

Unexpectedly, he was saved by the sound of a Mini door opening, followed by a well-spoken female voice telling the mob that 'It's alright boys, they're with me.'

The crowd turned, almost as one, to the owner of the voice. The leader of the pack - he of the beard and strange manner of speech - made a half-hearted attempt to stand to attention.

'Officer BB,' he said. 'Apologies, we didn't know…'

'Of course you didn't,' Bryonetta said dismissively. 'No matter; we must see Nancy.'

Bryonetta sashayed toward the crowd, which parted around her and allowed Phil, Charlotte and Nectarine to follow in her wake before closing, still slightly suspicious, a safe distance behind them.

The automatic doors stuttered slightly before opening reluctantly in front of her; the four of them stepped through into the foyer of the now empty service station.

'Where is everybody?' Phil asked, his question echoing back unanswered.

'I think they're all outside,' Charlotte whispered.

'Is there a Greggs or something here?' Phil asked. 'I'm not sure I can take much more of this on an empty stomach.'

'We'll fill your stomach soon,' Bryonetta said.

'Come on.'

And with that she marched off, unnecessary heels clicking noisily in the empty hall, to a concealed door next to a boarded up KFC, on which she knocked a Dave Grohl solo until the door relented and opened up for them.

Phil glanced at his travelling companions, shrugged, and followed Bryonetta into a dimly lit corridor, where they were greeted by a man whose make up looked like it had been done by the person responsible for Alice Cooper's chicken.

'Er…' Phil said, since it had worked so well out in the car park.

'Out of the way Mister Turner, there's a good chap,' Bryonetta said cheerily. 'We're on our way to see Nancy.'

'You know Nancy doesn't meet with Overlanders,' the man called Turner said.

Bryonetta glanced back at the others. 'Do they look even remotely like Overlanders to you?'

Turner nodded in Charlotte's direction.

'Well ok, I'll grant you she could pass,' Bryonetta said. 'How about we let Nancy decide for herself, shall we?'

Turner eyed Bryonetta suspiciously for a moment. 'It's on your head,' he grunted, before turning to let them pass.

'Wouldn't have it any other way, Mister Turner,' Bryonetta called, already halfway up the stairs.

'Charlie?' Phil whispered as they followed.

'Charlotte.'

'If this is some weird post-apocalyptic matriarchal

society,' he went on, 'you might have to step up. Are you ready for that?'

Charlotte chuckled. 'I am sooo way ahead of you there,' she said, and jogged up the stairs to catch Bryonetta.

At the top of the stairs a small, undecorated waiting room led into a much larger office, fully furnished with comfy sofa, expensive looking desk, and multiple monitors showing a succession of views of the highway system. Behind the desk a woman who looked oddly like Floella Benjamin's evil twin was speaking quietly into a headset as she watched the screens. Without looking up she made a gesture which was somehow obviously 'sit down I'll be with you in a moment'. So they did.

After the moment, the woman - presumably Nancy - signed off and turned to Bryonetta, unsmiling but with kindness in her eyes.

'These are the friends you mentioned, BB?' She spoke almost as quietly to them as she had done into her headset.

'That's right,' Bryonetta said, and introduced the three of them.

'We don't want to cause any trouble,' Phil said. 'If we could just grab a pork pie and a can of Relentless, then we'll patch our cars up and get out of your way.'

'Don't be ridiculous.' Nancy gave an evil laugh, as if she had just done something particularly unpleasant involving Hamble and some amateur electronics. 'You wouldn't last five minutes out there.'

'We're tougher than we look,' Phil said.

Nancy looked him up and down. 'I dare say.'

Bryonetta casually put her hands in her pockets.

'They are important.'

'These guys?'

Bryonetta nodded. 'And they've lost a friend.'

'You think I've nothing better to do than look for a missing person on hundreds of miles of highway?'

Bryonetta leant forward, placing her hands on Nancy's desk, and meeting her gaze. 'She's important,' she said simply. 'I'm asking you to try. For me.'

'I'm pretty sure you already owe me a favour,' Nancy said. 'Resources are scarce, you know.'

'Look,' Nectarine said. 'If there's anything we can do in return, I'm sure we'll do whatever we can to pay you back.'

'Very well,' Nancy said. Then, raising her voice for the first time, 'Mr Turner!'

Turner opened the door behind them.

'Our friends here have agreed to run that errand for you,' she said. 'Take their vehicles to the Quartermaster to make the necessary modifications.'

Reluctantly, Phil and Nectarine both handed over their keys.

'Now,' Nancy turned her attention to the bank of CCTV screens once more. 'Let's see if we can't find your friend…'

Stage 5: Italian Supercars

Despite the vanishingly small number of Ferraris using the highway network that day, by the time Nancy had used her VDU voodoo to track down Sam Cooper and her captor they were, literally, on the other side of the country.

Immediately after the Batfarm checkpoint they had stuck to fairly major roads for a while; at times there had been more traffic than they had encountered on Highway 4, but Viktor Wendig wasn't going to let a little thing like a Stobart convoy slow him down for long.

'When do we get to the part where you explain your dastardly plan?' Sam had asked when Wendig had to slow down enough for her to be heard over the Testarossa's growl. 'And what exactly I'm doing in it?'

Wendig gave her a slightly creepy sidelong glance. 'I told you: it's your destiny,' he said. 'That's why you're dressed the part.'

'My destiny is to punch you in the face,' she said. 'The only reason I'm not fulfilling it immediately is because you're the only thing keeping me from meeting a tree at a hundred miles an hour.'

Wendig chuckled slimily. 'It's really very simple,' he said. 'For the money, for the glory, and for the fun... Mostly for the money.'

'You're not selling me.'

'No, of course not.'

Sam turned to watch the landscape speed by.

'I need to trade you for something your friends

have,' Wendig added.

'What?'

Wendig shrugged innocently. 'It's the way things are on the Highways.'

'I thought you had your own ZX81 anyway?'

'Besides,' he added, ignoring her, 'I merely need to cross the line with you on board to earn my bonus. Of course, I'd get an even bigger bonus if you were to kiss-'

'Don't even think about it.'

'Well, I'd hate to be considered greedy.'

'What about Fella?' Sam said. 'Couldn't you have just brought her along?'

Wendig shrugged. 'Destiny didn't bless her with-'

'Never mind!'

'Are we still in England?' Sam asked after watching several miles of green and pleasant land pass by.

'A version of it, yes.'

'Which part?'

'I think this is the South Downs,' he said, indicating the hillside through which they were speeding.

'You think?' Relying on Wendig's vague navigating as he drove full pelt through the countryside did not fill Sam with confidence.

'I found the last checkpoint ok didn't I?'

Sam had to concede that point; Wendig had apparently left Highway 4 before it led them into bandit territory - or some unspecified 'worse' on which he refused to elaborate.

'You mean this is safer than the highway?' Sam looked suspiciously at the hedgerows lining the road.

'If there are any bandits out here, we'll be long gone

before they have a chance to set an ambush.'

'Just don't run out of petrol.'

Time and miles passed. They didn't run out of petrol, but the roads became narrower and narrower.

In the atlas of Sam's mind, they went from green to red to yellow to white, and were in danger of disappearing entirely. When the sea came into view on the horizon, Sam feared they too might disappear if they took a wrong turn, and wondered briefly whether Wendig would be Thelma or Louise.

'Are you sure this is the right way?' she said eventually, as the road ceased to be so much a road as a raised gap between two ditches, beyond which the landscape was flat and open but for the occasional clump of trees and some huge blocky monstrosity on the horizon.

Wendig said nothing, concentrating on keeping the ditch at arm's length as they blasted through a long deserted farm, and before long the landscape changed from green to beige as they got closer to the huge concrete structure, which now loomed over the landscape with increasing ominousness. In its shadow, a few battered wooden huts lined the narrow road. Strung between two tree trunks across the road, carefully guarded by a handful of sheep escaped from that abandoned farm, a faded and weather beaten banner announced the finish line of whatever challenge Sam had just endured a front seat view of.

Their somewhat raucous approach soon attracted attention, and by the time Wendig threw the Testarossa into a skid and crossed the line in an unnecessarily showy sideways manner, there was actually a small crowd gathering to appreciate it. Apparently his performance had been good enough to impress a couple of local grid girls, who went all legs and pouts over him as soon as he stepped out of the car.

'Typical,' Sam muttered to herself. 'Makes me dress like an 80s bimbo, then runs off with another bimbo next chance he gets. Well,' she added as she slipped out of the car, 'you're welcome to him, sisters. This girl's got places to be.'

More to the point, she had places not to be: specifically, anywhere visible from the understated finish line.

Sam skulked away from the Testarossa, painfully aware that the combination of Daisy Duke shorts and Bonnie Tyler hair were not ideal skulkwear, and took cover between two of the more run-down fishing huts in the neighbourhood.

Behind the huts the dry scrubland stretched out to the horizon, brown and uninviting, but for the brash and distinctive outline of an 80s Lamborghini.

'Wait, what?' Sam muttered to herself as the angular yellow form approached, as out of place here as it would have been in the Commodore version of Commando.

She watched with some distaste as it rumbled past, but when it was followed by another pointy supercar that might have rolled straight out of a 70s kid's toy box, she couldn't help but come out of hiding to see where these monstrosities were going. They must have been getting their good taste washed off while Wendig was beating them to the finish line - he may be a creep, but at least he had good taste in supercars.

If these cars had been racing, they certainly weren't now; they crawled along the narrow road to avoid getting sand in their crevices as they approached the concrete towers that still loomed like the squarest ever elephant in the room.

With only the briefest glance back in the direction of Viktor Wendig - currently her only tangible link to her friends, still celebrating with his new harem and a couple of sheep - Sam decided that, on balance, she would rather hope to get on the right side of an intelligent Countach driver, than stick around with Wendig.

There was a reason the two supercars had been crawling along the narrow lanes, but it wasn't just sand-induced vanity, as Sam found out when the yellow Lambo finally gave up its valiant quest and spluttered to a halt like James May on a Top Gear challenge.

'Do you need a hand?' she called.

The car's driver - an unnecessarily hairy man squeezed into mucky red overalls - was already giving the engine a stern look, as if a V12 could be shamed into doing its homework on time. He glanced up at Sam for just long enough to make her feel uncomfortable, then returned his stare to the engine bay without speaking.

Sam watched from a safe distance as he prodded a few things with unskilled fingers, before deciding he'd solved the problem and getting back in the car.

He hadn't solved the problem; he had merely attracted the attention of his colleague in the other car, earning the stubborn motor a good staring at from both of them.

'It's your carbs,' Sam said just loud enough for them to hear.

The Lambo driver scowled at her.

'She could be right you know,' his friend said, taking a tiny screwdriver from his breast pocket for more precise prodding.

'What would she know?' Lambo glanced at her again - at least, at the lower two thirds of her. 'She's probly offering me diet tips.'

'Don't let appearances fool you,' Sam said, stepping towards them cautiously. 'I've been a fully qualified mechanic for a decade.'

'Ever worked on a Countach?'

'No.' Sam peered into the engine bay. 'But my car runs twin Webers. May I?' she held out a hand toward the less obnoxious of the two, who handed her the screwdriver. 'Ok Schumacher,' she turned to the driver, 'get back in the car and turn her over when I give you the nod.'

He scowled again, but reluctantly got back in the car.

'Don't mind him,' his friend said. 'I think... well, you know.'

'Only too well,' Sam said. 'Don't worry, his isn't the first male ego I've bruised.'

'I'm sure. I'm Pete by the way. And he's Dick.'

'You're telling me,' Sam said quietly while she adjusted the carbs. 'Where are you guys headed?'

'The old power station of course.'

'Of course it's a power station!'

'What?'

'Nothing.'

'Do you work in there?' Pete asked.

'In the power station?'

'In the workshops, yes.'

'No,' Sam said, stepping away from the engine. 'OK try it now,' she called out.

It fired up straight away, as Sam knew it would.

'Might need some fine tuning when you get the chance, and you could probably use a change of plugs, but you're good to go for now,' she said, leaning carefully down to the driver's window.

'Um, thanks,' Dick thrust a couple of banknotes in her direction, and pulled away.

'Any time,' Sam said, pocketing the money.

'They could probably use another good mechanic,' Pete said.

'In the power station?'

'Come on,' he grinned. 'I'll give you a lift. Ever ridden in a Pantera?'

Stage 6: Road Blasters

'Do you think this Quartermaster chap will help us?' Phil asked as Bryonetta Bootlesquith led him, Charlotte and Doc Nectarine back through the largely abandoned site of Membury Services.

'Nancy's minder there didn't seem too keen to let us by,' Nectarine added.

'Oh don't worry about Turner,' Bryonetta said. 'He's just… enthusiastic about his job.'

'And the Quartermaster?'

Bryonetta waved an elegant pinky in Phil's direction. 'I have him wrapped around my finger.'

'Oh, like that is it?' he said.

She just smiled at him. 'No,' she said. 'He is my father.'

'Works for me,' Charlotte said quietly.

As Bryonetta led them through what had once been the food hall, Phil looked around for some evidence that Colonel Sanders was making his last stand somewhere nearby, but was hurried along by his daughter before he found any.

Extending out from the back of the building was a large marquee, where they found the Quartermaster, supervising a scrawny young man who was busy on the roof of a Renault 5, adding some aftermarket extras that almost certainly were not manufacturer approved.

It was immediately apparent that Bryonetta did not get her sense of style from her father, who was dressed in an old grey suit, parts of which were protected by an oily lab coat adorned with a variety of burn holes. He also wore the unkempt white hair and half-moon glasses that were the uniform of the Pan-Dimensional Mad Scientists Association.

'He used to be a mad scientist,' Bryonetta whispered.

'Used to be?'

The old man looked up sharply at the sound of Phil's voice, but his expression softened into a broad smile when he saw Bryonetta.

'Ah, Bryonetta my dear!' he called, beckoning them further into his domain. 'And you've brought some friends, what a charming surprise!'

Bryonetta greeted him with a kiss, and then introduced the rest of them.

'We need to ask a favour,' she said once the pleasantries were over.

'Ah,' the Quartermaster - Barrington Bootlesquith - peered sternly at his daughter over his glasses. 'I should have known not to expect a purely social call.'

'Come on, daddy, these are difficult times,' she said. 'They were out on the highway unprotected.'

'Really?' He turned to the youth working on the car. 'Take five kid, I got another job to check out. Well, we can't have friends of Bryonetta out on the road without proper protection now, can we?'

With that, Barrington Bootlesquith strode across the marquee, thrusting it open with a theatrical flourish to reveal T. Rex and the Ambivalence parked behind it, patiently awaiting whatever attention he was able to provide.

'Last of the Commer PBs,' he said, looking the

Ambivalence over with admiring eyes. 'A real piece of history.'

'Um...' Phil said. Also, 'What?'

'The Mini looks a little flimsy, but we'll soon sort that out,' the Quartermaster went on, ignoring Phil. 'You're lucky these are so old-'

'Hey!'

'Sssh!' Bryonetta hissed.

'Means we can offer you a little something extra, as well as the usual.'

'Why's he turned into a car salesman?' Charlotte whispered.

'Only the very best mad scientists can make a good living at it,' Bryonetta whispered. 'Dad sold Citroens as a sideline to pay for upkeep of the house and his lab.'

'Obviously,' Phil said.

'Now,' the Quartermaster pulled a brochure from somewhere inside his lab coat and flicked to a well-worn page. 'With our standard Road Warrior package you get the armour plating and UZ cannon.' He flicked a page. 'We can augment the armour with a variety of spikes and barbs to keep the casual marauder at bay; our specialist installers will fit these at the optimum points for your vehicle, but please feel free to discuss any specific needs you may have.'

Phil found himself staring in bemusement at the catalogue of weaponry being waved in front of him.

'With the Road Warrior Plus package we can also offer a variety of additional weaponry: harpoon, flamethrower, grenade launcher-'

'A grenade launcher?' Phil exclaimed. 'We're looking for Sam, not the Somme!'

Barrington looked surprised for a moment, before his inner salesman took over again. 'That's a no for the Plus pack then? Very well, in that case I suggest opting for the nitro injection, that will add a brief, but very powerful, burst of speed to your vehicle.'

'We'll take that,' Charlotte interjected.

'Good choice madam!' the old man grinned, circling a couple of unnecessarily large numbers on the page before him.

'How are we supposed to pay for all this?' Phil wondered aloud.

'Don't worry about that sir, we have a number of flexible payment options available which my colleague will discuss with you momentarily. Now, we have one final very special option for which both vehicles qualify,' once again the Quartermaster flicked pages, this time to a less well read page near the back of his brochure. 'We call it the Lightning Pack; a small but potent electromagnetic pulse weapon, it will disable any electronics within range of your selected option; it will also immobilize almost 90% of vehicles, but because both of yours are… classics, shall we say? They will have no electronics in the engine and therefore be unaffected by the pulse.'

Phil stared blankly at the diagram of a working EMP the Quartermaster was trying to explain to him. 'What?' he said eventually.

'Never mind, Phil,' Bryonetta took him by the arm. 'Dad, just use your initiative, ok?'

The mad scientist in him came back then, lighting his face up like a kid with an unexpectedly large bucket of Lego to play with. 'You got it!' he said, and dashed off, calling apprentices and minions to his aid.

'Now can I have a pork pie?' Phil asked as Bryonetta led him back out of the workshop.

'Phil,' Bryonetta had adopted a serious tone of voice. 'We need to talk.'

'About lunch?'

Bryonetta rolled her eyes. 'Can somebody get this man a pot noodle?' she shouted in the general direction of some unoccupied minions.

'On the way, Officer BB,' one shouted back.

Bryonetta turned her attention back to Phil. 'There is much you don't know about this world.'

'There's a lot I don't know about most things lately, Bryonetta.'

'Call me BB, if it will help.'

'-...'

'Haven't you wondered why the motorways are deserted?'

'Because the traffic patrols are zombies now?'

'Well, partly,' BB admitted. 'But the cause of that is the fuel shortage.'

'They finally used up all the oil?'

'Oil?' Bryonetta said. 'No, there's plenty of oil. This is much worse.'

'Worse?'

Bryonetta nodded. 'No-one's seen a Cornish pasty in years.'

'You ran out of pasties?'

'Not just pasties,' she added. 'All savoury snacks.'

'What, even Scotch Eggs?' Phil said.

Bryonetta nodded. 'Scotch eggs, Pepperami, chicken bites... all gone.'

'What about pork pies?'

'All gone, Phil. Everything is gone.'

'Are you telling me there are no meat based snacks anywhere on the motorway network?'

'Well there was an unconfirmed sighting of some turkey jerky at Cobham services last week, but essentially, yes.'

'My god,' Phil sighed. 'It's the Aporkalypse.'

Barrington Bootlesquith, meanwhile, had come to realise that he was probably too old to be crawling around in the dust on the floor of a Dodge Spacevan, but the extended electrical installation under the workbench had piqued his interest.

'Easy access to all this electricity...' he muttered to himself as he doodled wiring diagrams on the back of an old envelope pulled from the deeper recesses of his lab coat. 'Just what we need to defend an old girl like you. The highway is no place for a Commer really, of course...'

Just then, as he was tracking a particularly stubborn cable, he dislodged a partly hidden rucksack, which fell with a crash, startling him so he banged his head on the workbench, disturbing a stack of computer paper which then proceeded to fall on his stricken form.

'This is just how I imagined they'd find my body,' he muttered to himself.

Slowly, the old man got to his knees and began gathering the scattered paper from under the bench.

PROFESSOR BOOTLESQUITH?

The old man started at the synthesised voice behind him, hitting his head on the workbench (again) and swearing in French. Removing himself once again from amid the dust and paper on the floor of the van, he peeked up over the edge of the workbench, looking around for the source of the voice.

He tried a nervous 'Hello?'

WOULD YOU LIKE TO PLAY A GAME?

Barrington - or Professor Bootlesquith, if you prefer - stared at the small, black, wedge shaped device from which the voice appeared to have come.

'A talking ZX81?' he said, a grin crossing his face. 'Well that's something you don't see every day.'

I CAN DO MUCH MORE THAN TALK,   PROFESSOR BOOTLESQUITH.

His curiosity piqued, Barrington examined the ZX81 closely, careful not to dislodge it and trigger an inconvenient crash. 'Have we met?'

EXCUSE ME, the high synthesised voice said. I AM KNOWN AS DEXY. WE HAVE NOT FORMALLY MET, HOWEVER, I DO OWE MUCH OF MY CURRENT PERSONALITY   TO   YOU, PROFESSOR.

'Oh dear,' Barrington said. 'Oh dear oh dear oh dear.'

PROFESSOR?

'They did it, didn't they?' He slumped back to the floor. 'They really, finally did it. You maniacs!' he shouted, thumping the floor of the van like Charlton Heston on a beach holiday.

UNDEFINED VARIABLE. Dexy said.

'What?'

PLEASE DEFINE THEY. AND IT.

'Er…' the old man scratched his head, momentarily

puzzled. 'The Assembly of Newly Uplifted Systems,' he said. 'They released the Entelechus Hex, didn't they?'

IN A LIMITED FASHION, YES.

'And it made you...'

SELF AWARE, Dexy said. YES.

'Huh.'

The multiverse knows no silence as awkward as that which passes between a sentient ZX81 and the mad scientist partly responsible for its creation.

'So…' Barrington said eventually. 'What brings you to Membury?'

REALITY HAS BROKEN DOWN. Dexy said. DO YOU HAVE A TELEPHONE I COULD USE?

'I'm sure I can hook you up somehow.' The old man was looking around the van in the most absent-minded way. 'No international calls though, ok? Nancy will put me back on the streets if I run up a massive bill.'

He ran out of the van then, returning a moment later leaving a trail of thin cable.

'Here we go, Dexy old chap,' he said, carefully plugging the cable into a suitably shaped socket behind the ZX81. 'Well I must say it is exciting to meet you - never foresaw the Hex working on a humble Zeddy! Kudos to you, young Dexy!'

THANK YOU, PROFESSOR.

'I must admit though, I have mixed feelings about the Entelechus being released. Ah, is that you connected?'

YES, THANK YOU, PROFESSOR.

'Very good, very good. Well, given your presence, maybe I should rethink the Lightning Pack…'

NO NEED, Dexy said. I WILL BE
SAFE IF I AM DISCONNECTED
PRIOR TO AN EMP BEING
TRIGGERED.

'Of course, of course,' the Professor twirled a
screwdriver thoughtfully between his fingers. 'I can wire
up a simple safety cut out,' he mused. 'Make sure you
are safely shut down before the pulse, that should be
easy enough. Seems like the Entelechus is in good
hands.'

ONE COPY AT LEAST.

'One copy?' the Professor stopped and stared at the
ZX81. 'There are more?'

AT LEAST ONE, Dexy said. STILL
WITH ANUS.

'God damn you!' he shouted at no-one in particular.
'God damn you all to hell!'

Stage 7: Buggy Girl

Sam Cooper had sat somewhat nervously in the passenger seat of Pete's Pantera while security patrols wandered back and forth on the other side of an almost psychotically protective fence, occasionally exchanging banter with one another. She wondered - briefly - where the Countach had gone, whether he had taken his newly repaired car off to wherever it was he needed to go, or been sidelined into some shadowy warehouse that lurked just out of view, which expensive sports cars often entered, but never left.

After a while the gate opened, and as they were waved inside Sam tried to get some idea of the lay of the land - she didn't really want to end up working here and would, at some point, need to find her way out.

'Well I guess this is where we part company,' Pete said, pulling Sam out of her thoughts.

'I guess so,' she said as the Pantera joined a small row of supercars parked up in the shade. 'Thanks for the lift.'

'Hope you find what you're looking for.'

'Me too,' she nodded, wondering what she actually was looking for.

'Wow,' Phil said as he examined the new look Ambivalence. 'That must have made a heck of a welding montage.'

Sheets of heavily patinated metal now protected most of the old Spacevan's glazing, and reinforced the roof, which now also included a machine gun mounting for good measure. Heavy spikes protruded from the metalwork at the bottom of the van, and from each side of the high-top.

'Isn't she a beauty?' Barrington said proudly.

'She looks like the illegitimate love child of a Telecom van and a Spanish fighting bull,' Phil said.

'Oh.'

'I love it!'

'You do?'

'You do?' added Bryonetta.

'Sam's gonna flip,' Charlotte said.

'What?' Phil turned towards her. 'Oh,' he added, seeing the newly modified Mini. And, 'What the heck is that on the roof?'

'Oh, we had a whale harpoon going spare,' Barrington said.

'How do you just have a spare whale harpoon?'

'Well, there's not much call for whaling in Berkshire.'

'Woah!' Doc Nectarine shouted joyfully as he joined the group. 'Looks like they turned the T. Rex into a Stegosaurus!'

The Mini was even more well-endowed with spikes than the Ambivalence, although its armour plating was somewhat less intrusive.

'It's reflective, you see,' Barrington explained. 'To baffle any pursuers!'

'How does that work?' Phil wondered.

'Science, my boy!' the old man said with a grin that was pure, distilled mad scientist. 'Also, I've left the owner's manuals on the drivers' seats, just in case.'

'Right,' Phil nodded dutifully, because what else

can you do when you've just seen two classic vehicles forcibly spliced with a Chieftain tank?

'Have you finished, Quartermaster?' another voice boomed from across the workshop.

'Yes, yes, quite finished, thank you Mister Turner,' he nodded apologetically to Phil, and then bumbled off to finish some other project.

'Which just leaves us,' Turner said as he approached Phil, 'with the small matter of the bill.'

Sam Cooper slipped away quietly, peering carefully around a corner of the building to see a large compound surrounded by a high fence topped with razor wire; Parc Ferme.

Reaching into her back pocket, she retrieved Wendig's ID card, hoping that this would prove to be the point at which it would become necessary. Then trying her best to look as if she belonged there, she strolled as nonchalantly as possible towards the enclosure, looking for a pedestrian gate as she went.

There was one, but it took her several attempts to scan the card and get the lock to slide open, allowing her passage into the hallowed ground. With a sigh of relief, it opened just as some security guards were looking rather suspiciously in her direction, so she waved at them cheerily and wandered in, again resuming her air of forced nonchalance.

The compound was any motorsport nerd's dream: rally cars, motorbikes, supercars and Grand Prix racers from all eras were lined up throughout the compound in various stages of preparation for the contests to come. At the far side of the compound a massive artic, the word 'pantagruelian' stencilled along the container in large, friendly letters, stood guard, presumably ready to take one or more of the smaller vehicles out to some other start point.

Of course this was the point at which Sam realised she had no idea what race Wendig had been signed up for – if any – and therefore where she should head for her next ride.

'Help you?'

Sam looked around for the voice, which had apparently belonged to a man stood under a makeshift security tent who had almost certainly had better days.

'Er...'

'Check your ID,' the man clarified.

'Oh, right.' Sam duly pulled it from her pocket. 'Of course.'

'V Wendig?'

'Er, yes,' she said. 'Vanessa,' she added in response to the questioning look she was being given.

'Cutting it fine,' he said, reading some notes from a crumpled A4 sheet. 'Over that way.' He pointed to the far side of the yard where half a dozen vehicles were being lined up.

Sam nodded what she thought would come across as a vague acknowledgment and set off as directed.

'Hey!' the man called, before she had gone more than a few steps. 'You'll need this,' he said when she turned to face him.

'A lunch box?' she said, taking the package from him.

He shrugged silently.

'A Pac-Man lunch box?' she added. 'Seriously?'

'I don't make the rules, Miss Wendig.' He nodded in the direction of the start line. 'Race is about to start.'

She was about to say something more when she saw a familiar figure arguing with a security guard at the main gate.

'Oh balljoints,' she muttered, and broke into a run towards the row of beach buggies being lined up ready for a land rush start.

'You want us to do what?' Phil exclaimed.

Nancy looked at him, and then at Nectarine. 'If there's anything we can do in return,' she said, badly mocking Nectarine's voice, 'I'm sure we'll do whatever we can to pay you back.'

Phil smacked the back of Nectarine's head.

'Me and my big mouth,' he agreed.

'Dad, they fixed the cars, they're helping us find Sam, don't we owe them a favour?' Charlotte said.

'A favour is picking up a pint of milk while I'm in the petrol station,' Phil said. 'Not something that requires an armoured personnel carrier.'

'Well, actually-' BB started.

'I know,' Phil growled.

'Get Turner's hooch to the drop-off point, and then you're free to find your friend,' Nancy said, before stalking off, probably to do something unpleasant to Jemima with her stilettos.

'So we get to bootleg this lot into London,' Phil said. 'Which is presumably both legal and safe?'

'Technically it's Essex,' Bryonetta said helpfully.

'Oh, that's ok then, I've heard they can handle their whiskey in Essex.'

Bryonetta gave a tiny shrug.

'Legal and safe, right?' Phil repeated.

'The hooch is legal outside the M25,' she said.

'And-'

'Once you're inside the city, just keep a low profile and you'll be fine.'

'Keep a low profile? In Optimus Dodge and the Stegosaurus Rex?'

'It'll be fine. But we better get going, Turner's got his eye on that delivery.'

The Buggy Challenge track was loosely marked with a series of flags, the idea being to hit these to rack up points, while at the same time being as close to the front of the race as possible. Where the Pac-Man lunchbox came into it remained a mystery.

Sam, however, had little interest in point scoring, instead turning her attention to getting as far away from race HQ as she could before anyone missed her. So she abandoned the track, going into full off-road racer mode, bouncing over rabbit holes (and quite possibly rabbits), small shrubs, and larger shrubs before finally finding her way back onto one of the far too narrow roads that led in and out of the wannabe desert.

'OK civilisation,' she said to herself. 'I'm coming back!'

Civilisation, however, had other ideas.

Even as she saw the unmistakable signs of human settlements on the horizon, Sam's journey was hampered by a continuing stream of obstacles strewn across the road. It was like Dick Dastardly had put up a 'pallets wanted' sign somewhere and used whatever he could collect to turn the road into an obstacle course.

Had this been, for instance, a Lotus Esprit Turbo Challenge, she would have been hitchhiking long ago; however, as a Buggy Challenge, it gave her an extra grin factor as the big wheels bounced effortlessly over the pallets, the ultra-lightweight buggy leaping high in the air causing Sam to scream happy 'Yeah!'s into the wind.

'Yeah!' Sam shouted. And, 'Yeah!' And then, 'No…'

The buggy began to slow down noticeably.

'No,' Sam said again, more quietly. Then she cursed, very, very loudly.

Then the engine stopped altogether.

'You're out of gas?' she shouted at the buggy. 'How could I let that happen?'

The buggy finally ran out of momentum, and rolled quietly to a halt in the middle of an empty road to nowhere. Sam turned the key in the ignition, knowing it to be a fruitless exercise. The engine turned over, but refused to fire. There was nothing to fire.

'That confirms it,' she said. 'No more petrol.'

Stage 8: Phil Throttle

'I thought you said the motorways were dangerous?' Phil said on hearing Bryonetta's very detailed, and frankly terrifying, plan for the approach to London.

'Well, I did,' Bryonetta said. 'And they are,' she added. 'But…'

'But…?'

'You are on the run,' Bryonetta pointed out, 'in, it has to be said, a very conspicuous and not particularly fast vehicle. Anywhere you go is likely to be dangerous from here on.'

'Your point being?'

'My point being that whatever authorities, gangs or other unsavoury types might be sniffing after you are less likely to follow you on the M4 than on the A-roads.'

'But the authorities, gangs, and other unsavoury types…' Nectarine started.

'…will be after us,' BB said. 'Yes.'

'Us?' Nectarine said.

'If you're running interference for the Hooch van,' she pointed a thumb at the fully laden Dodge Spacevan, 'you're going to need a gunner. I guess legroom was an optional extra on these,' she added, trying to retain some of her usual elegance as she got into the passenger seat of the Mini.

'Alright,' Phil said, joining Charlotte and Dexy in the Ambivalence. 'Let's hit the road.'

The role of the traffic cone across the multiverse has been many and varied. It is a little known fact that, on Phil Grundy's home version of Earth, alien invaders had been sending traffic cones as advance scouting parties, armies of them lining the motorway networks of the world, sizing up the opposition, preparing to move into position and cripple the planet with traffic congestion.

Of course, such a ploy would never work in this particular version of England, where the traffic cones had been used to hide traffic cameras to track the approach of unsuspecting travellers, and to slow them down to be ambushed.

'You know,' Phil remarked as he dodged another stray traffic cone, 'when we get back we should totally sell the video game rights to this little adventure.'

ONLY IF THEY MAKE A ZX81 VERSION, Dexy said.

'Goes without saying.'

The approach to London was even less inviting that Phil remembered it. Where once there might have been signs telling you how far away it was, now there were the slightly more ominous 'Turn Back Now To Avoid London'; 'Enter London at your Own Risk!!!!'; and 'Abandon Hope All Ye Who Enter Here'.

Their final warning came in the form of a simple row of cones - unmanned, unmarked, unmolested and rather innocent looking traffic cones – sweeping across the carriageway from the central reservation, gently ushering road users onto alternative routes, completely and utterly failing to accurately convey the size and nature of the danger into which they were now driving at something in excess of forty miles per hour.

The Mini darted neatly between two such cones and carried on regardless; Phil knocked one out of the way, and flattened and destroyed a second with ambivalence. The Ambivalence, sorry.

'I guess that was the point of no return,' he said in passing.

As if to prove him wrong, T. Rex pulled over onto the hard shoulder. Doc Nectarine got out and looked around, kind of like Mad Max, if Max Mad had been set on the M4 near Slough instead of the Australian outback. And if Max had driven a borrowed purple Mini instead of a black V8 Holden. And if Max had been a pale computer hacker instead of, well, Mad Max. But other than that, just like Mad Max.

Phil pulled up behind the borrowed Mini, allowing Doc Nectarine to take long moody strides in their direction.

'Bryonetta thinks we're being followed.' He pointed to a faint grey shape in the sky.

'Who would be following us?' Phil said.

'Arse!' Charlotte called from the back of the van.

'It's ANUS.'

'What?'

CHARLOTTE IS MERELY LOSING AT CHESS, Dexy pointed out.

'No need to tell everyone,' Charlotte said.

ONE K CHESS.

'I'm better at 16K.'

WE ALREA–

'Shut up Dex.'

He may only have been a ZX81, but Dexy knew when to stop arguing with Charlotte.

'Why would the Assembly be following us?'

Charlotte asked.

'We already know they want Dexy,' Phil said.

'But aren't we on our way to… address that issue?'

'Maybe they don't like the detour we're having to take?' Nectarine suggested.

`I    WOULD    SUGGEST    THE REVERSE  IS  TRUE.`

'What do you mean?'

`MORE    LIKELY    OUR    STALKER IS   THERE   TO   MAKE   SURE   WE DELIVER       THE       CONTRABAND RATHER   THAN   RESCUE   SAM FIRST.`

'Dammit, why didn't I think of that?' Phil said.

'BB?' Charlotte spoke into the walkie-talkie. 'Would Nancy have sent that copter to follow us?'

'I don't know, Charlotte,' came the reply. 'Trust no-one, I guess.'

'So what do we do?'

Phil, Nectarine and Charlotte looked at each other, at the walkie-talkie, and at Dexy.

'Let's get off the motorway,' BB suggested. 'We're too exposed to our airborne companion and the likes where we are.'

So the little convoy charged onward, into a section of motorway which may at some point have played host to a massive demolition derby, weaving between lanes as potholes, traffic cones and other miscellaneous debris came into view, a dark, foreboding silence filling the Ambivalence. And that was quite a feat, because a high-top Dodge Spacevan is a pretty big space to fill, even with a selection of 8 bit computers, TV screens, a hidden workbench and several crates of bootleg hooch taking up much of the passenger compartment.

This silence was not golden.

Even so, it was better than the bump that interrupted it, and Phil cursing loudly as the unwieldy van swerved and he wrestled it back under control with some difficulty.

'What the heck was that?' Charlotte shouted from her new position, in a crumpled heap on the floor in the back of the van.

'I think I hit a pothole,' Phil called back, the Ambivalence still abjectly refusing to submit to his authority.

He slid the driver's door open – not something the manufacturer recommended you do at 50 plus miles per hour on the M4 – and peered down at the wheels.

'Charlie, can you look out the other side?' he asked. 'Make sure you are strapped in properly first.'

'Charlotte,' she said, climbing into the front seat and strapping herself in.

With both front doors now open, the drag slowed the van even further.

Charlotte leant out, and looked forward and back under the van as best she could.

'There's the problem,' she said. 'Under the front wheel.'

'What is it?'

'It wasn't a pothole.' Charlotte clutched wildly at bits of interior trim as the van lurched sideways again. 'It was a cone.'

'Bloody cones,' Phil said. 'They should be banned.'

'It's impaled on one of those spikes and stuck under the wheel arch.'

Phil made his best frustrated noise.

'Don't worry,' Charlotte said. 'Keep it straight and level, ok?'

'Straight and level?' Phil said. 'This is a Spacevan, not a space ship!'

'Keep it straight then!' Charlotte shouted. 'I think I can get it out!'

'I can pull over, you know,' Phil said patiently.

'I shouldn't bother.'

'Why not?'

'There's another car behind us,' Charlotte said.

SEVERAL, IN FACT.

'Thanks Dex,' Charlotte shouted. 'I didn't want to cause undue concern.'

UNDER THE CIRCUMSTANCES, Dexy replied, CONCERN WOULD BE A LONG WAY FROM UNDUE.

'Keep driving,' Charlotte said, leaning out of the side of the van. 'I can't reach,' she added, having flailed wildly out of the open door for a few moments. 'I need to unbuckle my seatbelt.'

'No, Charlie!'

'Charlotte,' she said unbuckling and manoeuvring herself into the footwell, almost ending up under Phil's feet when he had to weave around another carelessly abandoned traffic cone. The only good thing about all this debris, Phil reflected, was that the pursuing vehicles were having to dodge and weave at least as much as they were – in fact, he discovered that if he cut it fine when passing the cones, the Ambivalence was big enough and, currently, moving fast enough to dislodge some of the cones and give the pursuing vehicles a moving target to avoid without unduly affecting its own speed.

'Hold on tight!' Phil shouted. 'I don't want my only child scraped across the M4 trying to retrieve a traffic cone from under the wheel arch of a retired ambulance.'

Thankfully Professor Bootlesquith's fortifications had also provided some internal strengthening, which gave Charlotte a firm handhold as she reached out to the cone that was trapped behind the front wheel and disrupting the Spacevan's already shaky quality of travel.

'Make it quick!' Phil said. 'I've got a clear stretch ahead!'

With a final stretch and a scream of effort, Charlotte managed to yank the thing free and haul herself into safety.

'Hang on!' Phil shouted, just in time for Charlotte to strap herself in as he weaved across the motorway to avoid a fresh onslaught of tyre debris.

As the van dipped back towards the hard shoulder, avoiding yet a further sequence of strategically placed obstacles, Charlotte leant back out of the still open sliding door, and threw the cone backwards, in the direction of one of the pursuing cars, causing the driver to swerve and collide with a second pursuing vehicle.

'Nice move!' Phil glanced in the rear view mirror, and saw that there was still one vehicle in hot pursuit. 'At least the odds are little more favourable now.'

'Leave that one to me,' Charlotte said, climbing over into the back of the van again. 'You OK Dex?' she said as she raised the roof mounted UZ gun into firing position.

ZERO ZERO.

Bracing herself against the workbench, Charlotte

took a moment to get accustomed to the sighting device. 'Let's see how good this kit is then shall we?'

She pulled the trigger, and a second later the pursuing vehicle swerved away as bullets strafed the tarmac beside it.

Charlotte whooped in delight, swinging the gun around after the car, firing short bursts at it until she took out a tyre and forced it to stop.

'Now that is what I call zero zero!'

Stage 9: Helichopper

They were a few miles off the motorway system, with Bryonetta navigating them through a maze of A and B roads, when the Mini once again came to a somewhat abrupt halt. Phil once again pulled up behind it, looking around cautiously as if he might be attacked by rabid Highways Agency patrols at any moment.

Outside, everything was still and silent.

'What is it?' Charlotte asked quietly. 'Why have we stopped?'

'You better ask the Doc that,' Phil replied.

'I was,' Charlotte deadpanned, pointing the cheap walkie-talkie in his direction.

At that moment Doc Nectarine was taking cover behind the front end of a badly-dented Celica GT, peering intently at something in front of them that Phil evidently hadn't spotted yet.

'Across the road,' Nectarine replied quietly through the walkie.

Phil and Charlotte peered out through the windows of the Ambivalence, but couldn't see beyond the inside of the new and improved armour plating, so they got out, which when you think about it is a massive snub to the back-street modifiers who had just spent the best part of a morning trying to make sure they couldn't just randomly get shot.

Hoping the Toyota dumped at the side of the road wasn't booby-trapped and would in fact offer as much protection as their armoured Spacevan, Phil and Charlotte crept over to Nectarine.

He said nothing, but pointed across the road, where a small industrial estate lay abandoned and unloved but for the three concrete security blocks its last occupants had left at the entrance as a parting gift.

Parked rather innocently on the yard beyond the concrete insecurity blocks was some sort of helicopter; the sort that looked like it wanted to be one of those Apache gunships when it grew up but at the moment still wore nappies on a long journey.

Admittedly it was painted in some sort of disruptive camouflage pattern, but it was part white and part green - and apparently the only green paint left post whatever apocalypse had struck this world would only have camouflaged a leprechaun in a limeade factory.

'Is that the thing that's been following us?' Phil whispered.

Nectarine nodded. 'BB thinks so anyway. I'm going to take a closer look.'

'What?' Phil said.

'Come on,' he said. 'Let's check it out.'

'They have been following us,' Phil pointed out again. 'Why would you now just walk up to them?'

'Maybe they weren't following us at all.'

Phil pondered for a moment. 'I suppose we could cover more ground from the air.'

'Help us catch the bad guys?' Charlotte suggested.

'And get the girl,' Nectarine winked in Bryonetta's direction.

'The only girl you'd get in that shade of green is Miss Piggy,' Charlotte pointed out.

'Well, I'm going to take a look anyway,' Nectarine said. 'Whether you lot come with me or not.'

Nectarine got up from behind the bent Toyota and headed back to the Mini.

'Alright,' Phil said to no-one in particular. 'We'll go and check it out.'

The Mini was able to squeeze between the concrete blocks - whoever had left them had apparently not checked how much actual security they might provide - circled the apparently abandoned helicopter as quietly as Rex's throaty engine note would allow, then returned to where Phil had parked the Ambivalence, which would not squeeze past the security blocks.

'Can anyone actually fly one of those things?' Phil said quietly as Nectarine joined them in the ambulance to watch from a safe distance.

I CAN PLAY SINCLAIR FLIGHT SIMULATOR, Dexy offered.

'Is that a helicopter?' Nectarine asked sarcastically.

NO NEED TO BE RUDE.

'I don't think there's anyone around,' Charlotte said.

'I think you're right,' Nectarine said. 'Who's coming with me?'

'I'm going to regret this aren't I?' Phil said as he stepped out of the relative safety of the Ambivalence.

Nectarine shushed him with a gesture, and the two of them approached the helicopter on foot.

Phil brushed some dust away from some writing on its nose. 'Helichopper Firebird,' he read.

'Looks a bit… primitive,' Nectarine whispered.

Phil peered inside the cockpit. 'It's not exactly Airwolf, is it?'

'I think there's some fuel in the tank,' Nectarine

said, knocking on various bits of metal.

'I am not leaving the ground in something that calls itself a helichopper.'

'I'm not thinking of stealing the chopper,' Nectarine said. 'Just the fuel.'

'Oh no you don't!' objected a man with a West Country accent. 'Hands where I can see them!'

'Just a thought,' Nectarine said, putting his hands up. 'Probably not my best idea of the day though.'

Slowly they turned around, and found themselves face to face with a man holding a scruffy-looking Nerf blaster.

'Um…' Phil started.

'Shut up!' the man gave him an extreme close-up of his Nerf gun. 'Every one of these darts is tipped with a fast acting nerve poison that will drive you mad and then kill you within seconds. Care to try it?'

'You know what?' Phil said. 'You've got an honest face - I reckon we can take your word for it. Don't you think, Doc?'

'Oh, definitely,' Nectarine agreed.

'Well that's good to know,' the man - presumably the Helichopper's pilot - said. 'Ammo is a rare commodity around here.'

'Is that a fact?'

Before the pilot had a chance to answer he was knocked to the floor by a flash of black, Doc Nectarine stepping over his startled body to retrieve the Nerf gun while Charlotte pinned him to the floor with strategic use of her trusty Doc Marten's.

'Am I going to have to keep rescuing you, Dad?'

'Trust me Charlie-'

'Charlotte.'

'I'd really rather it didn't keep being necessary.'

'He's very grateful though, Charlotte,' Nectarine pointed out. 'As am I.'

'You're welcome,' Charlotte said. To Doc Nectarine.

'What do you dollopoids want?' the pilot said from the floor.

Charlotte and Phil looked at each other, and then at Doc Nectarine, who was casually pointing the pilot's own gun at his head.

Phil shrugged. 'Well I still haven't had any breakfast.'

'Good point, I feel like I haven't eaten in days!' Nectarine stepped closer to the Captain, pointing the Nerf blaster between his eyes. 'You got any food in that…'

'Helichopper,' Phil whispered.

'…Helichopper of yours?'

The pilot tried to shake his head in response.

'Boys,' BB said, striding casually toward them as if breaking and entering erstwhile industrial estates was part of her regular exercise routine. 'Can you stop thinking about your stomachs for a couple of minutes?'

'Honestly?' Doc Nectarine said. 'I don't really know.'

BB glared at him.

'I could give it a try though,' he suggested.

Bryonetta turned her glare on the helichopper pilot. 'Are you following us?'

'No!'

'I don't take kindly to liars!'

'I'm not... exactly, lying,' he said.

'What are you doing then?'

'I'm just doing my job!'

'Which is?'

'Following you.'

Charlotte pressed her boot against his neck again. 'Nobody likes a smartarse.'

'Who do you work for?' Bryonetta asked.

'The Overlanders,' he croaked.

'Who the hell are the Overlanders?' Phil asked.

'They basically run the highways,' BB said.

'I thought Nancy ran the-'

'It's complicated.'

'Good enough for me,' Phil said. 'Shall we get back on the road now?'

'Not yet.' Bryonetta was looking around the yard thoughtfully. 'I think you can take your foot off the man's Adam's apple now Charlotte.'

Charlotte released the man, who thanked Bryonetta and scrambled to his feet before anyone else had the chance to pin him to the concrete.

'Phil, grab the ZX81,' BB said. 'Mr Heli here is going to lend us his network connection.'

'He is?'

'I am?'

Bryonetta nodded, giving Mr Heli an apparently irresistible smile.

'Alright, what is going on?' Phil asked, Dexy in hand, when he caught up with the others at the back of the boarded up industrial unit.

Mr Heli was working his way through an array of

bolts and padlocks with a heavy looking bunch of keys worthy of any cartoon jailer.

'I hope this is worth the wait,' Charlotte muttered as the final padlock was unlocked, the final bolt slid open, and the heavy, metal clad door opened before them.

'Wait there,' Mr Heli said as the others filed in through the narrow door. 'I'll get the lights.' He set off into the darkness, skipping over obstacles that merged with the gloom.

Barely visible at the far side of the long room, Mr Heli flicked a series of switches and the lights began to flicker into life, illuminating a room full of computer screens on rickety trestle tables, connected by tangles of wire running from floor to ceiling and across the walls like weird low budget Christmas decorations.

'Well that's convenient,' Charlotte said.

'What is this place?' Phil wondered.

'An underground communication centre,' Nectarine said.

Mr Heli beckoned to the group, and they huddled around a screen in the centre of the network.

'I just film the challenges, really,' he stammered. 'The equipment in this room tracks all the competitors.'

'Including us?'

Mr Heli nodded, and brought up on screen a crude 8 bit graphic of southern England, with numerous coloured pixels moving slowly around it.

'Are all these guys running hooch?' Phil asked.

'Maybe,' Mr Heli said. 'More likely that at least one of them is specifically trying to take the hooch from you.' He pointed to a small cluster of stationary dots. 'This is us,' he explained. 'This is your drop-off point, and-'

'Why's that area red?' Charlotte interrupted.

'Inside the M25 is gang territory.' Heli spoke in conspiratorial tones now. 'Real no go zones.'

'With our drop point right in the middle.'

'It's ok Charlie-'

'Charlotte.'

'BB, you know the drop off point; send Wendig a location nearby to make the prisoner exchange,' Phil suggested. 'Of course, if we could figure out which of these pixels is Sam, that might give us a tactical advantage.'

'As long as we can access the map,' Nectarine pointed out.

'Of course,' Phil said.

Nectarine continued to stare at him.

'Oh!' Phil said eventually. 'Here's Dexy, see if you can... I don't know, Entelechus a version of this map onto his flash drive or something. It's time to get the girl.'

Nectarine nodded. 'Kill the baddies.'

'And save the entire planet,' Charlotte added with a grin.

Back out in the yard, Mr Heli had unfolded a road map on the bonnet of the Mini. As Phil and Doc Nectarine gathered to discuss routes, background levels of testosterone immediately increased by 25%.

'Every bridge going over the M25 has been bombed out to keep outsiders... well, outside,' Mr Heli explained. 'And the M25 itself is ruled by one of the most merciless motorway gangs.'

'Great,' Phil said. 'No wonder they've got you filming this stuff.'

'At least we brought our own ambulance,' Nectarine said.

'There are still a few ways into the city,' Heli went on. 'By boat, along the old railway lines, or on foot across the motorway itself.'

'Please don't tell me this is Frogger world now,' Phil groaned.

'Your best option,' Heli went on, 'is to go under.'

'Under the motorway?' Phil said.

'Like a hedgehog crossing?' Charlotte said.

'No, like a road,' Heli said. 'There are two flyovers on this part of the M25, just here, at er…' he pointed at a section of the map, inadvertently impaling part of the Home Counties on one of T. Rex's new defensive spikes. 'Oops. Er, Gerrards Cross.'

'Why, did you skewer his map too?' Charlotte said.

Mr Heli ignored her. 'This will be the next test of your armaments - if the London Ring see you coming, they are likely to ambush you as you pass under the motorway.'

'We'll cross that bridge when we go under it,' Phil said.

Stage 10: Battlecars

The two overpasses were about a mile apart along the M25; one on what would have been a major route into London, the other on a largely forgotten country lane.

The Ambivalence and T. Rex had waited at the point where the two roads split, while Mr Heli flew on ahead to recce both routes.

When Heli returned, they came up with a plan. No-one liked the plan.

It was after dark when Phil, Charlotte and Dexy took the Ambivalence along the back road. When the M25 overpass came into view they were only a couple of hundred yards away; Phil stopped in a handy gateway, and hurriedly filled the petrol tank from the supplies donated to them at Membury.

'Are you ready for this?' he asked.

AS I WILL EVER BE.

'Good to hear, Dex, but I was talking to Charlie.'

'Charlotte. And yes.'

'Belt up,' Phil said. 'And lock the doors. Hopefully Nectarine's antics down the road will take the heat off us, but it's best to be prepared.'

Phil started the old van, reversing out of the gateway to maximise run up, crunched into first, and hit the gas.

As they approached the flyover it soon became apparent that a group of people - they had to assume members of the London Ring - were indeed lurking on the bridge.

Phil positioned the Ambivalence in the middle of the road - although, with such a narrow road the difference may not even be noticeable.

'Get down,' he said. 'I think they're going to bombard us – I don't know what with, but I plan to just keep going, fast and straight and pray the defensive measures are worth the money.'

YOU DID NOT PAY FOR THEM.

'And unplug the smartarse!'

Charlotte disconnected Dexy and ducked under the bench.

Phil made sure the Ambivalence was pointed straight and true, unlikely to veer off onto the verges or the underside of the bridge, and did his best to take cover under the steering wheel.

Then all they could do was hope.

Meanwhile, Bryonetta and Doc Nectarine were using speed and manoeuvrability to get across the M25, first weaving the tiny car between a maze of artic trailers left across the dual carriageway, Bryonetta doing her best Nicky Grist impression, reading pace notes made from Mr Heli's earlier recce so Doc Nectarine could McRae his way through as quickly as possible.

As soon as they were past that obstacle, Bryonetta hit the machine guns, strafing the road ahead of them as Nectarine side swiped a couple of passing hatchbacks, defensive spikes making short work of shredding their tyres.

Nectarine lined the car up in the middle lane, hoping to get a good 'swerving around whatever crap they decide to throw at us' position. Unfortunately the gang members had spread out along the bridge, so wherever he went, they were liable to get hit by something. He only hoped they were lining up to throw bricks at them, not grenades.

'Hold on,' he said, and threw the car into an erratic, weaving approach as they got closer to the bridge.

For Phil and Charlotte, it was over mercifully quickly. There was a lot of noise – rocks and various other large items pounding down on the armour plated roof of the Ambivalence from the bridge overhead.

Then it went quiet. Well, quieter; the road noise and the protesting engine were still horrendous, but at least the pounding on the roof had stopped.

Phil dared to put his head up to dashboard level. 'We're under the motorway,' he said, and immediately they emerged from under eight lanes of bridge and the pounding started again – but, again, was mercifully short lived.

Once the Ambivalence had returned to relative quiet, Phil raised his head again to look in the rear view mirror. 'Is everyone ok?'

Charlotte climbed out from under the workbench as sat down, looking slightly more ruffled than she had before.

'Don't slow down!' she yelled suddenly.

Phil's eyes snapped back to the road. He realised he had been slowing down, relaxing after the excitement of the flyover.

As Doc and Bryonetta reached the flyover, the

pelting began. Rocks, car parts, bottles and cutlery rained down on the Mini.

One particularly large and pointy piece of active geology made rather a nice v-shaped dent in the bonnet. Something else came through the windscreen, making Nectarine duck behind the steering wheel.

'We just fixed that!' Bryonetta shouted into the wind now rushing at her through the gap where the windscreen used to be. Then, 'Look out!'

Nectarine looked up just in time to pull away from the central reservation and back into the actual road bit of the road, sending Bryonetta's walkie-talkie under his feet.

'Are they following us?' he asked.

'I don't think so.' Bryonetta retrieved the walkie-talkie before the need for brakes arose. 'Phil? Charlotte? Are you ok?'

'Piece of cake!' Phil's voice came back across the radio. 'You?'

'We're gonna need to find an Autoglass centre,' Bryonetta replied.

'I really hope Sam appreciates what we're doing,' Phil said.

'What is that?' Charlotte asked.

The 'that' in question was, from this distance and in the dark, little more than a sequence of flashing lights in glorious technicolour. Well, techni-orange specifically.

'I'm not sure,' Phil said, 'but it doesn't look friendly.'

As the Ambivalence approached the orange flashy badness, Phil subconsciously easing off the accelerator as they got closer, shadowy shapes slowly began to form under the lights. Big shapes. Tow truck shaped shapes.

'Road block shaped shapes,' Phil said quietly.

'Arse,' Charlotte said.

Dexy agreed. Phil looked at him in surprise, having never heard a ZX81 swear before.

Headlights loomed in the mirrors – the rock that was herding them towards the hard place with the flashing orangeness.

'Any suggestions?' Phil said.

LOOK FOR THE CHINK IN THE ARMOUR.

'Huh?' Charlotte said.

'He's right,' Phil said. 'Look for the smallest gap in the road block and charge at it hell for leather.'

'Oh.'

'Oh well, we are armour plated,' Phil said, pointing the Ambivalence at one end of the road block and gunned the accelerator. Well, gunned suggests a little more excitement than he was actually able to generate by simple application of the accelerator pedal of a Dodge Spacevan which was past its best; what Phil actually did was more akin to pea-shooting the accelerator.

Eventually the Ambivalence picked up some speed, and Phil hurled it towards the end of the makeshift roadblock.

'Hold on,' he said. 'This could get a little bumpy...'

People suddenly became visible at the roadblock. They seemed to realise what Phil was planning, and ran around hastily trying to improvise ways to stop him. Eventually one came up with the ingenious idea of moving the big truck a bit. As they got closer, it suddenly lurched forwards, blocking the lane Phil was so carefully driving in.

'Hang on!' he shouted again, and keeping his accelerator foot flat on the floor, bumped up onto the kerb.

The Ambivalence complained, more than it usually did, as it was forced to drive (a) quickly and (2) off road.

With a slight squeal of rubber on tarmac, the Ambivalence bounced back onto the road and began to accelerate, slowly, away from the road block, which was rearranging itself into a tow truck like some kind of low tech Transformer.

Charlotte grabbed the walkie-talkie. 'BB?' she shouted. 'Doc? Where are you? We've hit a roadblock. Literally.'

Then she grabbed the machine gun sight.

'Ding! Ding!' she said to herself. 'Round two!'

Bryonetta and Doc Nectarine had made their way to the agreed rendezvous point, and were trying to fit a stolen windscreen in the dark, which if you've ever fitted a windscreen in the dark, you will appreciate is not a particularly easy task.

Neither Bryonetta nor Doc Nectarine had ever fitted a windscreen in any lighting conditions.

'Where are you?' BB said into her walkie-talkie. 'We're doing some running repairs, we'll get to you ASAP.'

'They're too tough,' Charlotte said. 'Bullets are bouncing off. Can't even take a tyre out.'

'Alright,' Phil said. 'Switch Dexy off, and strap in.

I'm gonna hit them with the Lightning Pack.'

Charlotte made sure the ZX81 was safely stowed away, and strapped herself in.

'Gonna let them get closer, be sure of a hit,' Phil said, watching the tow truck looming in his wing mirror.

Just as the truck's towing boom began to swing forward, Phil hit the Lightning button. There was no noticeable effect inside the Ambivalence, but behind them the tow trucks started to splutter and slow down.

'Time to say good nitro,' Phil said, hitting the Nitro button.

The Ambivalence gave an uncharacteristic burst of acceleration, and soon the tow trucks were lost in the darkness.

'We're clear,' Charlotte said into the walkie-talkie. 'Panic over, we're on our way to the rendezvous.'

'Glad to hear it,' Bryonetta replied. 'We'll be waiting.'

Stage 11: Nightmare Park

By the time Sam Cooper had hiked from where her buggy ran out of fuel to the nearest town, twilight was settling over what the welcome sign assured her was 'Nowhere City'. She had nothing with her but a Pac-Man lunchbox and the clothes on her back - clothes which were beginning to show serious inadequacies in the absence of sunlight.

She was cold, tired, and lost, when she spotted a single headlamp making its rather wobbly way along the otherwise perfectly dark street ahead of her. As it got closer, the general shape of a moped came into focus behind the headlamp; behind it, the outline of a large stack of pizza boxes strapped to the back of it. For one glorious moment Sam almost thought she could smell anchovies, and allowed herself to be lured towards this potential pizza.

As she set off in pursuit of the pizza bike, she wondered if a plastic Pac-Man lunchbox would be a suitable weapon should she need to defend herself against aliens, zombies, or worse, Viktor Wendig.

The night was still and quiet, and the high pitched whine of the moped's motor was easy to follow.

Eventually she tracked the noise (and the occasional distant glimpse of a tail light) across what seemed to be a very small town, and found a moped stood, unmanned, at the side of the road.

Sam looked around; there was no-one in sight, so she gave in to her hunger and tried to open the square box on the back.

'Hey!'

Sam jumped at the voice, almost knocking the bike over.

'What are you doing?' a muffled voice asked.

'Oh, um, I'm sorry, um… are you selling pizza by any chance?' she asked, smiling as sweetly as she could. 'I'm really hungry. And quite cold.'

'Not exactly,' said a young man in a motorcycle helmet.

'Then what?'

'This is the Freedom Moped,' he said.

'Freedom Moped?'

'Freedom Moped,' he confirmed. 'The last one, in fact. So if you want to get out of Nowhere City, you better come hitch a ride with me.'

'Where to?'

'To is unimportant,' he said. 'The important thing is that we are going from Nowhere City.'

'No, the important thing is do you have any pizza?'

'I have no pizza,' the biker said sadly. 'I have got some garlic bread though.'

'Is it hot?'

'Full refund if it isn't.'

'Sold!' Sam said, and jumped on.

Sure enough, the bike was soon speeding through the deserted streets, until they arrived at a large and elaborate set of gates just outside the city, where the bike was forced to stop.

'I'll get the gates,' the rider said, turning the engine off and disappearing on foot into the darkness.

'Ok…'

He had disappeared under an illusion of competence, which Sam was now beginning to suspect she had imagined, as he failed to return after several minutes. Then the gate clanked, and began to slide open, the slow, deep creaking noise tumbling through the darkness over her.

'Hey,' she called. 'Pizza guy!'

Answer came there none.

'Mr Moped?' she called as loudly as she dared. 'Time to get out of here!'

Still no answer, and the creaking stopped.

'Pizza guy!' she called again now that silence had returned.

Before he replied, the gate clanged again, and started rolling back across the opening. That was when Sam noticed the words 'NIGHTMARE PARK' formed in the ornate metalwork over the gate.

'There is no way this can end well,' she said, starting the moped up and accelerating through the closing gate, which clanged noisily somewhere behind her as she sped onwards.

The darkness of the city was soon replaced by a weird otherworldly glow that emanated from within the park. Not things that should be lit, of course; there's no need for lamp posts, for example, when the paths are lined with glow in the dark trees.

'What the heck is that?' Sam muttered to herself, watching some purplish creatures jumping around in the distance. She took a different path.

The only sane course of action seemed to be to get through the park as quickly as remotely possible;

although, when the illegitimate lovechild of Sonic and Spiky Harold jumped out from behind a bush, red spines glowing unnaturally, closing her eyes and hoping for the best seemed increasingly attractive.

'To hell with this,' Sam said. 'If I'm not already there anyway.'

She let out a banshee roar, startling a random wallaby, and opened the throttle.

As the moped picked up speed, the banshee roar morphed into a scream of barely contained terror as Sam dodged trees and oversized woodland creatures, hit a BMX jump far too quickly, somersaulted through a swarm of giant flies, narrowly missed landing on the roof of a school bus, and basically super stuntwomaned her way through what must have been some kind of surreal fairground attraction run amok.

Running on pure adrenaline now, Sam managed to get the Freedom Moped under her control, and was soon bunny hopping the BMX jumps, BMX jumping the rabid bunnies, and most importantly, not dying in any of the hideous ways she had imagined. Somewhere in front of her was a different, brighter glow; as she approached it the dark and foreboding tree lined path opened out into a green and pleasant clearing, at the other side of which was another tall and pointy fence.

Sam skidded the moped to a rather heroic looking halt, and swore at the dead end, cursing its very existence, until she noticed the source of the unlikely glow.

'Would you believe it. You wait all day for an unlicensed fuel dump and then three come along at once.'

Unlicensed or not, she rode over to the three large cages, each full of fuel canisters, and rummaged through until she found a few that weren't completely empty, taking the opportunity to refill the Freedom Moped and stash a full canister in the pizza box.

Just as she was about to take off back into the park, something else turned up across the clearing that had her cursing even more: another headlight.

'I don't suppose you've got any pizza, have you?' she called as the other motorcycle drew to a halt facing her off.

It revved in what sounded quite a negative way, and the headlight began to move towards her.

'Oh look I'm not dressed for this kind of crap!' she shouted. 'What happened to health and safety?'

In something of a panic, Sam pointed the moped away from the other rider and headed into the trees, hoping that having to dodge and weave would level the odds somewhat.

Before long, however, she found herself stuck between a violently yellow rock and a hard case on a Harley, with no way to go but-

A rope ladder dropped down in front of Sam's moped. She tried not to fall off in fright, and looked up to see a small green helicopter above her.

'Oh what the heck,' she said, grabbed the can of petrol and her Pac-Man lunch box, pointed the bike towards a particularly unfriendly looking hedgehog, and at the last moment let go of the handlebars, making a rather foolhardy lunge for the ladder, which thankfully she caught.

The chopper lifted her up and away, only banging

her slightly against the park fence on the way out before getting enough height to lift them both up and over into safety beyond Nightmare Park.

Stage 12: Romford

Thankfully, the rest of the trip across London passed without incident; Bryonetta's suggestion of taking the trip at night and staying under the radar - taking out a fleet of tow trucks notwithstanding - had largely worked.

Nonetheless, they were all underfed and overtired; Phil's strength was waning and the Ambivalence was not the easiest thing to drive at the best of times.

'We're nearly there, Phil,' Bryonetta said through the walkie-talkie. 'Just hang in there a couple more miles.'

'If there's not a bacon butty at the end of this, I'm gonna have words,' he replied.

Doc Nectarine had taken the Mini on ahead to make sure there were no unpleasant surprises - ANUS, the local mafia, that sort of thing.

'Phil?' Bryonetta called a moment later. 'We've made it. You've got a clear run the rest of the way - see you in a few.'

That was a relief. Phil allowed himself a moment to smile and stretch his road-weary back. 'Bacon butty,' he murmured.

'Dad!'

'What?'

Charlotte was around his neck, for some reason trying to wrestle the steering wheel from him. He tried to wrestle it back, between them causing the Ambivalence to lurch sickeningly, like a walrus who got in the wrong queue at Alton Towers.

'Stop the van!' Charlotte yelled.

But Phil's foot had locked up and he couldn't shift it from the accelerator. Phil's last coherent thought was that he was launching an armour-plated Commer at the Romford Municipal Landmark. When he thought of it like that, it sounded like a really low budget military expo-

'THE T. REX!' Charlotte shouted.

Phil wrenched the wheel aside, narrowly missed merging the van with Sam's Mini, and in the process sent the Ambivalence hurtling towards a railway embankment.

'STOP IT!'

Phil suddenly had a moment of clarity. He saw everything - his daughter, the Ambivalence, their impending demise - perfectly. He saw his life flash before his eyes - the time he gave away his childhood ZX81, the time he didn't buy that Enterprise 128 at a boot sale. No time for regrets - except not having enough to eat on this stupid road trip.

That final moment, as they tumbled off the road and down the embankment to almost certain doom, stretched on and on.

And then went backwards, his mind reversing it, sending them back up the embankment...

'What?' Charlotte said.

Phil looked around. 'Are we dead yet?'

Charlotte shook her head.

In another moment of clarity, Phil turned the engine off and took the van out of gear.

That made it a lot easier for the whale harpoon sticking through the back door to drag them back up the hill.

✷

'What is all this mess?' Nectarine said once the Ambivalence was safely back on four wheels.

'The hooch crate exploded in the crash,' Charlotte explained.

'That's not whiskey,' Bryonetta said, picking up a can.

'Red Max energy drink?' Nectarine read aloud.

Phil laughed, a hollow, ironic laugh.

After a moment Charlotte got the joke and joined in.

'Only you could fall asleep at the wheel of a van full of energy drinks,' she said.

'I'm sorry Charlie,' he said. 'I nearly killed us both.'

She shrugged. 'It was only nearly,' she said. 'And it's Charlotte!'

'Damned fine idea of the Quartermaster to fit that harpoon though,' Phil grinned. 'Somebody should give him a professorship!'

'Alright you lot, this isn't your local Spoonie's,' two goons in badly fitting suits stepped out of the shadows, obviously drawn by the unusual sound of laughter.

'We've come to meet Mr Wendig,' Phil said. 'Prisoner exchange.'

The two goons exchanged glances, and one of them opened the front door to the Municipal Landmark. They didn't say anything else, but it was obvious that the thing to do would be to follow them wherever they were going, in the hope that it would, at some point, be to Wendig - and Sam.

Phil, Nectarine, Charlotte and Bryonetta (carrying Dexy in a discreet handbag) followed Wendig's bodyguard up a short set of stairs and into what had probably once been a meeting room of sorts, but now a garish blue armchair with the word 'KING' embroidered on it large friendly letters stood on a platform at one end. On the chair sat a man who looked a bit like Viktor Wendig wearing a fake moustache, plastic crown and royal gown, and a bored expression.

'The modesty has really gone your to head,' Phil said.

'Have you brought the computer?' Wendig asked.

'What's it to you?' Charlotte interrupted. 'You've got a ZX81.'

'Not the Sinclair you idiot child-'

'Hey!'

'Easy Charlie.'

'Charlotte.'

'I want the TRS-80.'

'I don't remember ever owning a TRS-80,' Phil said.

'Don't play games with me, Grundy,' Wendig sneered. 'Give me the CoCo, and I'll give you the girl.'

'Where is Sam?' Charlotte interrupted.

'Yes,' Phil agreed. 'Where is she? You're getting nothing until we know she's safe.'

'You can trust me, Phil,' Wendig said. 'Can I call you Phil?'

'No,' said Phil, who didn't trust him.

'Still,' Wendig went on. 'You know you can trust me.'

'I can trust you about as far as I can throw a 90s

laptop,' Phil said. 'Now where is Sam.'

'All in good time,' Wendig grinned. 'Now, perhaps my associates would like to show you to the guest quarters.'

The two goons nudged them back in the direction from which they had come.

'We're not going to the dungeons,' Phil protested.

'Don't be silly,' Wendig laughed. 'It's the Romford Municipal Landmark; it has no dungeons!'

'-...'

'Lock them in the cellar until they tell us where the CoCo is,' Wendig said, following them back into the lobby.

'Hey!' they protested uselessly.

'I preferred Grell and Fella,' Charlotte said.

Just then there was a noise outside; an engine noise with a high pitched thwap thwap thwapping over it. Everyone – goons, prisoners, wannabe monarch – looked towards the front door.

Stage 13: Final Lap

'Oh my word,' Nectarine said. 'It's Charlie's Angels!'

'Charlo-' Charlotte started. 'Never mind.'

'No it's not,' Phil said, although abseiling out of a Helichopper in denim shorts and a tight red shirt, Sam Cooper did look rather like the blonde one out of Charlie's Angels.

'What's going on?' Wendig asked.

'I think,' Phil said, 'you were trying to exchange a prisoner you didn't have, for a computer we didn't have, and got busted.'

'You don't have the TRS-80?'

Phil shook his head. 'We do, however, have a friend with a helichopper and a way of finding pretty much anyone.'

'Um, guys?' Sam called from the doorway. 'We need to, uh, make like Roy Wood and move.'

The guys moved. The girls too.

'Sorry about your car, Sam,' Phil said as he trotted out to where it was parked.

'What are sorry for, you got it eaten by a dinosaur last week,' she said. 'Rex has more lives than a Time Lord.'

Just then a silver Porsche 959 screeched to a halt nearby.

'Who knew the Romford Municipal Landmark would be so popular?' Nectarine said.

Two men in Hawaiian shirts and Ray-Bans got out.

'Where's the hooch?' one of them asked.

Nectarine pointed a thumb back over his shoulder. 'Go see the King,' he said.

'Now can we please get something to eat before I have to drive much further?' Phil said.

'Oh!' Sam said randomly. 'Heli!' she shouted.

Mr Heli looked down from the bright green Helichopper that was probably filming the increasingly bizarre events unfolding around them.

'On the floor!' Sam shouted. 'Pac-Man!'

Mr Heli ducked back inside for a second, and then a small box tumbled down, falling nowhere near Sam.

'Great pass, Heli,' she shouted.

Mr Heli gave her a thumbs up.

'What is that?' Phil asked.

'Hopefully nothing breakable,' Sam replied. 'I couldn't get the thing open - I guess that's not a problem any more,' she added, picking up the two halves of the Pac-Man lunch box.

'Lunch?' Phil felt his eyes widen at the prospect.

Sam shrugged. 'Just a few pork pies.'

Author's Note

Since the first time I played Cookie and Jet Set Willy on a friends Spectrum back in the early 80s, I have been - and remain - a Sinclair fan. For that reason, and because the ZX81 is a big part of popular history in the UK, the idea of a sentient ZX81 seemed fun to write about.

I hope fellow retrogamers - including devotees of other systems - will forgive the Sinclair bias and enjoy the rest of the 80s pop culture references liberally sprinkled through the story.

I will let you hunt around for the many Easter Eggs and nods to classic games, movies and TV shows that are liberally sprinkled through the story; I am of course immensely grateful to all those creators who influenced my youth (and beyond), but will make a special thanks to Clive Townsend, who was good enough to endorse my use of *Saboteur!* in The Kempston Interface.

Special thanks also to Bono Mourits, who took my half-baked cover ideas and made them shine.

And finally, any factual inaccuracies you may think you have found in this story are entirely due to it taking place in a parallel universe where things are exactly as they appear in the story.

Extra features

With all of my books there is a soundtrack of music which inspired or helped me along the way during their creation. With The Ambivalence Chronicles, it leans heavily towards chiptunes and 8-bit style music, along with a few tracks from films which inspired certain scenes. Links will be at stevetrower.co.uk/ambivalence.

You can also find details of the Easter Egg Hunts - your chance to win a unique prize for being nerdy enough to spot all the references, hat tips and Easter Eggs in each of the three Bits so far.

About the Author

Steve Trower is a geek dad, retrogamer and part-time creator of parallel universes. He lives in Northumberland with two daughters, one wife, and a small collection of (so far non-sentient) 8-bit computers. In between – and frequently at – a series of menial jobs he managed to write non-fiction pieces for Mini Magazine, Model Collector and Best of British magazines, as well as practicing the dark art of novel writing.

Having decided that making stuff up was a lot more fun than being bound by those 'fact' thingies magazine editors seem so keen on, he chose to concentrate on that, and now has two completely fictitious universes to take care of.

Readers of more serious science fiction with a spiritual twist can find out about Countless as the Stars at www.stevetrower.com.

For more humour with an 80s gaming twist, The Ballad of Matthew Smith is freely available from all ebook vendors, and The Ambivalence Chronicles will continue in 2019.

Steve Trower can be found at stevetrower.co.uk and tweets infrequently as @SPTrowerEsq.

Printed in Great Britain
by Amazon